T0208376

Once Upon A House

BY BOBBE TATREAU

iUniverse, Inc.
New York   Bloomington

Once Upon A House

iUniverse books may be ordered through booksellers or by contacting:

iUniverse
1663 Liberty Drive
Bloomington, IN 47403
www.iuniverse.com
1-800-Authors (1-800-288-4677)

Because of the dynamic nature of the Internet, any Web addresses or links contained in this book may have changed since publication and may no longer be valid. The views expressed in this work are solely those of the author and do not necessarily reflect the views of the publisher, and the publisher hereby disclaims any responsibility for them.

ISBN: 978-1-4502-2297-6 (sc)
ISBN: 978-1-4502-2298-3 (ebook)

Printed in the United States of America

iUniverse rev. date: 4/19/2010

Chapter 1

"This is it." Margo Waters swung her silver Mercedes into the driveway alongside the two-story clapboard house and shut the engine off. Her voice slid into selling mode. "It has great potential."

Rule One: Always be upbeat. "The lot is slightly over half an acre."

Rule Two: Point out minor imperfections, then quickly mention something positive. "Of course, the English-style cottage garden in the back needs some TLC, but the deck was rebuilt with treated redwood two years ago."

Rule Three: Get the buyer to picture herself living in the house. "Imagine having your coffee on the deck, enjoying the spring flowers."

Only half listening to Margo's sales pitch, the woman in the passenger seat leaned forward, peering through the windshield. "Is that the guesthouse? It looks smaller than what the listing says—and it isn't at the back." The major reason Dani Springer had wanted to see this house was the separate two-bedroom guesthouse at the rear of the property. None of the other houses Margo had shown her had one.

"Actually, there are two guesthouses. Senator Hamilton converted his elaborate workshop into the guesthouse you're looking at. One large bedroom with a bath, a living/dining room, and a small kitchen. Later, he built another guesthouse between the garden and the end of the property where the woods begin. A split level with two bedrooms, but you can't quite see it from here. The Senator and his wife did a lot of entertaining when he was at The General Court. Sometimes his guests were very important people who wanted their privacy. This past year, his widow has been living in the smaller one because the stairs in the main house got to be too much for her." Margo glanced at her client, weighing whether this was the time to be completely honest about Mrs. Hamilton and why the converted workshop didn't appear on the listing form. The truth had discouraged the other buyers who'd been interested in the property. Probably would this time too.

Because she'd been on floor duty at Krag & Krag Realtors the day the Hamilton daughter came into the office, Margo had gotten stuck with this listing. At first, it seemed like a terrific opportunity; selling this house would help make up for all the sales she hadn't made. But so far, there hadn't been an offer, and she was beginning to see the Hamilton house as something of an albatross. The rest of the sales staff made no secret of how grateful they were that it wasn't their listing.

"I have the keys if you'd like to go inside."

"Thanks, just give me a minute." Dani got out of the car and walked over to the wide, basket-weave brick path leading to the front steps so she could look at the house straight on. It had a rather old-fashioned charm, simple New England Colonial lines, with an all-weather sunroom on the left side. The house could definitely use a fresh coat of paint. Across the front, there was an inviting front porch with fretwork along the edge of its roof, arched brackets over the steps, a balustrade and turned posts. Deep enough for white wicker furniture in the summer. The front door needed refinishing, but it still had its original oval of frosted glass, a faint pattern of flowers etched around the edges.

She pulled the copy of the listing from her purse, comparing the picture to the actual house. Almost four thousand square feet, four bedrooms, four bathrooms, a half bath downstairs, another small bedroom and bath in the attic. Two fireplaces, one in the living room, one in the master bedroom. Some furniture included. The asking price had been reduced by $50,000. On paper, at least, a bargain. In Southern California, that amount of money might buy a three-bedroom, one-story house on a lot the size of a postage stamp. Might. Margo had hinted that, because this house had been on the market for a while, the owner could be persuaded to accept a lower offer.

Shading the porch were two beautiful maples, one on each side of the brick path and, between the sunroom and the driveway, three handsome evergreens. The yard looked like it was in better shape than the house. She slipped the form into her purse and glanced at Margo, who was tactfully giving her plenty of time to look and think. Dani liked that.

This house just might serve her purposes. Not too imposing, yet with a style tourists would expect New England houses to have—and with more bathrooms than most. A definite plus. Dani hadn't confided to Margo that she was actually looking for a house that could be converted into a bed and breakfast, a way of providing a job for herself and a home for Spence—if he chose to come back. No more working long hours at someone else's establishment with only a meager paycheck for her efforts. It was time to show her ex, and anyone else who had ever doubted her abilities, that she could be successful too. In the last three years, very little in her life had turned out the way she'd wanted it to. Even her son had defected.

She walked over to Margo, "Let's go in."

Smiling her best real estate agent smile, Margo handed Dani the key, allowing her to enter first.

Rule Four: Give the prospective buyer a sense of ownership.

Margo's first year in real estate had been rough. It had been nearly three months since she'd sold a house. Mr. Krag, Senior was not pleased, and she had taken to avoiding him as much as possible. Truth be told, selling houses had been harder than she expected. Some of the selling strategies she'd been encouraged to use made her feel like she was manipulating people, never lying outright but never quite telling the truth. She hated that part of the job. Even more troubling, a few of her colleagues believed she was just playing at being a realtor because, after all, her husband had a good job. Margo pretended she didn't know what they whispered behind her back.

The moment Dani opened the front door, she was hooked. The entry hall was spacious, the staircase curving down to an elaborately carved newel post. Not quite like the staircase in *Gone with the Wind*, but close. The centerpiece of the house. Guests would love it. A small room to the right, perhaps a sewing room at one time, had enough space for an office with a counter to check guests in. On the other side of the hall was a large living room with a fieldstone fireplace, perfect for late afternoon coffee or tea in the winter months. Opening off the living room was the sunroom which, according to the listing, was not part of the original structure.

Dani wasn't worried about what the rest of the house looked like—the porch and the staircase were enough to capture her. Anything else could be changed, painted or repaired. A building inspector, who would certainly be part of the process, could tell her what needed to be brought up to code. She'd had plenty of experience redecorating whatever Navy housing she and Ben had been assigned. She should have majored in interior design instead of psychology. As she walked through the house, she was already envisioning bright Southwest colors for the downstairs—different from the traditional flowered wallpaper and subdued New England colors. Perhaps some of her own oak furniture would fit in with the pieces being sold with the house. Whatever else the house needed, she could pick up at yard sales or second hand stores.

In spite of the fact that she was pretty sure she wanted to own this house, Dani took her time, walking through all the rooms as though seeing each one mattered, keeping her expression noncommittal. No sense letting on that she was ready to make an offer.

From the living room window of the smaller guesthouse, Clarissa Hamilton watched the two women enter her home—her real home, not this converted workshop she was reduced to living in because her knees would no longer tolerate multiple trips up and down the staircase every day.

For the first three months the house had been on the market, no one looked at it, and the listing expired. That was when Lorraine decided to list it with a larger real estate office in Lenox and lowered the price. Even so, this was only the fourth time the agent had shown the house. Clarissa was not impressed with her. Brassy blonde hair—she should try a softer, lighter shade—a French manicure, three-inch heels, and a flowered cotton dress that was in fashion but definitely not flattering. Today's client was probably in her thirties, khaki twill slacks, a chocolate blazer, probably faux suede, and low-heeled ankle boots, stylish but not terribly expensive. Clarissa knew clothing and style and measured the rest of the world by such things.

She was rather enjoying the fact that the house hadn't sold. No one was interested in making an offer once they learned that she was part of the deal: she must be allowed to occupy Judd's old workshop for as long as she wished, free of charge. Not many buyers would want a house that came with an eighty-three year old tenant in the side yard. Clarissa was counting on it.

Lorraine kept trying to talk her into moving to that dreadful assisted living complex on the south edge of town—Happy Hill—but Clarissa wasn't leaving the premises until she went feet first. She'd invested too much of herself in this house, and it was almost the only thing she cared about, except quilting and, of course, Lorraine. And so the house hadn't sold. With it empty, she could still go inside, wander around, dust a little and, for an hour or so each day, pretend Judd and the children would be home later, that nothing had changed.

The first time Clarissa saw the house, she wanted to cry. Standing on the sidewalk, holding ten month old Matthew on her hip, the only thing she could think of was that this house Judd was so excited about was a monstrous dump, a two-story clapboard that probably had been painted white at some point but now looked as though it was haunted. Broken windows, the front door screen hanging by one hinge. Weeds everywhere. Neglected and sad. How could her husband consider moving her and their son into this eyesore? One selling point, however, was that it was within walking distance of downtown Lee so she could do her shopping without waiting for Judd to find time to drive her. The only vehicle they owned was his truck, which he needed for work. She wandered around the outside of the house, studying it from all angles. There were young spruce trees in one side yard, a couple of alders on the other side, and a densely wooded lot bordering the back of the property. Plenty of room for children to play and space for flowers. She'd always coveted the gardens in other people's yards.

Judd was certain they could buy it cheap, before it was auctioned off for back taxes. "Then we can get out of this cramped apartment, and Matt will have room to run—after he learns to walk, of course." Judd smiled that dazzling smile of his, and all of Clarissa's arguments vanished. He could be quite convincing.

One of the reasons she'd married Judd Hamilton—besides the fact that he was drop dead handsome—was that he had more prospects than the other young men who wanted to marry her; there had been three serious proposals before his. Judd had an engineering degree from Amherst and was starting his own construction business. Because she suspected he was going to be successful—and he certainly had charm—she accepted his proposal.

The Depression had hit everyone in the Berkshires hard and, just when the economy was improving, most of the young men went off to war. Judd was one of the few who hadn't been drafted. Having lost the hearing in his left ear when he was a boy, he was classified 4F and was able to finish his education. As soon as the war ended and it was again possible to get building materials, Hamilton Construction took off.

The success factor mattered. Growing up, Clarissa Marie Malone had always been embarrassed by her parents. Her father had dropped out of high school at sixteen to go to work for the County Road Department and, a few years before his retirement, had finally been promoted to crew supervisor. To make ends meet, her mother worked as a seamstress at home while raising five children. There hadn't been many extras for the family. Clarissa hated being almost poor, hated living in a rented house with bare dirt and weeds instead of grass in the front yard, and she especially hated hand-me-down dresses from her sister and cousins. If her mother wasn't too busy making clothes for other women, Clarissa might have a new dress for Christmas. Since there was never any money for new books, she read library books that smelled of stale cigarette smoke, her mother always worrying about having to pay a few cents if the books were overdue.

When Clarissa was thirteen, she began baby-sitting so she'd have money for lipstick or a bracelet from the drug store. For hours at a time, she practiced her flirting techniques in front of the bedroom mirror. She knew she wasn't beautiful in the conventional sense, cute perhaps, but she had a good figure and a way of making the boys of Lee think she would put out more than she ever did. Even Judd had to wait for their wedding night.

Yesterday, when he told her about the house—told her he'd put in an offer without consulting her—he promised he would build a sunroom off the living room and add bathrooms upstairs. Clarissa knew he intended to do all those things, but his other construction jobs would come first. They always did. That was why he was so successful, why people said that, if Judd Hamilton gave his word, you could count on it. She, however, couldn't always count on him finding the time for the things she wanted him to do at the apartment. Maybe he'd be better about renovating their own house. When the time was right, she would insist that the attic have a room for live-in help because she had no intention of becoming a drudge like her mother.

Clarissa was still at the window as the two women left the house an hour later. It was hard to see their expressions from this distance, even though her eyesight was still good. Only four o'clock. Enough time to drive to The Sewing Basket where she taught a biweekly quilting class. She needed to use Phoebe's computer to order new quilting blocks for the students. Backing out of the driveway, she reminded herself to tell Evan what a good job he was doing with the grounds. When he took over the job, she hadn't asked him to work on her cottage garden, but now she was ready to admit that she wasn't able to keep up with it like she used to. Perhaps she'd have to get him to take care of that also. Nice young man, quiet, with a marvelous smile.

Back at the real estate office, Margo poured two cups of coffee and sat down at the gray metal desk she shared with another agent. Dani took the chair across from her.

"What do you think? It's one of a kind. Most of what needs fixing is cosmetic."

Dani interrupted Margo's sales pitch. "I like it very much. I'm prepared to make an offer contingent, of course, on what a building inspector tells me."

Margo knew better than to celebrate yet. "You are? Wonderful—that's wonderful." She sipped her coffee, gathering courage. "However, there's something you need to know before you make an offer, something that isn't in the listing."

Dani set her cup down and felt her stomach tighten. Margo's expression wasn't encouraging.

"Well, you see, the owner, her name's Clarissa Hamilton, well, ah—she's asking for the right to continue living in the smaller guesthouse—the one that's not on the listing—rent free for as long as she wants to." Margo rushed on, "I know it's totally weird. Her daughter is trying to get her to move into an assisted living facility but, right now, Mrs. Hamilton sort of comes with the house." She stopped herself. *Rule Five: Don't talk too much.*

For a moment, Dani struggled to get her mind around this strange request. "Is there something wrong with her?" Probably not the right question.

"No. Actually, she has all her marbles, still drives, teaches a quilting class in town. Just eighty-three and stubborn. Sort of intimidating and a bit of a snob, but then having been a state senator's wife probably has something to do with that. Likes to tell people how things should be done. The Senator's been dead three or four years. Both of their sons are also gone, but she has two daughters. Lorraine is local; the other daughter lives in Florida and seems to be estranged from her mother." Undoubtedly too much information.

Dani struggled to stay calm, not to let the news unsettle her. She wasn't in the mood for any more disappointments. She needed a house—needed a life. Before putting her San Diego house on the market, she had coolly analyzed her job options—and running her own bed and breakfast was the most practical, albeit risky, option. Unlike some of the people she'd met at the seminars on How to Run a Successful Bed and Breakfast, owning a B & B had never been something she'd had her heart set on; her heart was too bruised to be set on anything. She was tired of having her emotions shredded—first by her husband and now her son. Surely a house couldn't hurt her.

She chose her words carefully. "That certainly does put a different spin on the situation." Major understatement. Just once, why couldn't something in her life be simple? The house she liked and could afford came with the previous owner. What were the odds?

Dani knew she needed time to decide whether or not she could cope with this Mrs. Hamilton. Rethink everything. Daunting as the information was, having to accept a permanent, nonpaying tenant might work in her favor. She'd definitely need to meet the woman entrenched in the guesthouse before she made an offer. "Are you working tomorrow?"

"Yes, I have floor duty." Since she'd been saddled with the Hamilton listing, Margo'd begun to dread floor duty. She did not need a second albatross.

"I'll call you."

Before Margo could find the words that might save the sale, Dani thanked her for her time and left the office.

Rats. There probably wouldn't be a phone call. She threw out the rest of Dani's coffee, poured herself a fresh cup, and sat at her desk for a while, pretending she was busy. Actually, she was writing out a grocery list. She needed to shop for dinner on her way home. Edward expected his meals served on time. He didn't think she should be selling houses either.

Chapter 2

$\mathcal{D}$ani took the Mass Pike east, paid the exit toll at Springfield, then drove south on I-91 to Enfield. House hunting was stressful, even more stressful when her livelihood was at stake. By now, she should be getting used to stress. In the last three years, she'd faced divorce, entered the work force for the first time, and buried her father. Then, just when she thought she finally had all her ducks in a row, the most important duck moved—literally. In May, her son announced that he wanted to live with his father.

Full time.

On the opposite side of the country.

House-hunting in the Berkshires was driven by her need to make a living as well as wanting to be closer to Spence. Before the divorce, she'd never needed a job, never been especially anxious to have one. She'd dropped out of college when she married Ben and, as soon as he received his commission, they began their gypsy life in the Navy. Moving, moving again and again until they ended up in San Diego when Spence was eight. Going back to finish college never seemed all that important until the divorce made her face the fact that she had absolutely no work experience or college degree, and needed a job. Immediately. She'd suddenly been abandoned in a place without road signs or how-to instructions.

When another Navy wife mentioned that a friend, who owned The Sea Breeze Inn in La Jolla, was looking for an assistant, Dani applied and got the job. It didn't take her long to realize *assistant* really meant woman-of-all-work, preparing breakfast for fifteen when the regular cook didn't show up, handling on-line reservations, ordering supplies and, once, having to fire a maid who was never on time. In those years of long hours and keeping temperamental guests happy, she learned the hospitality business from the ground up and discovered she was pretty good at it.

A few months before the divorce was final, Dani's father passed away suddenly. As executrix of his estate, she spent several months sorting out his affairs, making two cross-country trips, and shedding countless tears as she cleared out his house. On balance, however, the money from selling the house in Enfield gave her enough cash to buy out Ben's share of the house in Pacific Beach so she and Spence didn't have to move. With his share of the equity, Ben bought a condo for himself and Sherry, the twenty-something girlfriend who had been in the picture long before Dani realized her marriage was over. Navy wives were used to being alone when their husbands were at sea but, this time, Ben was gone—permanently. As though being dumped wasn't bad enough, the lawyers moved in to slice and dice what remained of her dignity. When the battles were over, Ben was obligated to pay her five years of alimony, as well as child support until Spence was eighteen. The alimony wasn't even close to being enough to live on.

As soon as home wrecker Sherry became Mrs. Ben Ashcroft, Dani took back her maiden name. Since Ben no longer wanted her, she no longer wanted to be Dani Ashcroft.

Now that Spence was almost fourteen and had chosen to live with his dad, Dani was rearranging her life—again. His announcement at the end of the school year had shocked her—and hurt. She hadn't seen it coming, but then she hadn't seen the divorce coming either. Because Ben was being transferred to the Naval Academy at Annapolis to teach electronics, there'd be no more deployments for awhile. She'd had primary custody of Spence while Ben was assigned to Westpac, serving on ships in the Middle East for six or seven months at a time. When Ben was at sea, his only contact with his son was by phone or e-mail. Spence undoubtedly deserved some up close and personal time with his father. The whole male role model thing. However, recognizing that need didn't make accepting Spence's decision any easier. Every day she missed her son. The sand and salt in his surfing clothes, his surfboard strapped to the roof of her car. His laughter. Sending him to the East Coast all by himself was the hardest thing she'd ever done, and it was tempting to punish him for hurting her. Chapter 6 in the *Bad Mother's Handbook*: "How to Inflict Guilt." The first week after he left, she didn't answer any of his text messages. When she finally calmed down enough to be civil, she lied. "My phone wasn't working."

While she waited for her house to sell, Dani wallowed in self pity. In the weeks after Spence left, she walked and talked as though everything were okay, but inside she was empty, drained of purpose. For fifteen years, she'd been entirely focused on being a wife and/or mother. She couldn't remember who she'd been before Ben and Spence. Now, if she came home late, no one knew. If she ran errands all morning, no one knew exactly where she was or what she was doing, whether she'd been kidnapped or run over in a parking lot. When she wasn't crying or cursing the universe in general, she was throwing out the remnants of her life with Ben under the guise of packing to move, stopping just short of trashing their wedding photos. Someday, a grandchild might want to see them.

The only way to get even with Ben and, *admit it*, with Spence was to survive. And do it well. Without anyone's help. On the day her San Diego house went into escrow, Spence had been in Annapolis for a month.

And so she was looking at Clarissa Hamilton's house.

Thanks to the crazy Southern California real estate market, she'd cleared nearly four hundred thousand from her San Diego house. Though house prices were down, a house at the beach still brought top dollar. Start up cash. The alimony payments would keep her in groceries and gas. Since she no longer had the day-to-day responsibility for anyone else, she would put all her energy into this project, prove she could be successful too. Ben had always been the successful one. She was the one who hadn't finished college, who didn't work. When it suited him, he would throw those facts in her face.

As soon as the San Diego escrow closed, she put her possessions into storage, quit her job at the Inn, bought four new all-weather tires, and drove east.

Until she found the right house, Dani was staying with Abby Janow, her best friend in high school. Abby was still single, working her way up the corporate ladder at the Lego plant near Enfield, and dating her way through the match.com listings of men over 35 and under 50. "I have a spare room. Stay as long as you need to. Who knows, I might even be able to help."

Tonight, the hour plus drive to Connecticut sped by as Dani thought and rethought the reasons she should buy the Hamilton house—and the one big reason she shouldn't.

Abby's initial reaction to the guesthouse tenant was, "How bizarre! There ought to be a way to get rid of her—legally of course. Putting a contract out on her might be unwise."

Dani laughed, "And get me jail time."

"Have you met her?"

"No. I was too tired to deal with the issue this afternoon. I need to think through my next step. On the plus side, I should be able to get her to accept a substantially lower offer. Most buyers wouldn't even think of letting a stranger live on their property—rent free no less. The fact that I'm going to use the house as a business is a little different. The other guesthouse is big enough for me and Spence. Actually it's quite nice; the living room looks out on an English-style cottage garden that's seen better days, and the bedrooms, which are slightly below the living area, overlook the woods on the adjacent lot."

"Sounds like you're talking yourself into it."

"Maybe."

"So tell me what the main house is like."

The following morning, Dani called Margo to arrange an afternoon appointment with Mrs. Hamilton. Margo was amazed that Dani was still interested in buying the house. None of the other people who had looked at the house ever got beyond hearing that Clarissa was part of the deal. Margo lost no time getting someone to cover her floor duty.

To Clarissa, meeting with a potential buyer seemed entirely correct and necessary. After all, if she had to part with her beloved house, she wanted to know who was taking custody. The real estate woman—Margo something-or-other—arrived first, sitting in her Mercedes until another car pulled in behind her. Some type of hatchback, pale blue, maybe four or five years old, with California plates. By the time the women were on her porch, she had the front door open.

"Mrs. Hamilton, good afternoon." Margo took a moment to steady her nerves. "Umm, well, this is Dani Springer." Mrs. Hamilton always made Margo uncomfortable, as though nothing she could say or do would measure up to some invisible Hamilton standard. "She's thinking of making an offer on the house."

Clarissa shook hands with Dani. *Odd name for a woman.* She took stock of the woman's chestnut-colored hair, probably professionally streaked; not much make-up. The same boots and slacks as yesterday but a different jacket. Tasteful and practical.

"Thank you for meeting me, Mrs. Hamilton."

"I understand that you're curious about me. My request is unique. Please," she gestured toward the couch with an intricately designed quilt spread across the back, "have a seat." Clarissa had debated whether she should serve them something but decided that this was not a social occasion. Better to keep them at a distance.

Margo and Dani sat side-by-side on the couch; Clarissa took the upholstered chair opposite and waited to see what *this woman* had to say. She could afford to be polite, even gracious. It was still her house. She always enjoyed having the upper hand.

Dani waded in. "Mrs. Hamilton, I have a couple of questions and concerns about your house. First, is all the furniture in the house part of the sale?" Dani had given it only a cursory glance yesterday, no sense looking at it more closely if some of it was going elsewhere.

"The dining room table and chairs don't— my husband's grandniece wants those. And the antique four-poster in the bedroom with the striped wallpaper goes to my granddaughter, Rose. She's a CPA with a big Boston firm and just got married. Her husband is related to the Kennedys. She paused to emphasize the importance of that relationship. When neither woman responded, "Everything else goes with the house."

"And if there are pieces I can't use?"

Clarissa hesitated. She knew she couldn't very well force *this woman* to keep all the remaining furniture, but telling her to dispose of what she didn't want came hard. These were cherished pieces, each one an integral part of Clarissa's past life. Like the antique writing desk that had belonged to Judd's grandmother. Clarissa had battled Judd's sister for it when his mother's possessions were being divided up. As a result, her sister-in-law had never spoken to her again. Surely *this woman* wouldn't get rid of that.

At some cost, Clarissa forced herself to sound sensible, even disinterested. "You can make whatever decisions you wish." The words nearly caught in her throat.

"Thank you. As I understand it, you want to stay in this guesthouse, rent free."

"I have lived on this property for over half a century. I see no reason to leave." The subtext was clear. *It's my home regardless of whose name is on the title.* "Even when my husband—the Senator—was at The General Court, I lived in Lee, in my house, most of the time."

"Are you comfortable in this guesthouse? It must seem rather small after living in the other house."

"I have many of my treasures around me. I prefer living here to living in that institution my daughter wants to send me to." Clarissa cleared her throat, aware she was giving away more than she intended, inadvertently admitting that she and her daughter were at odds. She always tried to give the impression that her family was perfect. Whether it was or not.

It was time to go on the offensive. "Do you mind if I ask you a question?"

"Of course not."

"Why here? Why Lee? It's a fairly quiet town, even though that awful toll road and those outlet stores are practically on our doorstep. Most people who move to this area prefer Stockbridge or Lenox."

"I know. I grew up in Enfield, across the state line, so I'm familiar with the area. For me, the size and style of the house are more important than its location. Most tourists come to visit the Berkshires, not just a specific town. This house suits my purposes." And pocketbook.

"One more question. You are not wearing a wedding ring. Do you have a family?"

"One son, he'll be fourteen in October. Right now, he's living with his father in Maryland."

"Then isn't my house rather large for you?"

"Not at all. It's just the right size for the bed and breakfast I intend to open."

Surprise registered on both Clarissa's and Margo's faces.

For the briefest of moments, Clarissa wasn't sure she'd heard correctly. *This woman* was going to turn her beautiful house into a *business*! Of all the scenarios she might have imagined once Lorraine had become adamant about putting the house on the market, having someone use it as a business had never occurred to her. This was the house that held her memories, the house she'd helped renovate and decorate numerous times, the rooms in which she'd raised four children, mourned two of them and her husband. Now, strangers—uncaring strangers would be traipsing through her house, looking for a day or two of leisure, their luggage banging against the walls. Clarissa closed her eyes against the picture. Finally, "You're turning my house into a—a *hotel*?"

"A bed and breakfast isn't a hotel."

"I know what a bed and breakfast is. I won't permit it.

"No.

"Never.

"You cannot buy my house."

The instant she'd confessed her plans, Dani watched Mrs. Hamilton's face freeze. The sale just might be dead in the water. Obviously, this woman felt a deep emotional attachment to her home, not something Dani had ever experienced. She'd spent too many years in Navy housing to develop an attachment to any single place. Though she'd been sad when she sold her parents' house, the house she was raised in, that sadness was more about losing her father than about the house itself, and she hadn't been at all sorry to get rid of the house Ben had walked out of. Bottom line, a house was four walls and a roof. Necessary, but nothing to get emotional about.

Dani kept her voice even, searching for words that might defuse the situation, turn it in her favor. "I'm sorry you feel that way. This is a unique house." *A tiny white lie.* "Having guests coming and going would be good for it, keep it alive. No house should stand empty." *Perhaps too smaltzy.* But her other option was screaming, *It's just a house, dammit. Get over it!*

"I will never agree, and I'm certain the Town Planning Board will never allow a business on this street." Clarissa stood up, signaling the meeting was over.

"I checked with the appropriate offices and the County Zoning Commission before I looked at any of the houses Ms. Waters has on her list. There's no problem as long as I follow the town's guidelines for this kind of business." *Pages and pages of guidelines.*

Clarissa set her jaw, glared at Dani, but said nothing.

Checkmate.

The room was deathly quiet as Margo and Dani let themselves out.

Dani followed Margo's Mercedes back to the Krag & Krag office. Once they were again seated at the metal desk, Margo pulled out a packet of legal-sized forms.

"Do you want to put in an offer anyway?"

"You heard her." Dani couldn't hide her disappointment. No other house had caught her interest like this one. She'd spent last night mentally redecorating it.

"I did. I've also had several conversations with the daughter, who actually has Mrs. Hamilton's power of attorney. We're doing business with Lorraine Sessions, not her mother. I suggest we let Lorraine cope with Mrs. Hamilton." Margo sounded surer than she felt, but she desperately needed to sell this house. If that meant taking on Mrs. Hamilton, so be it.

Margo was showing a tougher side than Dani expected. "Do you think I've got a chance?"

"Who knows? It depends on how badly they need to sell the house. It was listed with another agency before they came to us, and no one else has turned in an offer. Are you really all right with the old lady living in the guesthouse?"

"If that's the only way I can buy the house, then yes. How much trouble can she be?"

Margo shrugged. "It's a gamble." Her pen was poised over the forms. "You said you've been pre-approved by the mortgage company?"

"Yes. I contacted them before I left California. I didn't want to run into any surprises. I've also had all my accounts transferred to the Bank of America in Springfield. The financial part shouldn't be a problem. I do, however, want some safety nets in the offer to make sure Mrs. Hamilton can't come back at me if I decide to dig up her garden or re-align the driveway, which I will probably have to do to add the parking spaces the zoning requires. I have a feeling she won't want anything changed. And let's get a building inspector out there as soon as possible.

I don't need to find out, after escrow closes, that the house is ready to fall down." Dani surprised herself. She sounded like a businesswoman, knowledgeable and confident. At this moment, she was anything but confident about this project. Terror didn't begin to describe what she was feeling.

"No problem. Now—is Dani your given name?"

"It's short for Danielle." She spelled it. "Middle name Ann, no e."

Margo began filling in the forms. An offer—even if it fell through—might make encounters with Mr. Krag, Senior easier for a week or two, and she was perversely looking forward to calling Edward to say she'd be late tonight because she was writing up an offer.

Chapter 3

For at least two decades, Clarissa had her hair washed and set every Thursday afternoon at Madeline's Salon in Lenox. But since Lorraine had decreed that Clarissa could only drive in and around Lee, she'd had to settle for Sissy Newcomb at the Snip and Curl on Lee's Main Street. A nuisance. There was no reason she couldn't drive to Lenox, been doing it for more years than Lorraine had been alive. Her daughter was getting bossier and bossier, thinking she had the right to run Clarissa's life. "I've never gotten lost and never had an accident," Clarissa reminded her. It was, of course, the speeding ticket she'd gotten a few months ago that had set Lorraine off—going fifty in a thirty-five mph zone. She'd been late for a bridge game at her friend Natalie's.

The Thursday after the meeting with *that Springer woman*, Clarissa came home to find Lorraine's sensible maroon Buick parked at the curb. Her daughter was all smiles as she walked up the driveway to Clarissa's car, a not-so-sensible black Lexus ES that Judd had bought two years before his heart attack. Something was up.

"Hi, Mom. Your hair looks nice. Sissy does a good job."

Clarissa wasn't fooled. Lorraine wanted something. "Madeline did a better job." Actually, there really wasn't any observable difference, but Clarissa was not about to give Lorraine the satisfaction. Better to keep her off balance. Lorraine tugged at the shoulder strap on her purse—a clear sign of nerves. Best guess, *that woman* had made an offer on the house.

"Let's go inside, Mom. I've been on my feet all day, and I had playground duty besides." Once they were inside, "We have an offer on the house."

Clarissa pulled out a chair at the small dining room table and sat down. Trying not to be unnerved by her mother's silence, Lorraine took a sheaf of papers from her purse and took the chair facing Clarissa, who was rather enjoying Lorraine's discomfort. She should be uncomfortable—the whole idea of selling the house was hers.

Adjusting her reading glasses, Lorraine studied the papers in front of her and began explaining the major points. "The purchase is contingent on a satisfactory report by a certified building inspector. He'll be here tomorrow or Saturday." She turned the page. "You can continue to live in this guesthouse for as long as you wish. You're lucky she agreed to that. Not many people would. However, the offer is fifty thousand under our current asking price. That is much too low." She looked up, "The rest of this paperwork details who will handle the title search and the escrow."

Clarissa had heard enough. Lorraine was acting as though the only problem with the offer was the amount of money. It was time to put a stop to this farce. "I made it quite clear to *her* that I refuse to sell my house so she can turn it into—a boarding house. I'll not have it. I want you to reject the offer!"

"It's the only offer we've had."

"What's your hurry?"

"It's been on the market for nearly six months. You aren't made of money."

"Your father left plenty for me to live on."

"No he didn't."

"Of course he did. When he went into politics, he had your Uncle Harold invest the profits from the sale of the company so there would be no question about a conflict of interest. He got an extremely good price. Then there's his pension from The General Court and the life insurance."

"He sold the company over twenty-five years ago. Inflation has crept up and up, and after the recent downturn in the market, there's not much of the original capital left. We both know Dad wasn't the most frugal person, and The Court's retirement for a beneficiary isn't all that much. You've already used up most of the insurance money. There's his social security and the house. You definitely need the money from this sale."

"I do not."

"I can show you the figures. The investment firm sends you statements every quarter. Don't you ever look at them? It's all there in black and white. If you have to move someplace else—well, there isn't enough money." Lorraine's face was flushed with the need, once again, to convince her mother that selling the house was necessary.

"I'm not moving anyplace, thank you. Refuse the offer."

"I've already made a counter offer."

"You can't do that without my permission."

"You know I can. I have your power of attorney."

"Lorraine, I demand that you refuse the offer."

"Too late, Mom. I countered at twenty thousand less than the asking price. I'm waiting to see whether there's another counter offer." This was one of the few times Lorraine had ever faced her mother down. She usually ignored Clarissa's decrees or figured out how to circumvent them.

Clarissa stood up—almost overturning her chair. "We'll just see about that."

If they'd been in the living room of the big house, Clarissa would have been able to make a more eloquent exit, striding up the stairs to make her point. In this dressed-up workshop, however, all she could do was walk into the bedroom and slam the door. No eloquence in that. More like a teenage tantrum. Unfortunately, Lorraine held the trump hand this time.

As soon as she heard Lorraine's car drive away, Clarissa walked over to the house and spent the rest of the afternoon in the living room, sitting in Judd's old leather chair, the shades pulled against the late summer sun—and against defeat. She detested losing.

She should never have given Lorraine her power of attorney. But then, Clarissa had done several idiotic things during that terrible period after Judd died because she hadn't been functioning very well. All the bits and pieces of settling Judd's estate had been turned over to her daughter because she was good at dealing with paperwork, and Clarissa had willingly signed over the power of attorney. Until now, Lorraine had always been the reliable daughter, returning to Lee after college and teaching in the elementary school. Just before her thirty-fifth birthday, she'd married a pharmacist who was ten years older and had been married before. Grant Sessions already had three grown children and didn't want any more, so Lorraine kept her teaching job and, since Judd's death, interfered in Clarissa's life. But at least Lorraine was here. Not like Aileen, who had come home the day of Judd's funeral and flown back to Florida the same evening. Supposedly, she had to get back to her business, something to do with wholesale beauty supplies.

As soon as the young Hamilton family took title to the house, Clarissa became obsessed with making it presentable. Finally something she could be proud of.

She insisted that Judd immediately send a couple of his workmen over to paint. She was determined the house would be the envy of her family and friends. Despite its rundown condition, she would transform it into a showplace. She chose pastel colors for the downstairs rooms. Massachusetts' winters were long and dark, no sense having dark walls too. Judd had initially been appalled that she'd had the living room painted a pale mauve. It was too close to pink for his taste, but he stopped complaining after their second confrontation about it and gave in. Since they'd bought the house, he was discovering that his wife—once so willing to please him—had become harder to deal with. It was simpler to let her have her way.

Clarissa converted the room on the right side of the entry hall into her sewing room. The one skill she'd acquired from her mother was sewing and, since her parents had scrimped to buy her the best Singer machine on the market as a wedding present, she intended to use it. She spent weeks pleating and lining the drapes for the living and dining rooms. The slipcovers for the old couch Judd's aunt had given them for their apartment were more complicated, but she was pleased with the results. Even though they didn't have much furniture yet, Clarissa was determined to use what they had until it could be replaced with good quality pieces. No more second hand.

When she met her high school friends in town, all she could talk about was the house.

Judd's building me the most wonderful sunroom—it'll be perfect in winter.

Judd's going to put in a bathroom or two upstairs.

Judd has promised to add a room in the attic for a housekeeper. It's such a big house. He doesn't want me to work too hard.

She'd spent most of her school years envying the clothes and boyfriends of the other girls and, of course, their houses. Now, she had a handsome husband with a good business and a house that would eventually be a graceful swan. She talked about the house morning, noon and night—and thought about little else. Even Matthew got less of her attention. One night, Judd accused her of thinking about the house while they were having sex. Her tears forced him to apologize, but he'd actually been right. She'd been debating whether the curtains in the kitchen should be yellow or white. What puzzled her was how Judd had known.

By the time they moved in, Matthew was walking and Clarissa was two months pregnant with JT. When she was seven months along, she cajoled her mother and older sister into giving her a shower so this baby would have new clothes of its own. Clarissa insisted on having the party in her house. It would give her an opportunity to show it off. She would have been too embarrassed to invite her friends to her parents' house with its worn furniture and faded wallpaper.

Judd still hadn't put in the upstairs bathrooms, but the sunroom was nearly finished and the exterior had a fresh coat of paint—white with dark green trim.

She borrowed some extra straight-backed chairs from her friends and polished the staircase railing until it was gleaming. They had a new dining room set with six ladder back chairs, and she'd made the last payment on the Turkish rug that was on layaway in Pittsfield.

"Honey, you need to pick up the rug before the party. I want the living room to look perfect."

"I do have a company to run," Judd complained. "We're pouring the foundation for a new barn at the Carmichaels' farm."

As though she hadn't heard him, "Maybe you should go on Saturday."

Chapter 4

*E*very other Saturday afternoon, Evan Murray took care of Clarissa Hamilton's yard. Last night, she'd left a message on his voice mail, instructing him—she never asked—to stop by her place today before he began working.

He'd taken on this job as a favor to his cousin Sam, who was fed up with her interference and complaints. Understandable that she and Sam were a bad combination. Because he had a wife and three kids to support, Sam was always trying to cram too many jobs into too few hours, and Mrs. Hamilton was always finding something extra for him to do without paying him.

Evan, however, had learned not to hurry. Two years in three different Third World countries working on open space projects had taught him the value of slow and steady. And unlike Sam, taking care of other people's yards was a sideline. He had only three customers—Mrs. Hamilton, his Aunt Joanna and his high school drafting teacher—and no family of his own to take care of. Instead of joining a gym, he did these yards. Cutting, trimming, fertilizing and weeding gave him time to think through whatever more complex landscape design projects were waiting for him in his studio south of town.

When he pulled into the Hamilton driveway, Mrs. Hamilton was sitting on her small front porch. He noticed a Sale Pending sign attached to the For Sale sign that had been in the front lawn for several months. Change was afoot.

"Good afternoon, Mrs. Hamilton," he rested his elbows on the low porch railing so he was at eye level with her.

"Thank you for being on time. Your cousin was never on time."

"Has someone bought the property?"

"Trying to." Her answer was crisp, discouraging further questions. "That is not what I want to talk to you about." When she stood up, he realized she was wearing denim slacks and a pair of canvas sneakers. She was usually dressed more formally. "I want you to rework my flower garden." Without waiting for his response, she headed toward the tangle of dead flowers and weeds that had once been her pride and joy. At its center was a small pond spanned by a decorative wooden bridge with fading red paint. "The pond and bridge need repair, and I would also welcome your ideas about what flowers to plant. I realize September isn't the time for planting but, if you could clear away what has died off and get the ground ready for planting in the spring, I would appreciate it. I don't seem to have the heart for it this year. Of course I will pay for your time. I want to make sure the garden is properly cared for; no telling what someone else might do to it. I trust you."

Evan held back the smile that tugged at the corners of his mouth. It wasn't so much that she trusted him, more that she didn't trust the new owners to take care of the garden. Predictably, she hadn't asked whether he had the time to do the extra work.

"If the house is sold, won't you be moving?"

"No. I'll be staying."

He considered asking whether she'd checked with the buyer but, in his experience, she did not always welcome questions. Instead, he gave her the answer she wanted. "I'll be glad to rework the garden. Give me time to figure out what's already here. I'll fit the project around my other jobs."

"No hurry." She had stopped alongside the pond. "The bridge needs painting."

"Some of the wood also needs to be replaced," he reached over and poked at the railing with his pocket knife. "Would you like me to design a new one for you?"

"Of course not. My husband built the bridge. I like the way it looks." She had a knack of closing off further discussion. Not an easy woman to do business with.

She spent the next half hour giving him a detailed history of what had been planted, what had failed, what had succeeded. In the time he'd worked for her, he'd never seen her so animated—almost likable.

"Do you know who the buyers are?"

"Buyer." Her voice sharpened. "*Some woman* from California who wants to turn it into a bed and breakfast." With that, she left Evan in the garden and returned to her guesthouse. He spent a few minutes taking measurements and making notes to himself on the pad he always carried.

He didn't envy the woman from California.

It was nearly dinnertime when he finished mowing and edging, and had pruned the roses bordering the deck and the front porch. He bought some ground beef and hamburger buns at the grocery store in Lee and headed south on Highway 7 to Murray Farms. While he was working abroad, his Grandmother Murray had died, leaving him this farm where his grandparents had raised him. When he returned from the last of his overseas jobs and started his landscape design business, he'd converted the old post and beam barn into a studio/workshop, installing state of the art drafting and computer design equipment, adding oversize windows so he'd have good light, even in winter, and then built himself a loft apartment upstairs. He was accustomed to living in small spaces. If he wanted to work in the middle of the night, all he had to do was go downstairs. He'd turned the greenhouses over to Sam and was renting the farmhouse to a family with three kids and innumerable pets. The house rent paid the property taxes, and he liked knowing there was someone on the premises when he had to be out of town.

Friends and family were always telling him he should open a proper office in town and hire clerical help, maybe even an apprentice so that he could concentrate on doing bigger design projects. But having a staff would only make his business and his life more complicated. He usually took on only one project at a time, doing all the designing as well as ordering the materials, hiring the crew, and overseeing the construction. Keeping a construction crew and clerical help on salary would push him to accept jobs just to meet the payroll. He simply wanted to focus on designing and then building what he designed. A bigger and more successful company was not part of his plan. When he finished a job, he usually took time off, hiking in the summer, skiing in the winter. Last year, he'd spent a month driving through Europe, visiting public gardens, studying the architecture and sculptures, storing ideas for future designs. Burying himself in his craft kept him from touching the pieces of the past that were still tender.

He fried a couple of hamburger patties, added onion slices, cheese, and plenty of mustard. He'd forgotten to buy tomatoes and lettuce. Hamburgers were his food of choice, one of the foods he'd missed when he was living in countries whose basic diet consisted of various rice and vegetable mixtures.

While he was eating, he sketched what he remembered of Clarissa Hamilton's bridge, then drew his own version. He just might get away with convincing her to make some changes, maybe add a mosaic to the surface of the pond. The garden rehab would be an interesting diversion so long as she didn't monitor his every move. Of course, he'd probably have to discuss his plans with the new owner.

As soon as the building inspector's report came in the mail, Margo called Dani's cell phone. "I have the results, and I've talked to the inspector about his findings. He also gave me the name of a local contractor you might want to use—bonded, trustworthy, and able to go to work whenever you're ready. I can meet you at the house at your convenience."

"How about one o'clock tomorrow?"

Abby begged to tag along. "I have scads of vacation time, and I'm dying to see the house."

Margo's car was already in the driveway so Dani parked at the curb; thankfully, Mrs. Hamilton's Lexus was gone. Dani had worried that her prospective tenant would be peering through the curtains, watching every move they made.

"Margo, this is my friend Abby."

Margo extended her hand. "Glad you came along. We can always use another pair of eyes for a walk through." She handed a copy of the report to Dani and opened her own copy. "Given the age of the house, it's actually a better report than I expected, but there are some problems." She paused, in case Dani wanted to ask a question, then went on. "Let's start with the porch." Dani and Abby dutifully followed her.

"Because you're going to have a greater liability with paying guests, he evaluated the house from an insurance company's point of view. With that in mind, the porch will have to be completely redone."

"But I love the fretwork and the balustrade."

Rule Six: Empathize with the buyer.

"I do too. Maybe it can be replicated, but this porch isn't safe—some of the posts and floorboards are rotten and the balustrade is loose in several places. He says it's too dangerous in the long run."

Of all things, the porch! Dani loved the way it looked. *Damn and double damn.* Then she reminded herself that she'd been the one insisting on the inspection. Be careful what you ask for. She took a deep breath, trying to locate her confidence. "What's next?"

When Margo left two hours later, Dani was exhausted and depressed. She'd known the inspection would uncover flaws, every house had them, but not this many. Besides the porch, the wiring had to be brought up to code and a new breaker box installed. There was some termite damage in the attic and, because there was water damage in one of the upstairs bathrooms, part of one wall would have to be replaced. She'd need a new commercial size water heater, and a new heating and air-conditioning unit. Dani had expected the kitchen would have to be completely upgraded and that everything inside and out would have to be painted. All the wallpaper would have to go, the floors sanded down and refinished. At least, the roof had another ten years in it.

Her cottage—she'd fallen into the habit of calling both guesthouses cottages—was in good shape except for the shower head and the bathroom faucet. A major outdoor project would be the grassy area behind Clarissa's cottage. For each guest room, Dani needed to have one parking space and, of course, she and Clarissa each needed one since Clarissa could no longer block the driveway with her car. In addition to the lot itself, the existing driveway, which presently ended at Clarissa's cottage, would be extended and curved into the asphalt pad at the back. New shrubs and trees would eventually hide it from the guests sitting on the deck or strolling in the garden.

Long after Margo drove off, Dani and Abby sat in the car, staring at the house. It wasn't just the renovation that was unraveling Dani's confidence. Now that the inspection was over, she'd have to decide whether to commit her money and her life to this house which, until a week ago, she'd never seen. Owning a house this size and creating a business—a 24/7 business at that—was on the verge of being terrifyingly real. *Dani Springer, this is your new life. Are you up for it?*

"Now I'm getting scared." Dani fingered the contractor's business card, imagining the thousands of dollars all this work would add up to.

"Having cold feet is natural. If it's any help, I like the house. Not elaborate—but very comfortable. Lots of possibilities, great staircase." Abby grinned at Dani. "You can do it. Remember when all our posters for the senior prom got wet because there was a leak in the gym roof, and you stayed up all night redoing them so we could put them up the next morning?"

"Yeah, so?" Dani hadn't thought of that night in years. She'd been totally exhausted the next day, but triumphant. It had been a long time since she'd felt that kind of satisfaction.

"That's the Dani who wants to make this house into a successful business. Not the Dani whose husband convinced her that his success was more important than anything she might do. You've been treading water for years. At the risk of mixing metaphors, it's time to turn a page."

Dani sighed. "This is way bigger than dance posters but thanks for reminding me. I've missed you Abby."

"Me too, been much too long. I'm glad you've come home."

"I'm starving; let's find something totally unhealthy and fattening. If ever there was a time for comfort food, this is it. Then I guess I should make an appointment with the contractor to find out just how much this will cost."

Backing out of the deal would be letting Ben and Spence win, and she'd feel even worse about herself. Right now, there was nothing else she wanted or knew how to do. Fear was doing battle with pride. For the moment, pride was winning, but it was a close call. She would be responsible for everything. No back up, no safety net. Walking a high wire. The only other comparable risk she'd taken was marrying Ben, and look how well that turned out.

As they were pulling away from the house, Dani saw Mrs. Hamilton's car turn into the driveway. They'd escaped in the nick of time. While she was in the midst of second guessing herself, she didn't need a conversation with her nonpaying tenant.

Later, Dani called Margo to report that she had an appointment with the contractor and, in spite of the repairs that had to be made— and the hollow terror that had taken up residence in her stomach— she wanted to go ahead with the purchase. To turn the page. Dani agreed to counter Lorraine's offer by offering five thousand more than the first offer. Take it or leave it.

Her meeting with Jacob Hilldebrand, the contractor Margo had found, went well. Dani was satisfied that she could work with him and, before she changed her mind about anything, she notified the San Diego storage company to ship her possessions. Even before escrow closed, Jacob would have access to her cottage so that the inside painting and repairs would be done by the time her furniture arrived. Once she had a place that was hers, she'd feel better.

Maybe.

While she waited for the paperwork to move through the system, she and Abby spent hours with paint chips and wallpaper samples. Jacob drew up plans for the kitchen, suggesting she add a walk-in pantry as well as space for a second refrigerator. Even though she would only be serving breakfast and light snacks in the afternoon, she'd need plenty of storage.

When he gave her the estimate for the renovation, which included the cabinets and new kitchen appliances, Dani gasped—silently. The twenty percent down payment on the house, as well as the fees and permits the town required, insurance premiums, especially the liability, and what the contractor estimated his work would cost, added up to over half of what she'd realized from the house sale. And she hadn't started advertising, furnishing the rooms, or making monthly mortgage payments. Ben's alimony check would have to cover her personal expenses. She couldn't afford to live on her capital.

Abby volunteered to set up the web page—a necessity for on-line reservations—and install the business programs in Dani's computer, once it arrived with the furniture. "Those are things I do at work all the time. Piece of cake. Your computer will probably need more memory and the house should have a wireless set up so guests can use their computers even though they're supposed to be on vacation. Have you decided on a business name?"

Dani shook her head. "Any ideas?"

"As a matter of fact, yes. How about The Maples? Those trees in the front yard are gorgeous. As soon as they turn red, I want to take some pictures to use on the web page." Clearly, Abby was excited about the house.

"Not bad. I'll think about it. I've got to visit Spence before all hell breaks loose around here." Even though it would probably be painful, she needed to see him in his new surroundings. She didn't want to be angry about his wanting to live with Ben, yet she was.

It had been nearly four months since Spence left San Diego. She longed to talk to him face-to-face—not on the phone, in e-mails or text messages—she needed to make sure he was okay, get a sense of what he thought about her plans. He only knew she was looking at houses near her hometown.

When Dani called Ben to check on Spence's schedule, he ruled out the upcoming weekend because Spence was going to a soccer camp. How about the following weekend? So she and Abby spent Saturday and Sunday at second hand furniture stores, searching for pieces that would fit in with her furniture and Clarissa's. In answer to a saleswoman's questions about the style she was looking for, Dani explained, "I'm aiming for eclectic with bold Southwest colors." She was pretty sure the woman thought she was slightly mad. New England usually did New England.

The following Friday morning, she boarded the Amtrak at Springfield. Cheaper than flying. As soon as she arrived in Baltimore, she rented a car, drove to Annapolis, and checked into the Holiday Express. Once she'd eaten, she called Spence, arranging to pick him up the next morning at the house Ben was renting.

Spence was sitting on the porch steps when she pulled up in front of the two-story brick house. Tears blurred her first view of him. When he stood up, she could tell he'd grown. So quickly, he was different. His hair was shorter; his military father probably hadn't approved of the shaggy surfer style Spence had always fought to keep.

Knowing he didn't like being hugged, she briefly kissed his cheek. "You've grown a foot or two." She was trying to coax a smile out of him and got one.

"My new soccer shoes are a half size larger."

Because Ben and Sherry were conveniently someplace else, she took a tour of Spence's room. Ben had bought him new bedroom furniture and, instead of surfing posters, now there were soccer posters. On the wall above the computer he'd brought from California was a new flat screen TV. Ben was becoming an indulgent father, trying to make up for all the time they hadn't spent together since the divorce.

Spence seemed hesitant with her—the whole "I want to live with Dad" confrontation in May had left scars on both of them. Before that ugly afternoon, she and Spence had usually been on good terms, but her distress over his decision changed that. He had been on the plane before she had time to repair the damage. Once he was at Ben's, their phone conversations and e-mails were on safe topics, informational only:

> I've sold the house.
>
> *I'm taking Geometry, History, English, P.E. and Chemistry.*
>
> I'm moving back to New England.
>
> *Can you send my skis and winter clothes?*
>
> I'm looking at houses in the Berkshires.
>
> *I made the soccer team.*
>
> I bought a house in Lee, Massachusetts.

Necessary conversation, but not comfortable conversation. She could tell that he had settled in for the long haul. Any fantasy she might have that he'd be unhappy away from her and want to move back was just that—fantasy. Huge losses in the last three years—her father, her husband and Spence.

He would be fourteen in a week. For his birthday, she'd bought him CD's of some of his favorite bands and a warm fleece pullover. An East Coast winter would be something of a shock to this Southern California surfer.

Spence showed her around the Naval Academy campus; then they had lunch in the historic downtown and later drove by his high school. She'd brought pictures of the house and cottage to make sure he knew there would be a place for him with her, that the changes in her life wouldn't exclude him—though his new life necessarily excluded her. She'd lost the chance to watch his soccer games, make sure his homework was done, buy his soccer shoes.

He asked polite questions about the town, studied the pictures, let her explain her plans, but a two-story house in a place called Lee had nothing to do with his day-to-day life—not really.

"Your dad agreed you could be with me at Christmas." But only after a long argument, with her reminding him they still had shared custody.

"That's great." His tone, however, didn't sound like traipsing off to Western Massachusetts would be all that great. He was already making friends in Annapolis. Ben had promised him a ski trip at Thanksgiving if the resorts had snow. Not fair. She couldn't afford those kinds of luxuries right now. Divorce was never 50/50. In this case, more like 30/70, and she was definitely the thirty.

By the end of the afternoon, she gave up hoping he'd missed her and wanted to come back. Leaving Annapolis wasn't on his agenda. He probably hadn't stopped loving her; he just didn't need her right now. Unfortunately, she still needed him. Mothering didn't have a shut off valve. Disappointment washed over her.

That evening, he was attending a birthday party for one of his soccer teammates, so she retreated to her motel room, making to-do lists and feeling sorry for herself. On Sunday morning, she drove back to Baltimore and caught the train to Springfield.

When she got to Abby's, it was almost seven. She made herself a sandwich and finished the rice salad she found in the refrigerator, complaining, "I don't have any part in his life."

"It's probably only temporary—everything in Annapolis is new and exciting. Keep in mind you had him almost exclusively for three years."

"You're right. But I don't feel like being fair or rational."

"What else would you do? Move to Annapolis and force the equal custody? He certainly can't move back and forth between Lee and Annapolis during the school year."

"I know." She really did know.

"You certainly don't want to move to Annapolis and stand around, waiting for him to pay attention to you. That really would make you pathetic. And in two years, Ben might be transferred again. Then what?"

"You can stop being right any time now."

"You need a life he can come to—if he chooses. Don't make it a contest."

"But why does Ben get to have him, like a reward for cheating on our marriage?"

"At least you had a marriage and still have a child. I have a good job—so good that there are several wannabes snapping at my heels, ready to grab it if I mess up. Let's see, oh yeah, a brother who packed up his family and moved to Florida. My life is equally pathetic. Sorry, I know this isn't about me."

Dani put her plate in the dishwasher. "We're a miserable pair. Was there a category for losers in the senior yearbook?"

Abby changed the subject. "Margo called this afternoon. She said you weren't answering your cell."

"I was probably on the train. What's wrong?"

"Nothing. Escrow will close on Friday."

"Good. My stuff should be here any day."

Chapter 5

The week after escrow closed, Clarissa erased each message Lorraine left on her voice mail, though she knew that her daughter would eventually drive over to give her hell for not calling her back. Sunday morning, in spite of Lorraine's decree about not driving beyond Lee, Clarissa phoned Natalie Wise and made a date for lunch. If Lorraine discovered Clarissa had driven to Lenox, she would be furious. Precisely the response Clarissa was looking for. She was determined not to forgive Lorraine for ignoring her wishes and letting the house sale go through. Next week, she planned to make an appointment with her lawyer to get her power of attorney back. But, of course, the house was already gone.

Clarissa couldn't admit to Natalie that the house had been sold without her consent. Could not. Most of her adult life, the house had been an integral part of who she was—her skin. Not owning it made her feel like she'd disappeared. She and Natalie spent their two hour lunch discussing the upcoming bridge tournament and Clarissa's quilting class, exchanging gossip about mutual friends, and complaining about the price of almost everything.

Natalie was a petite, fragile-looking woman with a voice that always seemed as though it should belong to someone much larger. "My son says that whatever prices you were used to when you were in your thirties are the prices you expect everything to be today. I still assume a loaf of bread costs twenty-five cents." Divorced once and widowed once, she had just turned eighty and was living with her daughter's family.

A few years ago, to save on expenses, Natalie had finally let her hair go gray. Clarissa thought it made her look ninety, at least, and promised herself she would never let her own hair go gray, regardless of the cost.

As they lingered over dessert, she turned the conversation back to quilting, something Natalie knew little about, so Clarissa could rattle on without competition.

She drove back to Lee just before dark to find a large, yellow moving van with California plates parked in front of her house. No one was around. Obviously, *that woman* was moving into the other guesthouse. Clarissa pulled into the driveway and hurried inside so she didn't have to look at the ugly vehicle that signaled the invasion of the enemy. She remembered when JT died and the priest had visited the family to counsel them in their grief. *When someone dies, first comes shock, then denial, anger and ultimately acceptance.* Over the years, Clarissa had come to agree that those stages did, indeed, follow tragedy—after all, she'd buried two sons and a husband. Now she was grieving for her house. She was probably in the denial phase. If she didn't look, it wasn't happening.

There was another message from Lorraine on the answering machine. "I'm coming over after school tomorrow because we need to go to the bank. You can't stonewall me forever."

Of all her children, Clarissa had loved JT the best. He had her eyes and his father's build, but his personality was all his own. He was curious about everything, loved everyone and, once he smiled, everyone loved him too. The year he was seven, he'd charmed her into letting him keep the Collie puppy he found in a vacant lot. It was hard to refuse JT. When Matthew complained that he should also have a dog, she was trapped into taking him to the animal shelter to choose his own, an eight year old Beagle that he named Herman. Two dogs in one week.

JT was the risk taker who would jump off of or into anything, making fun of his more cautious brother, who was given to analyzing his every move. Having two older brothers who enjoyed making her life miserable, Lorraine quickly learned to stick up for herself and get even when they were least expecting it. But when Aileen came along, Lorraine changed her allegiance, usually siding with her brothers against the baby of the family. Clarissa refused to think about Aileen. Scarlett O'Hara wasn't the only one who could ignore painful topics.

Judd was never one to help take care of the children or clean up after the dogs. Not part of his job description. He expected Clarissa to handle the household and have the kids sorted out when he got home so he could enjoy them. After Lorraine's birth, Clarissa started pressuring Judd about his promise to install a bathroom upstairs, maybe two. She was sick and tired of taking the kids up and down the stairs in the middle of the night. Judd finally made good on his promise, deciding that every bedroom would have its own bathroom. Effectively shutting down Clarissa's complaints. He used the original walk-in closets in each bedroom and took a little extra space from the rooms themselves to make each bathroom en suite, then built modern closets with sliding doors. Each of the girls had her own bathroom, the boys shared a bedroom and bath, and Clarissa and Judd had a slightly larger bathroom with double sinks. If Clarissa's friends had been envious of her house before, four and a half bathrooms made her the talk of the town. Judd turned the original bathroom downstairs into a half bath, using the rest of the space for a laundry room. Clarissa was always doing a load of washing.

By the time Aileen was born in 1955, most of the major renovations on the house were complete. The attic also had a bedroom and bath, which they used as a guest room for a few years, then as a room for the live-in housekeeper they hired because taking care of such a big house and four children had increased the level of Clarissa's nagging.

Judd had always assumed one of his sons would come into the business: Hamilton and Son—or Sons—Construction. But Matt's decision to study law and JT's death destroyed that dream and, by the mid-seventies, Judd was losing interest in the company. Two years after JT died, Judd decided to run for Town Selectman and, four years later, ran for senator of The General Court in Boston. When he won the seat for Berkshire, Hampshire and Franklin counties, he sold Hamilton Construction. As usual, Clarissa hadn't been consulted but, because being married to a state senator would provide more status than being married to a building contractor, she didn't protest. Instead, she bought herself a new wardrobe and set about decorating the condo he'd leased in Boston.

She didn't, however, enjoy her new role nearly as much as she'd expected. In the hierarchy of senators' wives, she was the new wife on the block and would have to earn her way into the inner circle. After a few months in the condo overlooking the Charles River, trying without much success to make friends, she told Judd she was moving back to Lee where being a senator's wife had more clout—and she at least had a few friends. He didn't argue.

The loss of his second son pushed Judd even deeper into the legislative world. His outgoing personality and reliability, qualities that had made his business a success, earned him seats on the important Court committees. For the rest of his years at The Court, he divided his time between Boston, when the legislature was in session, and Lee, to fulfill commitments to his constituents and make the prescribed social rounds. Clarissa was very good at hosting teas and smiling for publicity shots. And when he was up for reelection, she was at his side, the dutiful senator's wife. It was during those years that he built the guesthouses so he could entertain colleagues and constituents. If Judd needed her to be visible at formal Court events, she drove to Boston. They had a long distance marriage even before the term was coined. Clarissa often wondered whether he saw other women. He was still good looking, his dark red hair just beginning to show some gray, and in good weather he played tennis two or three times a week.

Rather than watch *that woman* move in, Clarissa got up at six and was at The Sewing Basket by seven. She let herself in with her own key and began working on the appliqués for next Monday's class.

Dani was at the house at eight to meet the movers. She'd been too keyed up to sleep. Since there was so much work to do inside the house, she had the movers put everything other than the furnishings for her cottage in the basement of the main house. She hoped it didn't flood in wet weather. Mrs. Hamilton could answer that question, but her car wasn't in the driveway. Dani also needed to know when the dining room table and chairs and the four-poster were going to be moved out. Perhaps, she could ask Margo to call Lorraine about both issues and skip Clarissa altogether.

It was nearly three o'clock when the van was completely unloaded and Dani signed off on the delivery. She had a home again, smaller than the San Diego house, but a home nonetheless. Hoping the packing boxes had been marked accurately, she opened the one that said linens, made up her bed, took a shower, then drove into town for something to eat. Unpacking the boxes that said kitchen would be pushing her energy level. Besides, some of the kitchen equipment would eventually be going into the main house, and she wasn't ready to make those decisions.

Tomorrow morning, Abby would drive over from Enfield. She was taking vacation time to help with the move-in. "I'm as excited about your project as if it were my own. I didn't realize how boring my life has been. I want to play too."

With Abby's help, the unpacking went quickly, not quite play but enjoyable. Once the cottage was put together, they started getting the main house ready for Jacob's crew. They took down all the drapes and began stripping wallpaper off the living room walls. It would save the painters time and maybe save Dani money. She couldn't decide whether to buy plantation shutters or vertical blinds for the downstairs windows, but she definitely wasn't replacing the curtains. Since she wasn't going after a period look, contemporary styles would be easier to keep clean. She was fairly sure she didn't want to hang new wallpaper downstairs, but guests would probably expect wallpaper and curtains in the bedrooms. A cozier look. It had been several years since she'd done any decorating. She'd forgotten how much she liked visualizing the way a room should look and then making it happen. Abby went back to Enfield Sunday night, promising to return the following weekend to work on the upstairs bedrooms.

Monday afternoon, Dani noticed a man in a dark blue windbreaker crouched alongside the pond in the garden. Clarissa was standing beside him, a shawl pulled around her. He was holding a sketch pad, showing her something about the bridge that spanned the pond. When he stood up, Dani could see he was tall, wearing hiking boots and much-washed Levi's. Clarissa was smiling up at him.

Curious, Dani joined them in the garden. "Hello."

Clarissa's smile disappeared. No surprise there. The tall man who could make Clarissa smile, smiled at Dani. A slightly crooked smile that began at the right corner of his mouth, then slowly lit his face. She smiled back, taking note of his burnt sienna eyes and the thick auburn hair that tumbled over his head in no particular style.

"Hi. I'm Evan Murray."

"Dani Springer."

They shook hands; he held hers for just a fraction of a second longer than she expected.

"You're the new owner."

"Guilty."

"I promised Mrs. Hamilton I'd rework the garden. I'm trying to convince her to let me change the design of the bridge," he handed Dani the sketch pad, "and resurface the pond with a mosaic of crushed glass or maybe broken tiles—jazz it up a little."

Dani compared his drawing to the old bridge. "Your bridge has a more graceful arc. I like it." Those sienna eyes roamed her face, perhaps checking to see whether her comment was sincere. Her eyes assured him it was.

The dialogue their eyes were having was interrupted by Clarissa. "I don't want anything changed." Her voice was close to petulant.

"Mrs. Hamilton isn't a fan of changing things." Did Clarissa know he was teasing her? Probably not.

"Change can be a good thing."

Clarissa was not about to be sidelined, "Don't talk about me as though I were not here. Since I'm paying him to do this, what it looks like is my business." Clarissa clipped off the words.

"But it's on my property so it's my business too, and I like his new design for the bridge." It was time to assert herself; otherwise, Clarissa might assume she could treat her like an inferior being. "A mosaic would be beautiful."

"I saw a pond last week that had a mosaic of flowers—kind of a complement to the real ones surrounding it."

Clarissa frowned, obviously annoyed that he agreed with her enemy. He bestowed another smile on her. "Do you trust me to make the garden look better than any other garden for miles around?"

Dani wanted to laugh. He knew how to smooze Clarissa, play to her snobbery. Clarissa's body language shifted imperceptibly.

"Of course, but—"

"Then let me do what you hired me to do." The smoozing stopped.

Clarissa didn't answer right away, then raised her chin ever so slightly. "Fine, but don't destroy my husband's bridge."

"Where do you want me to—"

Without waiting for him to finish, she almost marched back to her cottage.

Watching Clarissa cross the lawn, Dani had to give her style points. "Great exit. I suppose she expects me to store the damned bridge in the basement."

"Probably."

"She's driving me nuts, peering out her window, watching everything I do, parking her car in the middle of the driveway so I have to park on the street."

"She's not easy."

"I'm discovering that. What are you going to do with the garden itself? I hope it'll have paths for my guests."

"It will." He briefly outlined his plans, which included two short paths and a bench so the guests could sit and enjoy the flowers in comfort. "Of course, I can't plant anything until spring, but I want to work on the pond and the bridge when I have free time this winter, get the ground ready for planting. I have some ideas I'd like to experiment with."

"And she's paying for it?" One thing off her list.

"That's what she said. When I started taking care of the yard in the spring, she wouldn't let me touch this garden. But it's obviously gotten to be too much for her, so she gave in and asked for help."

"Because she figures I'd wreck it."

"That too." Now he was teasing her. She liked that.

Though she was enjoying their conversation, she needed to be in Pittsfield. She glanced at her watch, "I have to go. I look forward to seeing how my garden turns out."

"Better not let her hear you say *my*. She still thinks it's hers."

"Okay, it's hers until she pays you. Do you have a business card?"

He reached into his shirt pocket and pulled out a leather card case. "Nice to meet you Dani Springer."

Chapter 6

Dani had forgotten that the weather was such a major topic of conversation in the Northeast—life dictated by Mother Nature. Everywhere she went, the Berkshire locals were complaining about the poor fall color. Not like last year. Last year had been perfect.

Everyone had a theory: It had stayed warm too late, there hadn't been enough rain in August, and of course global warming. The pundits were right about the poor quality of the colors. The leaves changed slowly, the yellows taking their time, the reds arriving only after the yellows and golds had faded to a dull brown. Bad timing all round; thus, fewer leaf peepers than usual. The tourist trade was hurting.

As long as the weather didn't interfere with the construction on the house, Dani didn't care about the color—this year. Next year, she'd be watching the fall foliage reports too. The weather watchers were also predicting a hard winter, already building up their woodpiles and laying in supplies of salt to break up the ice. At least there was always something new to talk about.

The day after Dani met Evan in the garden, Jacob's crew gutted the kitchen and tore off the front porch. There was no turning back. She couldn't decide whether she should be terrified or exhilarated. Next Monday, the porch reconstruction would begin. Jacob had taken detailed photos of the original porch, promising to imitate it as closely as possible. There were suppliers who specialized in copying the traditional posts and spandrels; everything had been delivered and was ready for installation.

The old kitchen cabinets were lined up on the brick walk, waiting for Drew, Jacob's foreman, to load them into his truck and deliver them to a house his nephew was renovating. Putting The Maples' new kitchen together would, however, have to wait until bad weather drove the workers indoors. For now, paving the parking lot, rebuilding the porch, and painting the exterior of all three buildings were more important. A roll-off dumpster was being delivered tomorrow and would stay until it was full—or the job was finished.

Clarissa hadn't been able to watch the rape of her house. Piece by piece, it was being piled on the lawn, like trash. She finally closed the curtains but couldn't keep out the sounds that penetrated the walls. When the noise stopped late that afternoon, she gathered her courage and opened the curtains. *That Springer woman* and one of the workers were standing in front of the house, looking at the old cabinets and the piles of discarded wood. How embarrassing. Everyone would see the rotten wood from the porch and the old enamel double sink perched on top of it all. Once it had been the best sink on the market. She and Judd had made a special trip to Springfield to pick it out.

She was rapidly approaching meltdown. Forgetting to put on her coat, she hurried across what was left of the lawn, stopping in front of *her*. "Tell them to clean up this—this mess immediately."

Dani silently counted to ten. Counting was better than exploding. "Don't worry. It'll go into the dumpster tomorrow."

"A dumpster? One of those ugly metal things that look like an old railroad car?"

"It'll be parked at the curb." Dani was pretty sure this news was unacceptable and was perversely enjoying the horrified expression on Clarissa's face.

"You can't do that—it'll look like, like a construction site."

"It is a construction site." From the corner of her eye, Dani saw Drew edge out of the line of fire and take refuge in the house.

"This is all Lorraine's fault. All her fault."

At least, for the moment, Lorraine was sharing some of the blame. "Mrs. Hamilton, you aren't wearing a coat, and it's very cold. Why don't you go home and try not to look at the front yard. Truthfully, this is none of your business, and I have better things to do than put up with your interference." She almost said behavior but decided against it.

Clarissa pulled her lips together in a tight line and slowly walked back to her cottage, her heart pounding in fury. There was no explaining to *this woman from California* that precious pieces of her life were being discarded and put on display for everyone to see. On top of everything else, the lawn she'd been paying Evan to take care of was probably ruined. Memories of her parents' barren front yard, never more than dirt and weeds, rose up to taunt her.

It wasn't just the debris piled in the front yard that was fueling Clarissa's tirade. It was the fact that her house—HER house looked naked, no better than the first time she'd seen it sixty years ago. She knew she'd neglected making repairs since Judd wasn't around to fix things or hire someone. It had gotten easier and easier to avoid looking at the fading paint and the wobbly balustrade. Like not noticing that someone you love is aging.

As soon as the workmen went home that evening, she made certain the blue hatchback wasn't parked at the curb, then walked out to the sidewalk to inspect the damage. Across the front of the house, a horizontal scar, at least two feet wide, was etched below the second floor windows; a parallel scar stretched along the foundation—the siding ripped away, black insulating paper dangling.

She stood there, her hands in her coat pockets, ignoring the early evening chill. Her place in the world belonged to someone else. All those years spent creating a home, and now there was no space left for her. *That woman* was creating her own version of Clarissa's house, and she could only watch from a distance.

Ironically, all the males who had lived in this house had been ripped away like the porch. Aileen, however, had removed herself. Clarissa's younger daughter had always been an enigma, had specialized in defying her mother. If Clarissa chose a sweater or a dress for her, Aileen refused to wear it, preferring to slouch around in torn Levi's and oversized sweatshirts. Too many battles to count: boys, clothes, chores, food, homework. The final break came when Aileen dropped out of Boston University in her junior year and flew to Europe, working at a series of temporary, menial jobs, hitchhiking from one country to another, staying in hostels. Occasional postcards confirmed that she was still alive. Ashamed to admit her daughter was a college dropout who was living like a hippie, Clarissa told people Aileen was studying abroad. The lie sounded better than *my daughter is hitchhiking around Europe with a forty-something artist named Nils.* Not long after Matt died, Aileen returned to the states and, a year later, was living on a boat in the Florida Keys with a man twice her age.

As an adult, Clarissa had kept her parents in the background of her married life. Similarly, Aileen wanted nothing to do with the kind of lifestyle Clarissa had worked so hard to provide. Judd kept in touch with his daughter, but he didn't always share what he knew about her life with Clarissa. He didn't need to hear his wife's lecture about how ungrateful their youngest was.

Only a few days into the house renovation and Dani was already buried by to-do lists.

One for the trail of paperwork to get the permits and inspections required by the town, though Jacob did the actual legwork.

One for Jacob and Drew, with construction questions/changes. Two days ago, the Zoning Commission had notified her that the house would need an exterior fire escape at the rear of the house. She and Jacob were still trying to figure out how to make it look like a decorative stairway instead of a fire escape. More money.

One list was for Abby, who was handling all things promotional—including designing the web page, getting bids on the sign for the front yard, and listing The Maples with B & B organizations. In this business, networking was central to finding new customers. Thank God Abby liked doing PR and knew her way around computers.

One list was for things Dani needed to buy for the house. That list was endless.

Since the mailbox on the front of the house had been removed along with the porch, it was the perfect time to solve the ongoing problem with the mail. Actually, the mail itself wasn't the problem. Clarissa was. She still believed the mailbox and what was delivered to it were her province. Most days, Dani tried to be home about the time the mail came, but it wasn't always possible and, if Clarissa got to the mail first, she would hold it hostage until Dani came after it. Chasing Clarissa down and asking for her own mail was seriously annoying. Clarissa, on the other hand, seemed to enjoy disrupting Dani's life. When Dani got to the mail first, she sorted Clarissa's back into the box, not because she wanted to be above such petty maneuvers but because she didn't want Clarissa to come looking for her. A bad day was a day she had to deal with her permanent tenant. Dani was already sorry she'd agreed to let her stay.

Determined to put an end to Clarissa's game, Dani first considered getting a post office box for The Maples, but that would mean she'd have to go to the Post Office every day—giving Clarissa sole possession of the mailbox at the house. At that point, Dani reminded herself that the house was now hers, not Clarissa's. The next day, she filled out the required paperwork to assign Clarissa's cottage a separate number: It was now 22 1/2 Orchard Circle.

Game. Set. Match.

The fun part was that Clarissa would have to notify all her accounts and friends of her new address. The not-so-fun part would come when Clarissa found out what Dani had done. In the meantime, Dani was immensely pleased with her solution. She stopped at the hardware store to buy the new numbers and a mailbox identical to the one that had been on the main house, asking Drew to have one of the workers put them on Clarissa's cottage, then left a message on Clarissa's voice mail, explaining that, for business reasons, they needed separate addresses.

The morning after the new numbers were installed—the morning that the work was to begin on the parking lot— Dani looked out her kitchen window to see Clarissa sitting on a folding lawn chair in the middle of the grassy area that was going to be the parking lot. Wearing a heavy wool coat, a scarf covering her hair and a blanket over her knees, she was calmly reading a book.

"God help us!" Dani grabbed her new fleece jacket and went to confront Clarissa, planting herself directly in front of her. "Mrs. Hamilton, what do you think you're doing?"

"Sitting in my yard."

"I beg your pardon, but you are sitting in my new parking lot, and the guy with the grader will be here in an hour to dig out the grass and level the pad so the paving company can start work tomorrow. The pad has to be finished before bad weather sets in." Like Clarissa would care. And how had she known today was the day the grader was coming?

"I will not have *asphalt*," she almost spat out the word, "behind my house."

"Mrs. Hamilton," Dani paused to take a breath, "shall I call your daughter about this?" The threat sounded hollow and childish.

"She's working."

"Then I'll call the police station. You're trespassing." Clarissa would probably know Dani was bluffing; the police had more important crimes to worry about. There was no way to physically remove her. That would be assault.

Because the guy on the grader couldn't work around her, he'd go to some other job, putting the parking lot behind schedule. As Dani was walking back to her own cottage, she remembered she'd kept the gardener's business card—the rather good looking gardener with the sienna eyes—because, once the lot was finished, she'd need to talk to him about new bushes and trees to camouflage it, another zoning requirement. Clarissa seemed to like him. In lieu of dragging Lorraine out of school, Dani decided to gamble on calling him. The card was clipped onto the outside of the folder with the contractor's estimates. *Evan Murray, ASLA, Landscape Architect.* A fancy title for a gardener. He answered on the third ring: "Murray."

Dani explained about Clarissa as briefly as possible. "I'm sorry to bother you. This isn't your problem, but I can't contact Lorraine right now, and the workmen will be here at ten-thirty."

His first response to the rising panic in her voice was laughter. "That woman is a piece of work sometimes."

"It's not funny. It's going to cost me money to have the guy with the grader come back another day."

"Sorry. From your perspective, it isn't funny. I'm at a job over in Stockbridge. I can be there a few minutes before ten-thirty."

"Thank you, thank you." She looked at her watch. It was nine-thirty.

Clarissa was delighted that *the Springer woman* gave up so quickly. If nothing else, the sit-in would spoil a day's work, and the crew would have to reschedule. She'd given up imagining she could completely stop the work being done on her house. Every day, workmen came and went, and the hideous dumpster was already half full. She could no longer

47

get inside the house because the locks had been changed. The only way she'd be able to see what was being done to the interior was to admit curiosity and go in during the day. Not an option yet. She was left with finding small ways to be a nuisance, like a summer fly buzzing around without ever landing. So far, it had been rather entertaining, though she hadn't expected the house number change. However, since the Post Office would forward her mail for a year, she wasn't in a hurry to send out address cards. No need for her out of town friends to know she was no longer in the big house. She tucked the blanket tighter around her legs. She'd have to stay put until the grader guy went away—another hour or so. Clarissa turned a page in her book. Her life had been reduced to small acts of sabotage.

The news of JT's death came at 11:15 a.m. on Wednesday, November 7, 1970. Clarissa had never been able to erase the icy shock of opening the front door to find two uniformed Army officers on the front porch, solemn strangers in dress uniforms, asking to come in, asking whether there was someone else at home. Judd was at his latest construction site, somewhere near Housatonic. He was never around when she really needed him.

All by herself, she listened to their voices delivering the hideous message, telling her how sorry they were, explaining that JT had been on a special operation to rescue two downed pilots inside North Viet Nam, that she should be proud of his bravery. Before leaving, they gave her a phone number to call about having his body shipped to Lee. How had her sweet boy become a *body*, an object to be shipped in a pine box, instead of the laughing young man who was proud of his new Army uniform, eager for the adventure that would kill him.

After they let themselves out of the house, she sat rigidly on the sofa for an hour—too frozen to move or cry.

Aileen had come home from school and found her.

"Mom? Mom, what's wrong with you?"

Clarissa stared vacantly at her daughter, unable to form the words, unable to say *dead* and *JT* in the same sentence. She wondered objectively if the news was going to kill her, if she would die sitting here thinking about how to tell Judd, who should have been here. Her perfect son, her perfect family—gone.

When he was a teenager, JT would burst into the kitchen and kiss Clarissa's cheek. "Hey, Beautiful, what's for breakfast? I'm starved." How many sons called their mothers beautiful? She was putty in his hands. He'd always been able to charm any female—except his sisters, who would have none of it. They'd been taken advantage of once too often. JT was totally different from his father and older brother, both of whom could be charming but were more often serious and practical. JT's mission was to enjoy all of life. Until Matt left for college, he'd kept a steadying hand on his younger brother. Whatever JT earned cleaning up his father's construction sites disappeared before his next paycheck, usually on something for the '55 Chevy he was rebuilding. Once he had his own wheels, Juddson Thomas Junior was ready for action. Without Matt's oversight, JT began acquiring a reputation as a player, barely managing to avoid getting in trouble with the law and the fathers of the girls he dated.

The fact that JT graduated from high school was something of a miracle. Only because he made an eleventh hour effort to get a C-average, was he able to walk with his class. Intelligence wasn't the issue. His teachers had always assured his parents he could do the work—but chose to avoid it. School was too boring. No college for him.

The Tuesday after his graduation, he kissed his mother's cheek, told her she was beautiful and that he'd enlisted in the Army. He wanted to get into the Special Forces, be a Green Beret, take part in daring rescues and special ops. It was bad enough that he'd be half a world away from her; that he was deliberately choosing one of the most dangerous jobs in the military twisted her heart.

"What do you think Dad will say?"

"I don't know." A lie. She did know Judd had always hoped one of the boys would come into the firm, but Matt was finishing up his law degree and putting in applications at prestigious law firms. Construction wasn't in his future. Now JT was leaving, might never come back. Judd would be quietly devastated but wouldn't interfere.

Because JT was eighteen, he hadn't needed his parents' permission to enlist. He'd already signed the papers—would leave for North Carolina in four weeks. A done deal.

"Tell me you're happy for me, Mom."

She did. Another lie. Her sweet boy was going to boot camp, then to fight a war in a tiny country no one had even heard of when she was a child.

Pretending to concentrate on her book, Clarissa heard a truck pull into the driveway but didn't turn around.

"Okay, Mrs. Hamilton, the jig is up."

Startled, she looked up from her book into Evan's face. For once he wasn't smiling. Not a good sign. *That woman* had outmaneuvered her. "What are you doing here?"

"I'm the cavalry and I've come to liberate the back yard."

"I don't want asphalt in my yard."

"You already have an asphalt driveway alongside your cottage. What's the difference?"

"People will be parking behind my house."

"You really need to watch the "my" word. Nothing on this property is yours any more, except what's in your guesthouse."

"So I've noticed." She pulled the flap of the book jacket out to use as a bookmark and closed her book.

He settled himself in front of her on the grass. "What's going on?" She could tell he was going to try to talk her out of her chair. *On that terrible day in 1970, Aileen had tried to make her get off the couch, go upstairs and lie down.*

She shot him a look. "I hate *her* and I hate *her* B & B and I hate—everything. Did you know *she* had my house number changed without my knowledge?" Clarissa stopped speaking because she could feel herself choking up, and she never wanted anyone to see her cry. She'd unintentionally confessed too much. "You can't make me move." Instead of sounding determined, she came off sounding foolish. She turned as she heard another truck stopping in front of the house. A small bobcat grader was chained to the trailer the truck was towing.

"You know you're going to upset your daughter when she finds out you're interfering with the renovation. Ms. Springer is just trying to earn a living."

"It's not fair."

Evan stifled the smile that threatened and stood up. "You sound like you're seven. Come on. Let's go inside so you can fix me a cup of coffee, and then I have to get back to my job in Stockbridge."

From where she was standing on the front sidewalk, Dani could see Evan talking to Clarissa. In a few minutes, they both stood up, Evan picked up the lawn chair, and they disappeared into Clarissa's cottage. "Thank heavens." She turned to the men. "The back yard is yours; just be very careful of the garden. Otherwise, she'll probably come out and throw herself in front of the grader."

While the sod was being scraped off, Dani fixed herself a bowl of cold cereal and a mug of coffee, then brought everything outside and settled herself on the steps to make sure her grading instructions were followed. Getting this job done was as important as painting the outside of the house and rebuilding the front porch. Winter would soon freeze the ground, effectively halting the outside work until spring. Though there had been rain a couple weeks ago, autumn had been kind to her construction projects. But the window of opportunity was getting smaller. Tomorrow, the paving company would lay the asphalt foundation and, as soon as that had set up, the finish coat would be put on and the lines painted. The last step would be widening and extending the driveway beyond Clarissa's cottage, curving it into the pad at the back.

An hour later, when the grading was done and the grader had been loaded onto the trailer that delivered it, Evan came out of Clarissa's. Pulling keys from from his jacket pocket, he walked over to where Dani was sitting, drinking her second cup of coffee. "She'll live."

"To fight another day?"

He laughed—Dani liked his laugh; it held nothing back.

"No doubt. Best guess is she won't try anything else today—can't guarantee tomorrow though."

"How did she know the grader was coming this morning?"

"She asked the guy who put out the survey stakes."

"Crafty. Thanks for intervening. She hates me, and I didn't know who else she might listen to. The paving company will be here tomorrow."

"Happy to help, but I do need to get back to Stockbridge. The floodlights surrounding the park are being installed, and I want to make sure everything is where it should be. Like you, I'm racing against bad weather."

"Lights? I—well, I thought you were—"

"A gardener? No. I'm a landscape architect. I design open spaces."

"But you've been mowing this yard."

"As a favor for my cousin Sam. He really is a gardener. He and Clarissa didn't get on."

"Not surprising."

"I promised to get him off the hook until she found someone else. But once I started, she assumed she didn't need to look further. I do two other yards—special friends. It's a way of getting exercise when I'm working on a project."

"Like the park?"

"This one is a playground specifically for preschoolers. Very classy, if I do say so."

"I was going to ask your advice about what to plant around the parking lot so it's hidden from the back of the house, but that's not what you do."

"I can help you with that." Since their first meeting in the garden, he'd been trying to figure out how to see her again without being too obvious. Her call for help was the perfect opportunity. "I'll be working on the bridge and the pond anyway."

"Perhaps I should ask your cousin to take care of the yard in the spring."

"Good idea. Sam needs the work. Lots of mouths to feed."

"You don't have mouths to feed?" She surprised herself by wanting to know.

"Only Zack's and mine. Zack's my black Lab. He eats plenty but not as much as Sam's three kids." He paused, "Mrs. Hamilton's just scared, you know. I suspect this house has been the center of her life for a very long time. It's like losing another child; she's already lost two of those."

"Margo said both sons are dead."

"The younger one was killed in Viet Nam. The older one was killed in a plane crash."

"Pilot?"

"No, a lawyer on a business trip." Clarissa had told him about her sons one hot afternoon when she'd fixed him a glass of lemonade.

Suddenly, neither knew what the next topic should be. Evan took a step back, "I need to check on the lights."

"I owe you."

"I'll collect."

Chapter 7

$\mathcal{W}$hen she saw Ben's name among the four voice mail messages on her cell, Dani caught her breath. Spence? But the brief message assured her there was no emergency, just a scheduling problem. *Just.* Her antennae went up. That meant the holidays. *Damn.*

One of the other messages was from Evan Murray, returning her call to him. She wanted to talk to him about what to plant around the parking lot—and when. As good an excuse as any to see him again.

She turned the phone off and dropped it into her purse. Now was not the time to return any of the calls because she was on her way to a Chamber of Commerce meeting—her first since joining. Making contacts in the business community was important. Time to meet and greet. Since Jacob would be working on the house for another four or five weeks—perhaps an optimistic estimate—she needed to use this time to start marketing her business. She'd already ordered plantation shutters for the downstairs and selected the new appliances for the kitchen, as well as a heavy duty washer and dryer. There would be low solar lights along the paths so guests could safely walk from the parking lot to the house or into the garden. Abby had almost finished the website and was in the midst of installing the spreadsheet programs The Maples would need. Learning to use them wouldn't be easy, but Abby promised to be on call. With luck, everything should be in place so The Maples could open sometime after the holidays. Dani wasn't ready to set a date yet.

After checking in at the registration table near the front door of the Chamber's headquarters and pinning on her name tag, she found a seat off to the side and pulled out a pad for notes. She had a lot to learn about how Lee's business community was run and who did the running.

As its newest member, she was introduced during the meeting: *Please welcome Dani Springer, the owner of Lee's newest B & B, The Maples.* Afterward, while the members drank coffee and sampled pastry furnished by the local bakery, Dani talked to an insurance agent who was probably hoping for new business, the owner of one of the hardware stores that was already getting plenty of her business, and a fiftyish woman who, with her husband, ran one of the other bed and breakfasts. Instead of viewing Dani as a competitor, the woman was eager to offer help.

"I remember how hard our first year was—even though we bought an established business. When do you plan to open?"

"Early next year. But there's still a lot to do."

"All the B & B's in the area try to help one another—it's good for everyone's business. We'd be glad to show you around our place, answer questions. We close down during January. Not much going on then, so we take some time off." She handed Dani a business card and encouraged her to call.

After living in the shadow of Clarissa's constant disapproval, it was refreshing to find someone who was actually welcoming. Dani needed to get out more. She looked at the card— George and Louise Quill—and tucked it into her increasingly fat daily planner. She'd call the Quills when the major construction was almost done and she was confronted with the nuts and bolts of putting the inside of the house together. Now was too soon.

Later, sitting in the grocery store parking lot, Dani returned Evan's call but got his voice mail again. Phone tag. She left a message, telling him that she'd be home this evening, then hit the speed dial for Ben. Even after three years, three and a half years, anger tightened her stomach as soon as she heard his voice. He wanted to take Spence skiing in Switzerland at Christmas instead of Thanksgiving. Would she mind trading holidays?

Yes, she minded.

A lot.

In her head she was yelling *No! No! No!* He'd trumped her, knowing full well she wouldn't cheat Spence out of skiing in Europe because she wanted him to spend Christmas with her. And so she agreed. Having Spence at Thanksgiving meant she'd see him for only four or five days instead of two weeks. Not the visit she had in mind. She hated having to compete for her son.

After putting the groceries away, she did her usual afternoon check on what work had been done at the house that day. The exterior of both cottages had fresh paint and, as soon as the porch was finished, the main house would be painted. The floors had been sanded but wouldn't be refinished until all the interior painting and wallpapering had been completed. Today, they'd started installing the new furnace and air conditioning unit. At least the house would be warm when the seriously cold weather arrived. Jacob had proved to be a good choice for the renovation. He was reliable and listened to what she wanted; however, his original estimate on the costs had been too conservative. It seemed that every time she saw him, he needed more cash—usually in thousand dollar increments.

While she was fixing herself scrambled eggs, asparagus and fried new potatoes for supper, Evan showed up at her door, his boots and pant legs splattered with dried mud.

Holding a spatula, she motioned for him to come in. "Did you find my message?"

"Yes I did and, since I was in Lee anyhow, I decided to answer it in person and see what the parking lot looks like with the asphalt." He perched himself on one of the barstools at the kitchen counter that divided the kitchen and living room. "That smells great."

"I'm just frying potatoes."

"I didn't have time for lunch today."

A hint if ever there was one. She didn't really feel like having a dinner guest. She was still upset about Spence coming for Thanksgiving instead of Christmas. But not feeding Evan was probably not being generous of spirit. "Do you want some? I'm going to scramble eggs."

"Is there enough?"

"It'll stretch." She had plenty of potatoes and some fresh bread. Adding sour cream to the eggs would dress them up a little.

"I'd like that." There was that smile.

"What were you doing that you missed lunch?"

"Sloshing around the edge of a very cold lake where the County is thinking of putting in a fishing pier and picnic area. Not the most creative project, but it's a job."

"Thus the mud."

He glanced at his boots. "Sorry, did I track some in?"

"No. I just noticed, that's all. Why don't you take a look at the parking lot while I finish cooking?"

Once he was gone, she stashed the breakfast dishes in the dishwasher, sliced more potatoes, and added the sour cream to the eggs. It had been a while since she'd cooked for two. She found a jar of jam for the bread and measured out decaf for fresh coffee. Before he returned, she took a minute to wash her face and put on lipstick, telling herself that she'd do the same even if her guest were female. Almost true. Since her divorce, male companionship hadn't been a priority. Still wasn't. Might never be. Getting over Ben's infidelity had been hellish.

Evan Murray, however, was—interesting.

She stopped herself.

Feeding Evan Murray was just about feeding Evan Murray—and about trees.

Their dinner conversation actually was about trees as well as the work on the house and the County's fishing pier. "At least the County pays its bills promptly. I've worked for them a few times."

Before he left, she gave him her new e-mail address so he could send her his suggestions about the landscaping. While thanking her for dinner, he added, "Now we're even."

Standing on the porch watching him walk to the parking lot, Dani thought she saw the curtain in Clarissa's kitchen window move. She'd been watching them.

While loading the dishwasher, Dani realized she was humming, remembering bits of their dinner conversation. Feeding Evan Murray had possibly been about more than trees and food. She'd have to consider that possibility.

Evan didn't often invite himself to dinner, except at his Aunt Joanna's, especially a dinner being cooked by a woman he hardly knew. No excuse other than hunger and the fact that, from the moment they shook hands in the garden under Mrs. Hamilton's watchful eye, he'd felt a connection with Dani. She was attractive, almost beautiful, intense eyes, probably a few years older than he was, certainly not afraid of hard work or, for that matter, of Clarissa Hamilton. She was refreshingly direct, yet he sensed a reserve in her, keeping her guard up. Maybe she'd been hurt, had lost something or someone. He understood loss.

When their job in Northern Thailand was finished, he and Fiona and Stuart, along with Kanya, their Thai translator, had decided to spend a week in the south on Phuket's famous tropical beaches, their Christmas present to themselves. This would be the last time they'd all be together for a while. Evan already knew about his grandmother's death, knew that the farm was now his and needed his attention. It was time to head home. Stuart and Fiona had been with him on two previous UNESCO jobs, one in Sri Lanka and another in Nigeria, working with local officials on ways to develop and maintain public space, using local resources. The three of them had originally met when they were graduate students at Heriot-Watt in Edinburgh. Though Kanya had only been with them for the final six months of their work, in that time, she and Stuart had fallen in love. After their holiday, Evan would return to Massachusetts for the first time in nearly four years; Stuart was headed for more graduate work in Edinburgh. Kanya had a new translating job that would begin in early January but, as soon as she could get a visa, she would be joining Stuart in Scotland. Fiona had to return to Scotland so she could apply for a U. S. visa and plan a spring wedding for herself and Evan at her family's home in the Borders. Evan would fly over for the wedding in early May.

Because they'd made their vacation plans at the last minute, they hadn't been able to get reservations at any of the hotels directly on Patong Beach. Their hotel was about fifty yards behind a larger, upscale resort. A one block walk to the ocean. The weather was glorious and they all had sunburns. On Boxing Day morning, two small earthquakes shook the hotel. Since no one seemed especially concerned, the other three took off for the beach while Evan stayed at the hotel to see if he could send some e-mails to his family, letting them know he was coming home as soon as he could get a plane ticket. He'd tried to get on-line the night before, but the internet connection wasn't working.

Half an hour later, having had no luck getting the hotel's computer to cooperate, Evan went up to his and Fiona's room to change into swimming trunks. A few minutes later, what sounded like a huge explosion sent him to the balcony overlooking the grassy area between his hotel and the one directly on the beach. What he saw sent sharp terror through him. A wall of water at least two stories high was slamming against the other resort, pushing debris and water through its first floor, tearing out part of one wall and racing toward his hotel. He felt the three-story concrete structure shudder as the surging water rammed its wall. The concussion might have been stronger, might have crushed the wall, had the beach front hotel not taken the initial impact of the water, diffusing some of its power. For several minutes, Evan could only watch in disbelief as cars and palm trees and people were hurled into the space between the hotels, a small SUV coming to rest in the overflowing swimming pool. Then, as swiftly as it had shoved everything out of its path, the ocean reversed itself, being sucked back toward the shore, scouring deep troughs in the sand. Not until later did Evan make the connection between the earlier earthquakes and the monster wave. This was a tsunami.

He remembered frantically running toward the beach, ignoring the possibility there might be another wave, intent only on finding his friends, finding Fiona. But it was impossible to ignore the injured, frightened people trapped in the debris, screaming "Help me! Help me!" The dead had been dumped like grotesque rag dolls on what had so recently been a pristine beach. He'd never seen this kind of brutal, indiscriminate death. Happy, healthy tourists on holiday one moment, battered corpses the next. In the space of minutes, the beach had become a war zone, cars piled on top of one another, trees jammed inside buildings. Kanya, Stuart and Fiona were nowhere to be seen.

Then came the hysterical rumors that another wave would arrive, fueling a chaotic evacuation to higher ground.

Evan stayed on the beach. Searching. Hoping. When the predictions about another wave proved false, some people returned to what was left of the hotels, others camped out all night on the high ground. In the early hours of the morning, he found Kanya, in shock, huddled in the littered lobby of their hotel. She clung to him, sobbing, telling him that Stuart and Fiona had already been beyond the breakers when, in an instant, the water swept everything and everyone away. Because she hadn't been in the water yet, she'd had enough warning to take refuge on the roof of a nearby restaurant, too terrified to leave until one of the restaurant's waiters found her, took her hand, and led her back to the hotel.

For several days, he and Kanya forced themselves to look at the rows and rows of already decomposing bodies that hadn't been identified yet. Because Kanya spoke the language, it fell to her to ask the agonizing questions of those who had been on the beach and survived. Evan checked the lists of the dead and the longer lists of the injured taken to hospitals. Nothing. Stuart and Fiona were suddenly and completely gone.

Exhausted and brokenhearted, Evan finally called Stuart's and Fiona's families. Stuart's father flew into Phuket on the same day that Evan was assigned a seat on a plane that had been chartered to take foreign survivors to Singapore, so they missed one another. He barely had time to call Kanya's cell to tell her goodbye. Though she was devastated by Stuart's death, she'd offered her translating skills to one of the hospitals. She promised Evan she'd meet Stuart's father at the airport.

From Singapore, Evan began a series of hop-scotching flights that ultimately ended in Boston on January 9. Physically and emotionally drained, still in shock, he phoned Sam for a ride. Not a happy homecoming. Liz Murray was gone and his beautiful Fiona had been swallowed by the sea. He blamed himself for suggesting the trip to the island.

The farm was a soft place to fall. His aunts and their families gave him plenty of space and time to recover but made sure he had company when he wanted it and kept food in his refrigerator. A year of hard physical labor to renovate the barn and the farmhouse kept him from completely succumbing to his grief. He wasn't sleeping well, often waking up yelling, trying to warn them to get out of the water. But the water just kept coming and coming and Evan could only stand and watch. The nightmares happened less often now.

While he was converting the barn into his studio, he lived in his grandparents' farmhouse, more or less camping out. He turned the greenhouses over to Sam. Taking care of other people's yards was a seasonal business; with the greenhouses, his cousin could supplement his income by supplying local florists with flowers year round.

Evan and Kanya e-mailed occasionally. That summer, she traveled to Scotland, staying with Stuart's parents for five months. Back in Thailand now, she was working for the Thai government in Bangkok.

In the months before the tragedy, as soon as Fiona had agreed to marry him, Evan had begun outlining plans for starting his own design business, poring over whatever catalogs he could lay his hands on. By the time he was back home, he already knew what equipment he needed, what he wanted to specialize in. His studies at Penn State and later at Heriot-Watt, as well as the undergraduate internship he'd had with a Philadelphia firm and his work for UNESCO, had provided him with skills he was anxious to use in the public sector. He loved the challenge of taking a raw piece of land and figuring out how to make it and its surroundings both beautiful and functional. He could probably make more money designing open spaces for housing tracts or corporate office buildings, but he wasn't interested.

Though he loved the work, Fiona should have been part of it.

Even after all this time, he wasn't sure he was completely healed, but he'd enjoyed having dinner with Dani. He was definitely attracted to her. He wondered if she felt the attraction too.

While Jacob's crew was rebuilding the front porch, Clarissa's curiosity forced her to find ways of watching their progress without seeming to. From her living room, she could see only the edge of the porch, so she invented excuses to leave her guesthouse. She ran unnecessary errands, made extra trips to The Sewing Basket and the grocery store. On Friday, before it was completely dark, she put on her heavy coat and walked to the front of the house. The new porch was finished but hadn't been painted yet. It was an amazingly accurate reproduction of the original, with the same balustrade and brackets, but squared posts. Gambling that no one would see her, Clarissa climbed the wide, shallow steps onto the porch, running her hand over the smooth, freshly sanded wood of the balustrade. It was sturdier than the old one. At least this much of the house would look the same—maybe better. The outside of both guesthouses had already been repainted a deep blue-gray with white trim and shutters. She and Judd had always favored white with green trim. The new color would take some getting used to.

After Friday's successful porch reconnaissance, Clarissa decided the time had come to go inside the house. The following Monday, when *that woman* drove away with the tall blonde who owned the sports car with Connecticut plates, Clarissa crossed the lawn and paused for a moment on the brick path. A plumber's truck was parked at the curb; the house must be unlocked. How embarrassing to have to sneak into her own house like a criminal.

The front hall was the same, yet not; perhaps it was the absence of the striped wallpaper that had only been up seven or eight years. The sewing room was now divided by a counter with a swinging gate. She'd spent hours and hours in that room, sewing for the children so they could be well-dressed without it costing a fortune. After Aileen was born, Clarissa had asked her mother to teach her how to tailor.

The wallpaper in the living room had also been removed, the walls were primed, ready for painting or perhaps wallpaper, and the floors were awaiting a new finish. The kitchen was completely empty, just four walls and exposed plumbing, a large pantry to one side. Why had she never thought to have Judd put in a pantry? It would have made cooking for four children easier.

She remembered the first time Judd had taken her through the house, remembered the ugly wallpaper with garish pink roses, circa 1925, the hideous dark stain someone had used on the oak floors. It had taken Judd's crew days and days to sand the floors and restore the beauty of the oak wood.

Judd had promised that the horrible wallpaper would be gone when they moved in. Promised that there would be a new screen at the front door and that the inside would be painted before their friends helped them move in what little furniture they had. True to his word, everything had been done, even though the paint smell was so overpowering that they had to leave all the windows open for the first week.

Because Judd was busy building a warehouse in Pittsfield, the rest of the move-in preparation had fallen on Clarissa. Leaving Matt with her mother, she scrubbed kitchen cupboards that hadn't been cleaned for years. Using an old toothbrush and a bowl of ammonia, she scoured the tile grout in the bathroom, chased cobwebs from every room. At the end of each day, she was filthy and exhausted.

Once everything was as clean as she could get it, she shopped for towels and rugs that looked more expensive than they were. She was good at ferreting out bargains, knew quality when she saw it. A day at a time, one room at a time, the house—her house—began to come to life. She kept back part of each week's grocery money, setting it aside to pay off the Turkish rug she'd put on layaway for the living room and the Monet print she'd seen in a second hand store. Since Judd didn't really have a lot of interest in the furnishings, she chose what she liked.

It was getting dark. She'd probably stayed long enough. For now, seeing the downstairs satisfied her curiosity. Too much trouble to drag herself up all those stairs to the bedrooms. Some other time perhaps.

Chapter 8

A week after Evan had dinner at Dani's, he called her. "Are you busy this morning?"

So casually, as though calling her was something that he did all the time. His voice sent a jolt of pleasure through her. "Nothing pressing— why?"

"I have to go over to a nursery in Great Barrington. If you want, I can show you what I have in mind to hide your parking lot." It had, truthfully, taken him a few days to come up with a plausible reason to call her.

"Sounds like a plan. Should I meet you there?"

"It's tricky to find, dirt road and such. Might be easier to come by my place and we'll go from here." He gave her instructions. "South on Highway 7; two miles after the Stockbridge junction, turn left at the white sign with green lettering that says Murray Farms. The sign's badly weathered, but I hate to take it down."

"If I get lost, I'll call."

At exactly two miles, she saw the square sign hanging from the inverted L-shaped post. *Murray Farms, founded 1952. Ross and Elizabeth Murray.* His parents? By the date, probably grandparents. Hanging beneath was a newer sign, *Evan Murray, ASLA. Landscape Design.*

The dirt road that turned off had recently been graded. He'd said the greenhouses—*Brunello Wholesale Flowers*—were a quarter mile from the highway, the barn just beyond. "I rent out the farmhouse. The barn is my studio and apartment."

Painted dark red with white trim, the barn had large mullioned windows in the wall that she parked beside, skylights in the gambrel roof. A handsome structure.

At the north end of the barn, the original doors were still in place, but an ordinary house sized door had been inserted into one of them. Alongside the door was a carved wooden sign, Evan Murray, and a brass knocker instead of a doorbell.

No answer. His mud-splattered, white pickup was in the yard, so he was here somewhere. She tried the knocker again.

"I'm over here, Dani."

She couldn't see him. "Which is where?"

"The front porch." And then she saw him sitting on the steps of the farmhouse with a petite, dark-haired woman holding a baby.

Dani crossed the lawn already brown from recent frosts.

Evan stood up—his wiry height making Dani at 5' 7" feel short. "Dani, this is Cathy and Peanut."

Cathy smiled but Peanut scowled, hiding his face in his mother's shoulder.

"Nice to meet you, Dani. Don't mind Peanut; he's in a clingy stage. He won't have anything to do with Evan either."

Evan pulled keys out of his jacket pocket. "And I used to be his favorite." He leaned over and kissed Peanut on the head. "We're going down to the nursery. Tell the plumber to send me the bill for the water heater."

At the truck, Evan opened the passenger door for her. She couldn't remember the last time any man had done that. "Chivalry is alive and well."

"My grandmother was from the old school. She worked in the gardens as hard as my grandfather, but she still expected him to open doors for her. She insisted I do the same."

He slid behind the wheel, turned the key in the ignition, and adjusted the heat. "Let me know if it's too warm—or cold. The heater is temperamental."

"Your grandparents raised you?"

"I was seven months old when my mother died. They legally adopted me a year or so later. And to answer everyone's next question, I have no idea who my father was." No bitterness, just a statement of fact.

"I wasn't going to ask."

"My grandmother was a stickler for discipline. Sam and I ran her ragged with our energy and curiosity. A tough lady. Fortunately, my grandfather was our ally. A pretty good childhood."

"The Sam who didn't do well with my tenant?"

"The same." Evan pulled onto the highway and headed south. He liked the way she asked questions—and knew when not to ask.

At the nursery, he showed her various bushes and trees that, in a year or two, would effectively camouflage the parking lot. He explained when they could be planted, how tall or wide each kind would get. As they walked around the nursery, he wrote out a tree shopping list for her, the prices, and the number she'd need. Then he took her over to a warming shed that had a coffee pot and a few folding chairs. "I have some other things to talk to Rolf about. I'll pick you up when I'm done."

A man who knew what he was about. Not trying to impress her, flirt with her or put her down, none of the usual male behaviors. He seemed comfortable with who he was. Ben was always the military officer, always in charge, making sure everyone knew he was in charge.

Before heading back to Lee, they bought sandwiches in Great Barrington and found a vacant bench on the River Walk. "Not fancy, but a good view. Is it too cold for you?"

"No. In spite of being spoiled by California, my Connecticut genes seem to remember this weather—so far. Of course, it isn't deep winter yet. I may have to retract that statement."

"My two years in warm climates didn't seem to hurt me either."

"Where were the warm climates?"

"Nigeria, Sri Lanka, then Thailand."

"Much more exotic than California. What were you doing?" There were intriguing layers to him.

"I was part of a team working with small communities, teaching them how to design and build public open spaces. Sort of education and construction all in one. UNESCO awarded the project to the Built Environment graduate program I was enrolled in. I was lucky to be assigned to the team. I probably learned more about design and function in those two years than I ever did in a classroom."

"So you liked working overseas?"

"Absolutely. A once in a lifetime adventure. The geography and the people were fascinating. On the downside, the bugs, the humidity and our primitive living conditions made every day a true challenge. Those two years left me with a permanent craving for hamburgers and an inability to toleratre the smell of Deets."

"What's Deets?"

"A really potent mosquito repellent."

"Why did you come home?"

"The project ended. My grandmother had died and left me the farm. I needed to decide what to do with it. With myself. And there were other," he hesitated, "well, other reasons." He was staring out over the river; momentarily, he'd gone somewhere else—then, "I need to get back. I have an appointment with a guy from the County at two o'clock—more fishing pier conversation."

She wondered what the other reasons were. But she wouldn't ask about those either.

Dani hadn't been able to work out just how she wanted to entertain Spence over the Thanksgiving weekend. He was flying into Albany late Wednesday afternoon, a shorter drive than going to Hartford. Picking him up was about as far as she'd gotten. She kept planning and unplanning—that was nerves. She was somehow afraid Spence would be even more distant than he'd been when she saw him in Annapolis. Never would she have imagined she could be uneasy about spending four days with her own son.

The first two years she and Spence had been alone on Thanksgiving, they'd shared their holiday dinner with servicemen who listed their names with the local USO. The third year, she'd worked at the Inn that day, so she and Spence had dinner in a restaurant. Not at all the same. No enticing smells or leftovers. This year, she'd definitely cook dinner. Since this would be their first holiday in Massachusetts, she wanted it to be as memorable as possible.

Unfortunately, Spence didn't know anyone in Lee. It would help make his visit more appealing if he knew two or three guys his age. At fourteen, he might not want to hang out with his mother for four days. The closest movie complex was in Pittsfield, but it had only two theaters. She checked the listings. Perhaps they could see a movie one day.

The Sunday before Thanksgiving, while Abby was putting the finishing touches on the new spreadsheet program, Dani asked her if she'd like to share their holiday dinner.

"I'd love to—I haven't seen Spence since he was ten or eleven. I can do some of the cooking here or bring things from my place."

"Great. Company is always more fun."

"Would you mind having another guest?"

"No problem. Who?"

"Drew—Drew Baldwin."

"Jacob's foreman Drew?" It took her a moment to connect the dots. "You've been keeping secrets."

"Not exactly, just not advertising."

"Abigail."

"Don't start. That's why I haven't said anything. His ex has their daughter on Thanksgiving, so he's on his own, though he does have family in the area—a sister. I thought about inviting him to my place, but that seemed—oh I don't know—like I was assuming too much. I don't want to scare him off. With you and Spence in the middle, it'll be easier."

"Oh God. We're your chaperones." Dani was struggling to focus on the news. "No wonder you spend so much time in Lee. And all along I thought it was my brilliant conversation."

Abby ignored the teasing. "Can I invite him?"

"Of course. Spence will at least have another male at the table. But I thought you were still doing match.com. Nothing?"

"Very nothing." Abby pulled her blonde hair back, twisted it into a loose knot and fastened it with a silver clip. "Drew is—nice. Such an empty word. But he is. Doesn't care that I probably make more money than he does, that I went to college and he didn't. No games, no agendas."

"And just how far has this—relationship—gone?"

Abby grinned and shut down the computer, pushing back the chair. "None of your business, my friend. What kind of pie does Spence like?"

A week before Thanksgiving, Lorraine found a voice mail message from her sister on the answering machine. Except for a card at Christmas, and not always that, Aileen had kept her distance from the family for over thirty years, selfishly leaving everything concerning their parents in Lorraine's hands. But then, as Lorraine reminded herself, Aileen had seldom thought about anyone but herself. She was always the pretty one, with their mother's fair hair and slender figure, a string of boys wanting to date her. Every school morning, she spent hours choosing what she'd wear, begging her mother to make her a new dress for the next dance.

In those days, Lorraine hadn't cared about clothes or how she looked. And she didn't date. She resembled her father's side of the family, had his nose and high forehead, features that looked better on him. Over the years, Lorraine had convinced herself that graduating *magna cum laude* and having a tenured teaching job was better than being pretty. Twenty years ago, recognizing that Grant Sessions' proposal was probably the best offer she'd ever have, she accepted it. Not the love story of the century, but a match built on solid affection.

She waited twenty-four hours before returning Aileen's call.

"Hi Lor, thanks for calling back." Aileen hesitated, "How are you? How's Mom?"

"For her age, okay."

"And you? Are you still teaching?"

Lorraine didn't feel like making small talk. "What do you want?" Since their father died—everything had been piled on Lorraine's plate.

"You left me a message a month ago—about getting my stuff out of Mom's attic. I've been out of the country, just got back. Is it still there?"

"No. The boxes are now in my attic." And Grant had not been thrilled about Lorraine moving whatever her mother's guesthouse couldn't accommodate into their attic. There were boxes of Aileen's high school keepsakes, as well as boxes of treasures that her mother wouldn't part with, hand-painted, yellow dessert plates, boxes of vinyl records, tablecloths and pillow cases with crocheted edges—even their baby shoes.

"What are they doing at your place?"

"The house was sold a month ago. When I called you." *And you didn't call me back.*

"Then where's Mom?"

"In the small guesthouse."

"The old workshop? That's a comedown. Why'd she sell the house? It's always been a huge part of her life." A fact all four siblings had recognized when they were children.

"She didn't want to. It was necessary."

"Wasn't she furious?"

"Of course. Still is. But she needs money, and I don't recall you sending checks or making sure she has enough to live on." To be fair, Lorraine hadn't given her mother any money either—just time and attention—but she didn't feel like being fair.

The line went silent. At least Aileen didn't try to argue or offer excuses. The young Aileen would have tried to put Lorraine in the wrong. "We're planning to drive up to Lee to take my stuff off your hands. Bart's coming with me. He wants to meet my family."

"Bart?"

"I got married. We've been in Jamaica on our honeymoon. Bart has a house on Big Pine Key, so I finally have room for my things since I'm not living on a boat anymore. Bart owns a resort, and I'm helping him run it."

Trust Aileen to land on her feet. Bumming around Europe, working as a beautician in Florida, shacking up—could you shack up on a forty-foot boat?—with a man twenty years her senior. Starting her own business with the money he left her. And now she was married to a man who owned a resort while Lorraine was still in Lee, jumping to her mother's tune, married to a man who thought a weekend in Boston was a vacation. Grant couldn't imagine why anyone would want to leave New England.

"When are you coming?" She knew her voice was cold.

"Bart and I will leave here on Sunday morning and should be there sometime the day before Thanksgiving. I made reservations at the Berkshire Inn outside of Lenox. We don't want to intrude on you."

"You're just going to waltz in here on a holiday and pretend we're one big happy family?"

"Lor, I know—"

"You don't know anything."

"We'd like to take you all out for Thanksgiving dinner—if it's not too late to make reservations."

Because Lorraine hadn't felt like cooking for Grant and her mother, she had made dinner reservations at Rumplestiltzkin's in Lenox ten days ago. At least Bart and Aileen would be picking up the check. Grant would like that. She'd have to call the restaurant, tell them there would be two more.

And of course, she was stuck with telling their mother Aileen was coming. Same old pattern.

After Lorraine's phone call about Aileen's impending visit, Clarissa couldn't get to sleep. She was uneasy about seeing her youngest child. With a husband, no less. Aileen had certainly waited long enough to make an honest woman of herself.

Clarissa finally got up at one in the morning and fixed herself a cup of hot chocolate. She needed to figure out how to handle this unexpected reunion. There was always the chance that her daughter would reveal the contents of the letter Clarissa had sent after Aileen's announcement that she'd dropped out of college—was taking time off to see the world. Hopefully, both of them would pretend the letter had never been sent or received. Lorraine had said Aileen was coming to pick up the boxes she'd left behind and introduce the new husband. Of course Lorraine didn't know about the letter, about the real reason Aileen had chosen to stay away. Even Judd hadn't known, unless of course Aileen had confided in him.

To this day, Clarissa didn't regret what she'd written. She felt justified. Aileen was the one who needed to apologize for her actions. All the years of parenting—time, effort, money—and Clarissa had nothing to show for it. Aileen had been the daughter who could have made a good marriage, who would have been beautiful on her wedding day, who would have made her mother proud. Clarissa's own wedding had been simple; there hadn't been money for anything splashy. In her frustration with Aileen's cavalier behavior, trashing Clarissa's dreams for her, Clarissa had written that Aileen was an ungrateful daughter and that, if she ever wanted to come home, she must apologize. Then she listed all Aileen's college expenses—even the cost of her braces when she was twelve, the cost of summer camps and violin lessons, trying to make her youngest feel guilty about throwing away everything her parents had done for her—what Clarissa had done and Judd paid for.

Aileen's reply—arriving two months later from London—had been short and to the point: *I'm only an itemized list? I'm surprised you didn't send me a bill.* She didn't sign it. And she never wrote to her mother again. Just occasional Christmas cards, usually sent to Judd's Boston address, later to Lorraine's.

Aileen had never been one to back away from a fight. There wasn't anything Clarissa could do if Aileen chose to discuss the letter. But she would not apologize for what she'd written.

She went back to bed just before five, not bothering to put her cup to soak.

Chapter 9

Except for the hordes of holiday travelers and the impossible parking at Albany International, Thanksgiving weekend went better than Dani expected. By the time she and Spence pulled into The Maples' driveway, he'd almost returned to being her Spence, not the distant Spence of her visit to Annapolis.

He dropped his new L.L. Bean duffle bag on the bed. "Hey, my room looks like it did in California."

"It's smaller." For just a second, Dani contemplated apologizing for its size, but didn't. *Stop competing with his new life.*

He ran his hand along the edge of his old surfboard propped against one wall. "Sure can't surf in this part of the world. Dad took me to the coast one day. Just ankle slappers and really cold water."

"Do you miss it?"

"Not so much. Anyway, I'm getting better at soccer."

Kids were lucky. The present and future were always beckoning, letting them drop off the past. A skill she coveted.

She glanced at her watch. "I need to pick up the turkey. Want to come or would you rather look around without me breathing down your neck? The main house is unlocked if you'd like to go in." She knew what he'd choose; following her around any store had always bored him.

"I'll skip the shopping."

"If you're hungry, check the fridge."

He grinned, "If?"

"See you later." She fled before he could see the tears well up. His "if?" told her that their old relationship was still intact. After all these months away from him, she'd been afraid that she'd somehow lost him. As though he couldn't still love her and want to live with his father. For the thousandth time, she reminded herself that parenting wasn't a contest. He could love both his parents equally, a lesson she'd probably have to learn over and over.

She wiped her eyes and headed for the grocery store to collect the twenty pound turkey she had on order. Large enough for plenty of leftovers. Abby was bringing cranberry salad and two pumpkin pies. Tonight, Spence would help chop celery and onions for tomorrow's dressing. He actually liked to cook, had often hung out in the kitchen at the Inn. The cooks enjoyed showing him how to crack an egg into a bowl, flip a pancake and, to her horror, how to use sharp knives safely. Even though she and Spence now lived different lives in different places, perhaps the rituals of the holiday would erase some of the distance.

As it turned out, Thanksgiving Day was one of the best holidays they'd had since Ben's departure. Drew and Spence bonded over soccer. Spence told funny stories about the coach of his high school soccer team and, since Drew coached the men's soccer team in Lee, he also had amusing stories about the players and the games. They kept each other entertained all through dinner. As Drew and Abby were leaving that evening, he invited Spence to watch the soccer match between Lee and Great Barrington the next afternoon. The rivalry among the local men's soccer teams was fierce, and this game would determine who went into the championship game in Pittsfield. The weekend was saved—Spence had guy stuff to do.

Drew was quick to include her, "You should come. It's at the high school. Abby'll be there too."

Tempting—more time with Spence. But going to a soccer game with his mother might embarrass him.

"What time does it start?"

"One."

"Umm, I have an appointment. I'll come by if I get finished early."

There was, of course, no appointment. She'd kept the weekend clear.

Sharing Thanksgiving dinner with Aileen had been uncomfortable for Clarissa. She kept waiting for her daughter to give her away. When Aileen came for Judd's funeral, she'd barely spoken to her mother, fleeing as soon as the service was over. During dinner at Rumplestilzkin's, Clarissa took time to study her youngest and the new Jamaican husband, a brown-skinned son-in-law with a Hispanic last name that Clarissa couldn't quite pronounce. Leave it to Aileen to fly in the face of convention. She was still pretty in spite of the crow's feet around her eyes and some gray threading through her fair hair. Since Aileen'd been a hairdresser, surely she knew how to touch up the gray. She was wearing denim slacks—at least they had a designer label—and a cowl-necked cashmere sweater. Expensive but too casual for Clarissa's taste, especially for a restaurant on a holiday.

For once, she kept her opinions to herself. Too many battles about clothes when Aileen was living at home. Her younger daughter's choices about almost everything had always frustrated Clarissa—as though Aileen were some sort of changeling that didn't belong in the Hamilton family. Maybe one of Clarissa's wild Irish ancestors had been reincarnated in this daughter. Clever, rebellious and ungrateful. Aileen's phone call, telling her parents that she'd dropped out of the university and had bought a ticket on a student charter to Europe was, for Clarissa, the last straw. Thus the angry letter. In all the years since, Clarissa had used her hurt and anger to justify what she'd written.

Judd, however, had never seen Aileen's departure as anything other than a declaration of her independence. "You don't raise kids to stay home all their lives. You raise them to be on their own. A kid doesn't ask to be born. She doesn't owe us anything. Let her be. She'll find her way back when she's ready."

Easy for him to say. The father who didn't father very often. Clarissa, however, felt owed. She'd never been good at losing or looking bad. Ask any bridge partner who made the wrong bid.

The year after Aileen left was the year Clarissa bullied Judd into redoing the kitchen. At least the house couldn't buy a ticket to Europe.

When they got back from Lenox, Bart and Grant decided to watch what remained of the Packers/Lions football game while the sisters dropped Clarissa off at her place. Once their mother was inside, they sat in Lorraine's car across from the house they grew up in—talking. During dinner, they'd made tentative, polite conversation but in the dark of the car, talking was easier.

This older Aileen was an improvement over the twenty year old Aileen that Lorraine remembered. Quieter, able to let Clarissa dominate the dinner conversation with thirty years of gossip that Aileen probably had little interest in. Time and distance had leveled the playing field between the sisters.

"The house looks good. I like the darker color, though I wish the new owner had gotten rid of that sunroom. I always hated it. Ruins the proportions."

"Mom's the one who wanted it. Guess sunrooms were a big thing in the fifties."

"She always did like to have the newest and best."

"Without paying top dollar. Good thing Dad was a contractor. Remember how many stores she'd drag us to—looking for just the right bath towels or shoes or dishes, comparing prices, going back to stores we'd already been to, making sure she got the best quality for the best price."

"She'd have made a great comparison shopper."

"She still exchanges the gifts she receives. Nowadays, I give her a gift card for one of her favorite stores. Saves the annoyance of knowing that whatever I choose will never be quite right. Made me hate shopping."

"Me too. Bart will shop and shop until he finds exactly what he wants, but he doesn't mind shopping alone. And he never returns a gift unless it doesn't fit."

"Grant assumes shopping is my job."

"In spite of the sunroom, I've always liked our house. It has— had—a comfortable feel. If only Mom had learned to enjoy it instead of obsessing over it."

"She's really pissed off that it's being turned into a B & B and has been giving the owner a hard time. So far, Dani has been able to sidestep Mom's interference and complaints. Been rather fun to watch, except I get all of Mom's angry phone calls. Thank God for caller ID and voice mail."

"I'm sorry you've been the one to deal with Mom."

Lorraine heard sincerity in her sister's voice. "Not nearly as sorry as I am. Grant ran out of patience long ago. He won't come over here because she always has something that needs fixing. Grant hates playing handyman. When she was still living in the house, the list was endless. Now Dani will have to fix things, though I don't think Mom has played that game with her yet. That's probably next." Lorraine filled her sister in about the house numbers and the parking lot sit-in.

"Mom never changes. When I was in high school, my friends thought she was so nice and pretty, and I wanted to tell them they wouldn't think she was so nice if they had her as their mother. Hard to explain the kind of tyranny she's so good at."

Lorraine started the car. "I need to run the heater; I'm freezing."

"What's the garden look like?"

"She let it go last year—always was a lot of work—wouldn't allow the gardener to touch it, but now she's paying Evan Murray to redo everything in the spring. Even Dad's bridge."

"Why is she paying him?"

"Bragging rights probably. Control. I don't know. Her story is that *that woman*—aka Dani—won't do it right. She never uses Dani's name."

"Figures. Do you know Dani?"

"I've met her a few times, seems nice enough. A hard worker. Grew up over in Enfield."

"Do you think Mom should still be living alone?"

"I've given up trying to talk her into moving. She's the one who forced Dani to accept her as a permanent, nonpaying tenant." Lorraine put the car in gear and pulled away from the curb. It was actually rather comforting to be able to talk to Aileen about their mother.

Friday morning, Spence and Dani slept in. After breakfast, she gave him a quick tour of the house. He was and wasn't interested, but he'd spent enough time at the Inn to at least understand the business.

"Who's the old lady in that other house by the driveway? She keeps looking out the window."

"That's Mrs. Hamilton."

"Why's she living there? I thought you owned all of this."

"She was part of the sale. I got a good price, partially because she came with the deal. Mostly, she's just annoying. Still thinks this place is hers and I'm the great intruder."

"Is she crazy?"

Like a fox.

"No."

"Does she have a family?"

"A couple of daughters."

"Maybe she's just lonely." One of Spence's nicest qualities had always been a warm heart. Hopefully, Ben wouldn't squash that.

When Dani got to the high school soccer field at 2:30, the game was almost over. Great Barrington 3, Lee 1. She found Spence sitting at the top of the bleachers between Abby—the same Abby who had always maintained she hated sports of all kinds—and a boy with red hair, maybe the same age as Spence. Dani needn't have worried about her son—he already had someone to hang out with.

"Hey Mom, this is Ross. His dad and his uncle are playing for Lee."

"Hi Ross."

Ross smiled and mumbled "Hello" but quickly turned his attention to what was happening on the field.

Abby slid over to make room for Dani. "Not a game with a lot of scoring. Just back and forth and back and forth. Spence assures me there's more to it, but I'm not convinced."

Dani laughed. "I can't believe you're even here. The planets must be out of alignment."

"Believe. And it's cold."

"You're such a good sport."

Abby stuck her elbow in Dani's ribs. "Cut the sarcasm. I'm in need of liquid refreshment, the kind they don't serve here."

"Did you go all the way home last night and drive back?"

Abby gave her a long look. "There are children present."

"This *is* serious."

At that moment, a shout went up in the section where Great Barrington's supporters were sitting. The game was over.

Ross stood up. "My dad's gonna to be bummed. No play-offs."

Spence stood too. "Mom, we're going to stay for a while—kick around some balls with his dad and uncle. I'll walk home later."

It was tempting to ask whether he knew the way back to the house, but she caught herself in time. No sense shaming him in front of his new friend. "Have fun."

She'd planned to take him to the movies after the game. Maybe they'd do that on Saturday.

When the boys were out of hearing, Dani sighed. "I wish he were still nine and actually wanted to spend time with me. I suppose this independence thing is only going to increase."

"Probably. But if he has friends here, he'll be more willing to visit."

"Is that why you come here? You have friends."

Abby didn't answer.

"Sorry, it was too good to resist. Drew's a nice guy."

Silence.

"Okay. I can take a hint."

"It's just—going so fast and I've never been, well the whole thing makes me nervous."

"How old is his daughter?"

"Eleven. He has her every other weekend. The ex lives in Springfield."

"Have you met her, the daughter?"

Abby shook her head.

"And you'd like me to shut up?"

"For the time being. Oh, there's Drew. Come on. We're going over to The Locker Room for a drink. Come along."

"I don't think I should—"

"Spence has a key?"

"Sure."

"Come on."

The Locker Room was packed with both soccer teams and some of the fans. Half an hour later, Dani saw Evan Murray and a redheaded man walk in. Both were wearing Lee team jerseys covered in grass stains and mud.

She turned to Drew. "Evan Murray's on the team?" She hadn't paid attention to who was playing. At that distance, her vision wasn't all that good.

"Yeah, Sam too. Ross is Sam's son—as you can easily tell by the red hair."

"You engineered the Ross connection?"

Drew smiled. "A little. Ross is a good athlete, plays junior varsity soccer. I thought Spence could use someone to sit with. Don't worry. Ross made the contact with Spence without my help. Kid-to-kid."

"Thanks." Dani was beginning to understand why Abby was so taken with Drew. He wasn't the kind of man you'd necessarily pick out of a crowd. A fraction shorter than Abby, stocky, thinning black hair that already had some gray. Thoughtful and deliberate, he managed the day-to-day construction details at The Maples with good humor and firmness. The men liked him.

Finishing her beer, Abby asked, "How do you know Evan?"

"He's the landscape architect I told you about. He's redoing the garden, rebuilding the bridge and the pond, all on Clarissa's tab. She's afraid I'll screw up the garden."

"And?"

"And nothing. Evan helped me get Clarissa out of the yard during her great sit-in."

"Oh he's the one. God, I'd love to have witnessed that."

"Next time she does something like that, I'm calling you."

"Attached?"

"Who?"

"The architect, dummy."

"I have no idea. Not interested in anything except what he does with the garden." Not entirely true. "It'll be a great draw in the spring and summer."

Abby was not to be deterred. "Perhaps a bit younger than you. How old is he Drew?"

"Don't drag me into this discussion. All I know is he's a year younger than Sam, spent four years abroad, two in graduate school, two working for UNESCO, been back here about that long. You do the math." He slipped his arm along the back of the booth and let it drop down onto Abby's shoulders. She smiled at him and moved closer.

Half an hour later, when the three of them left the bar, Evan saw Dani and raised a hand in a half wave. She waved back but kept moving, unsure whether she should have stopped to talk.

Early Friday afternoon, Aileen and Bart drove over to her mother's guesthouse to say goodbye. Standing in the driveway, Aileen and Clarissa were being careful with each other. Neither ready to risk trouble.

"The house looks good, better than it did three years ago."

"You came by the house?" Clarissa thought her daughter had gone straight back to the airport.

"I drove by."

"But you didn't come in." There had been a huge crowd, some locals, many driving from Boston to pay their respects to Judd's memory.

"I assumed I wasn't welcome."

Clarissa couldn't remember whether Aileen would have been welcome on that day. Actually, she wasn't too sure about today. Yet here they were, face-to-face, talking instead of arguing. Clarissa opted to discuss the house rather than the day of the funeral. "*That woman* changed the color of the house and put that ugly parking lot at the back. But I'm paying Evan Murray to redo the garden in the spring. I want it done properly."

"Of course you do. Who's Evan Murray?"

"The grandson of those people that had the truck farm out on Highway 7. Ran a roadside vegetable stand in the summer."

Bart fingered his car keys, "Honey, we need to leave if we're going to get as far as New Jersey by tonight."

Hesitantly, Aileen kissed her mother on the cheek, and Bart briefly took Clarissa's hand. Then they were gone, their mini-van filled with the bits and pieces of Aileen's childhood. Now that there wasn't anything of Aileen left in Lee, perhaps she wouldn't come back.

Clarissa reminded herself she didn't care.

Spence's flight left Albany at three on Sunday. He wasn't thrilled being sent off in the care of the flight attendants. "I'm too old for this!" He tugged at the plastic cardholder identifying him as an unaccompanied minor. Nevertheless, he let her kiss his cheek as they said goodbye. It had been a good weekend. She felt better about their relationship than she had in months. Maybe she'd visit Annapolis after the holidays. Take him into D.C., away from Ben's turf.

By the time Dani got home, it was almost dark. Shorter and shorter days. Evan's truck was in the parking lot with its tailgate down. She found him on his knees in the garden, removing the bolts that fastened the old bridge to the concrete berm surrounding the pond. Clarissa was nowhere in sight.

Without preamble, Dani asked, "Do you have permission?"

He twisted the last bolt out of the concrete and looked up at her. "I called her first. You don't think I'd do this on the sly. She'd like as not shoot me on sight." He slid the bridge away from the pond.

"Just wondered." Dani set her purse down. "Want some help? I assume it's going into the truck."

"Yeah. It's not all that heavy, just unwieldy."

Each of them picked up an end, carried the bridge a few feet, stopped, carried it a few more feet. At the truck, they hoisted one end onto the truck bed and slid the bridge forward. Too long.

Evan swung himself into the bed and studied the situation; then he lifted the front end of the bridge onto the top of the cab. "Can you close the tailgate now?"

She slammed it shut.

"Good. I'll have to tie this end of the bridge through the truck windows, to keep it from sliding sideways."

Fifteen minutes later, he finished securing the bridge with the ropes he'd brought with him. "I ought to be able to get this to my place if I go slow."

"Maybe I should follow, just in case you need two more hands."

He thought for a moment, "Not a bad idea. If you think it looks like it's going to slide off, honk twice."

"Give me a minute. I need to go inside." She changed into her running shoes and her heavy jacket, taking time to go to the bathroom and put on lipstick.

Though it was late when Clarissa got home, she walked out to the garden. A few days before Thanksgiving, decorative lamps had been installed around the deck and along the path leading to the garden and the parking lot so it was easy to find her way. In the last year, she'd begun to be more careful about where she walked. She wasn't afraid of falling; she wasn't unafraid either. She stopped at the pond. Evan had truly taken the bridge away. Without it, the pond looked shabby. Judd had built the bridge and pond to celebrate Aileen's birth. That meant it had been in the garden over fifty years.

So long. More than half of her life.

So many losses.

Except for the physical reminders, like the bridge—and the house of course—little of that life remained. As a young wife and mother, she'd been sure nothing would ever change. Instead, everything kept changing and changing. She should've been able to make certain parts of her life stand still—wait until she was ready for change. She wanted the life she'd had when the boys were little. When JT was learning to walk and Judd sometimes came home for lunch. Her happiest time. Before the people in her life left and the house replaced them.

Now she'd lost the house too.

Chapter 10

$\mathcal{T}$he week after Thanksgiving brought a cold, persistent drizzle. Normally, when Evan finished a major job like the park in Stockbridge, he'd go hiking for a few days, shake out some of the stress, make room for fresh ideas. This time he couldn't seem to decide where he wanted to go. Instead, he walked Zack, cleaned up the studio, made a few repairs on the farmhouse, and walked Zack some more.

He knew what the problem was.

Who it was.

The night Dani Springer had followed him back to the farm and helped him unload the bridge, he'd offered her coffee and a quick tour of his workspace. He seldom brought people into his studio. He generally met clients at their offices or the sites they were developing. The barn had been his sanctuary when he first came home and, when he was working, he craved its solitude. But showing her how and where he worked felt natural—oddly necessary. In spite of his disarming smile and easy rapport with people, he was—at a personal level—deeply private. Unable or unwilling to share the important parts of himself. Fiona had been an exception. And Sam. Sharing his workplace with Dani was a silent admission that he wanted her to know him better. And he wanted to know her better.

Though she claimed to have little understanding of computer graphics, she'd asked smart questions about how he did his designs, asked about the Stockbridge park. "I'd like to see it sometime." She said it like she meant it.

"I'll take you—sometime." And he definitely meant it. He was looking for reasons to spend more time with her.

Perhaps sensing they were tiptoeing into risky territory, she looked down at her watch. "I need to get home. I have an early appointment tomorrow."

Wanting her to stay but not knowing how to tell her so, "I'll store the old bridge when I'm finished with it. Then you won't have to put it in the basement."

"Thanks. She'll probably forget all about it."

He smiled. "Don't count on it."

Since that evening, her face insisted on following his memory around. No woman had gotten inside his head this way since Fiona. The first year after Thailand, he'd been a monk—mentally and physically. The second year, he dated occasionally, pretending a few of the women were important, instinctively knowing they weren't, at least not long term. He'd still been having nightmares about that terrible day, the water pulling him under, suffocating him. Spending a night with a woman had been problematic.

To distract himself, he'd joined the town soccer team, spent more time with Sam's family, and took a month off to visit Stuart's and Fiona's families. The trip was long overdue. Time to face his pain and theirs. When he returned, he felt more settled. The word closure probably fit, but nothing was ever completely closed. Fiona would always have a piece of his heart, but he was alive and she wasn't. Two months ago, if someone had asked whether he was ready to make room for another woman in his life, he'd have hesitated. But since that day with Clarissa and Dani in the garden, he'd subconsciously been moving pieces of the past into storage, making emotional room.

When the drizzle let up on Thursday afternoon, he drove to The Maples. Dani's car was in the parking lot; instead of looking for her, he walked to the backyard, took out his notebook, and began stepping off the outside dimensions of the garden. He didn't want her to think he'd come just to see her, didn't quite want to admit to himself that he actually had come to see her.

Making a list of which plants could be saved and which couldn't, he experimented with a couple ideas for two short paths into the garden.

He'd been working for nearly half an hour when he heard the back door of the main house close and looked up to see Dani walking toward him, wearing paint-stained Levi's, a faded blue Old Navy sweatshirt, and running shoes. Her hair was longer than when she'd arrived in Lee, the sharp wind blowing it across her face. She looked happy to see him.

"I was working in the attic. How long have you been out here?"

"Not long. What's going on in the attic?"

"Fixing up the bedroom for Polly Netherland. After Christmas, she's going to move in to be my combination housekeeper, waitress, and house sitter. All of that for a small salary and room and board. Her dad's company is transferring him to New Jersey, but she doesn't want to change colleges. Do you know her?"

He shook his head.

"Margo found her for me. I'm going to need someone in the house at night even though Jacob is working on an intercom for my cottage. Polly's in her first year at the community college, majoring in Hospitality and Travel. Margo says she's good with people and responsible." She leaned over to look at the notebook. "What are you working on?"

In that moment, he was tempted to touch her hair, to feel its silkiness on his fingers, but forced himself to say casually, "Making a diagram of the layout so I can see which flowers should stay and which need to go before I start reworking everything." He handed her the notebook, settling for the warmth of her fingers during the exchange. She studied what he'd drawn on the graph paper. "I'll get Ross to help clean out the old plants and rework the soil. I doubt Mrs. Hamilton has taken care of the soil in a long time." In truth, none of those tasks had occurred to him until just now. He was scrambling to find something plausible to talk about, establishing excuses to come back.

"I like the design."

"How's the work going on the house?"

"Jacob's almost done. Mostly waiting for the final inspections. Do you want a tour?"

"I thought you'd never ask."

An hour later, they were standing on the front porch. Dani had just finished telling him why Mrs. Hamilton's cottage now had a separate address. Though it was clear Dani was still annoyed about the battle for custody of the mailbox, she made the story funny. He liked that.

"This coming weekend is Stockbridge's Main Street at Christmas celebration. Would you like to go with me on Sunday?" *Please say yes.* "The town turns itself into a Nineteenth Century Christmas card. Santa Claus and the whole bit. It's probably more for families with young children, but you'll be seeing Stockbridge at its best. Next year, you can tell your guests all about it."

For the briefest of moments, she seemed uncertain about accepting his invitation, then "Sure, I'd enjoy that."

"I'll pick you up about eleven. Let's hope the drizzle stays away." Though she was tall, he was taller and could look down into her eyes—a translucent blue-gray. No question about it, he liked her. Maybe more than liked.

Dani wasn't sure the afternoon in Stockbridge had been a date or just two acquaintances on an excursion. Whatever it was, she'd had fun. No working on the house, shopping for the house, or fretting about the house. Evan made a good tour guide. She vaguely remembered having visited Norman Rockwell's studio when she was in high school, but it was all new to her this time. Afterwards, she and Evan strolled the Main Street, loitering at the handicraft booths, having lunch at the Red Lion Inn—waiting a half hour to get in—and ending their afternoon at the botanical garden.

Everywhere they went, Evan met people he knew. After he'd spent ten minutes talking to the cashier in the garden's gift shop, he apologized. "I didn't mean for that to take so long. His dad used to work for my grandfather."

"When you live in one place most of your life, that happens. I used to know lots of people in Enfield but, because I moved around the country so much when I was married, Abby's the only one I kept in touch with. I'd forgotten how nice it is to belong to a place."

"But tricky. They know too much about you and your family. One false step and you're in the midst of gossip central."

"Did you make false steps when you were a kid?"

"Not many I got caught at. Sam and I made our false steps in other towns. Otherwise, our grandparents or Sam's parents would have killed us. Drag racing at night on back roads, drinking too much beer, and having a few encounters with guys from other towns who thought we were moving in on their girlfriends."

"Were you?"

"Yeah." The slightly crooked smile. "I've tried to clean up my act since high school. You?"

"With parents who were teachers and knew most of the other kids in town, it wasn't easy to get away with much. I had the same boyfriend my junior and senior year; then I went off to college in another state, and we broke up." That had been Jared, a track and field jock who joined the Marines right out of high school. Military types had played a major role in her past love life. "Where did you go to college?"

"First Penn State, then Heriot-Watt in Edinburgh. You?"

"University of Maryland at College Park. But I never finished. I got married my junior year. My son was born the next year."

"Ever think about finishing?"

"It's been fifteen years. I'd have to make up a lot of units and would still need to find a job."

Evan did the math. She was four or five years older. Not that he cared. Hopefully she wouldn't. He was fairly sure she hadn't realized he was interested in her. That was okay. There was no hurry.

What had been on and off drizzle all afternoon finally settled into a steady rain. "Perhaps we need to head back." The afternoon had flown by. A lovely afternoon in spite of the weather.

Chapter 11

The week before Christmas, the National Weather Service began tracking a powerful storm that was moving across the Great Lakes, predicting it would sweep into Southern New England on Christmas Eve. The one day of the year no one wanted to deal with dangerous weather. Abby drove over from Enfield on Christmas Eve afternoon, not only to keep Dani company but because Drew's daughter was spending the holiday with him. Discretion was advised.

By the time Abby arrived, the temperature had dipped below forty, and the wind was tearing the remaining leaves off the maples, hurling them into untidy mounds against the porch. While they were unloading Abby's car, the rain started. They made sure the car windows were rolled up and ran for the cottage. Santa was going to have a nasty night.

Just before dark, Dani went over to the house to make sure everything was closed tight, nothing lying around the yard. Clarissa's car wasn't in the parking lot; she was probably at her daughter's for the evening.

Three days ago, Jacob and Dani had done a walkthrough of the house, scrutinizing everything. Over-all, Jacob, Drew and all the other workers had done a great job. She could hardly wait to get the furniture in and start decorating in earnest.

Several times in the last few weeks, Abby had pointed out that Dani had fallen in love with the house.

At first, she'd defended herself. "I'm simply trying to do a good job with this project."

"You're obsessing," Abby accused.

"I just want everything to be—"

"If you say perfect, I'll know aliens have stolen your soul."

"What's wrong with," she hesitated, "loving the house?"

"Isn't that part of Clarissa's problem? She loves the house too much?"

Oh hell. Maybe she'd caught some sort of psychological virus from Clarissa.

Remembering the conversation with Abby, Dani tried to be coldly practical while she and Jacob were making a list of what still needed fixing.

The switch plates she'd chosen were on back order, and somehow three of the kitchen cabinet handles had disappeared; she'd have to order more. The paint on the baseboards in the front hall needed touching up, and one of the faucets in the master bathroom insisted on dripping, a new faucet at that. And the Wi-fi still had problems. Unfortunately, the computer guy who installed the system was out of town until the first of the year.

Dani was tentatively planning to open for Presidents' weekend. With luck, there'd still be snow at Butternut, the ski area near Great Barrington. She was anxious to get started. Thinking about how she would do things wasn't doing them, and she definitely needed some cash flow. She'd made arrangements with the Quills to visit their place before they shut down in January. Seeing their operation when it had guests would help her visualize guests at The Maples. The last week of January, The Maples website would go on line; only then would she find out whether people would make reservations or whether all of this had been a fool's errand, rooted in her anger and frustration about her son preferring to live with his father.

Dani was grateful she didn't have to spend Christmas alone. Spence had already called from Gstaad, Switzerland, to wish her Merry Christmas and thank her for his gifts. He and Ben—and of course Sherry—were on their way to a midnight church service. A new behavior. When she was married to him, Ben had seldom set foot in a church. Was that Sherry's influence or was he trying to set a good example for Spence?

As the wind howled and rain lashed the cottage windows, Abby and Dani microwaved popcorn and watched the DVD of *Australia*. About ten, Drew called Abby's cell. She went into Spence's room for privacy. When she returned, Dani commented "Thoughtful."

"Yeah."

"You're in deep."

"Oh yeah."

"Have you met the daughter?"

"Stephanie. No. That happens sometime tomorrow. They'll be with his sister's family in the morning. I'm nervous about meeting her. I don't have much experience with kids. I only see my brother's boys once a year."

"If Spence is any measure, kids seem to deal fairly well with their parents' new partners. From the first, Spence accepted Sherry and Ben's new life—no fuss, no muss. Personally, I'd have preferred a little less acceptance."

At midnight, they wished each other Merry Christmas and went to bed.

Dani had no idea how long she'd been asleep—maybe she was still asleep. The roaring, at once shrill and rumbling, raced at her from somewhere in a dream; a huge truck or maybe a train seemed to be driving right through the bedroom, bringing with it a cracklingandcrashing that went on and on. Slow motion sound.

Then eerie silence.

Half awake, not sure whether the sounds had been dream or reality, Dani grabbed her robe and hurried outside. The cold instantly sliced through her clothing, sending her back for her heavy jacket. Outside again, she rounded the corner of the house and stopped in disbelief, trying to process what she was seeing. The sound had been very real. One of the evergreens alongside the driveway had broken off about six feet above the ground and the top nine or ten feet of the tree, branches and all, had landed on the sunroom—was IN the sunroom—pushing the longest wall out. Another big branch had come to rest on the trunk of Clarissa's Lexus which she'd parked in the driveway. Served her right. Dani had asked and asked her to use the parking lot, without success.

All this destruction from the wind, yet now the frigid night air was perversely still, pretending none of this mess was its fault.

Abby came up behind Dani. "Oh my God!"

91

At that moment, Dani saw fat snowflakes drifting gracefully into the sunroom. "Damn! It's starting to snow." *Merry Christmas.*

"We need to call someone to—" Abby stopped, "but it's Christmas. No one will want to—wait a minute." She disappeared into Dani's cottage, reappearing with her cell phone against her ear, listening. "Okay—yes—thanks."

"Who'd you call?"

"Drew. He'll be here as soon as he can."

Dani hugged her jacket tighter, fighting the temptation to cry. "It's ruined." Her mind could go no further. She could only stare, hypnotized by the tree resting in her house, her beautiful house.

Fortunately, Abby wasn't hypnotized. "Get the keys. We need to see what it's like inside, find something to cover the floors at least."

Like a robot, Dani obeyed.

All the money, the time. Now she wouldn't be able to open and there'd be haggling with the insurance people. She didn't know if she was covered for acts of God—why didn't she know? She should know. Her mind created worst case scenarios. Higher insurance rates, a later opening, more months with no income. She found the keys on the kitchen counter and went back outside to join Abby. The tree had missed the porch, one branch lightly resting against the balustrade. Probably just paint damage.

The interior wall dividing the living room and the sunroom was scratched and muddy but seemed solid. The sunroom's three outer walls and roof were, however, pretty much destroyed, the snow already collecting on the hardwood floor.

In the basement, they found the canvas tarps the painters had used. They dragged them upstairs and began stretching them over the floor where they could. There was no way to get beneath the tree itself.

Just as they were finishing, Drew's truck pulled into the driveway, right behind it was Evan's, then a third one with Sam and Ross. Drew's truck had sheets of old plywood stacked at an angle; Evan's had a chain saw and a gas can. He smiled at Dani as he got out of the truck. "Interesting Christmas present."

She was not amused. "I could have done without it."

Drew planted a kiss on Abby's hair as he passed. "Put on some warmer clothes. The two of you are going to freeze." Watching the men unloading the plywood made Dani want to weep with relief and gratitude.

As soon as she'd put on her heaviest sweats, socks, and tennis shoes, she was warmer. Then she made coffee and hot chocolate. Thank goodness Abby had brought muffins and donuts for their holiday breakfast In times of tragedy, food and drink helped. Certainly a miserable way to spend Christmas. She heard the chain saw start up. The noise would probably wake Clarissa. Her damaged car would be a crisis of major proportions.

One thing at a time. She poured coffee into the largest thermos she had and left the chocolate in the pan on the stove. Ross might be the only one who'd want it, though if he was anything like Spence, he'd prefer a soft drink, regardless of the temperature outside.

She was carrying the tray with coffee, mugs, and food over to the house when Clarissa appeared in front of her.

"You've damaged my car." Clarissa-the-terrible was awake and ready to do battle.

"The tree did."

"You own the tree."

"You owned it first." Such a ridiculous argument. "I have bigger problems than your car."

Dani went on offense, her voice rising. "And if you'd parked it in the parking lot like you're supposed to, it would have been safe."

Holding her satin-quilted robe off the wet ground, Clarissa almost stomped back to her cottage. Not easy to do in bedroom slippers.

Muttering "As if things aren't bad enough," Dani joined Abby in the house to watch Sam and Drew hammer plywood over the doorway between the sunroom and the living room, then set about drying the floor. Luckily, not much snow had drifted into the living room. But the sunroom looked pitiful, the long wall sagging around the gaping hole. The roof had an even bigger hole. All three walls would probably have to be rebuilt and of course there'd be a new roof. Drew and Sam spread tarps over the sunroom's flooring, though the damage had already been done. While they worked on protecting as much of the floor as they could, Evan cut up and removed the part of the tree that had fallen, and Ross began stacking the usable wood. Eventually, the rest of the tree would have to be cut down and the root ground out.

It was just getting light when Sam and Ross went home, the back of their truck piled with some of the wood from the tree. It was, after all, Christmas morning and the rest of the Brunello family would be waiting to open their gifts. Drew headed home to make sure Stephanie was all right. Abby had invited the two of them and Evan for breakfast, small payment for the middle of the night rescue operation.

After Evan finished cleaning and oiling the chain saw and loading his truck, he found Dani sitting at the bottom of the staircase, her arms hugging her knees, finally indulging in the tears that had been threatening ever since she first saw the fallen tree.

He sat beside her. "It's freezing in here."

"Don't care." She sniffed, fumbling for the Kleenex in her pocket.

He put his arm around her shoulders. "Eventually you will. Come on back to your place. Abby's mixing pancake batter and scrambling eggs. Food will help."

"We were done." Tears continued to slip down her cheeks.

"I know." He wished he knew how to comfort her. Crying would probably help. Fiona always said that crying, when she was angry or scared, was therapeutic. Dani was both angry and scared. He risked tightening his arm. She didn't pull away.

They sat together, neither knowing what to say, until Abby came after them. "Drew and Stephanie are here. Breakfast's ready."

Dani had thought her worst Christmas was the first one after Ben left and her father was at death's door. But having a tree destroy the sunroom came in a close second, and—to make matters worse—the insurance agent's message on his answering machine said he was taking a four day holiday. Nothing could be done right now. Predictably, Clarissa had been on the phone twice, asking about the insurance. "Just how am I supposed to get around? I have a new quilting class starting on Monday. I need transportation."

Dani was not impressed by a quilting crisis. "Is the car drivable?"

"I have no idea. The trunk has a huge dent. It looks terrible."

If only the sunroom's problem were a dent. "Well nothing is going to happen before Monday. Try driving the car. Then you'll know." Dani was close to losing it.

"I need to drive to my daughter's this afternoon, so I want you to come over here and make sure it's safe to drive."

"Good grief!"

Anything to shut her up.

Abby had been cleaning up after the impromptu breakfast she'd cooked. Evan, Drew and Stephanie had gone to their separate family celebrations. "What's she want?"

"Me to check out the car. I suspect she's hoping it'll explode with me in it; otherwise, I can't imagine why she's trusting me to touch her fancy Lexus."

Abby dried her hands and turned on the dishwasher. "I'll ride shotgun. Then, if it does explode, I can pull you from the wreckage."

"You watch too much television."

"It's probably lack of sleep."

As Dani and Abby set off in the Lexus, Clarissa stood on her porch, hands on her hips. Most of the snow had melted as soon as the sun came out, so the streets were wet, but clear. A benign morning on the heels of destruction. The kids with new sleds couldn't try them out, but the ones with bikes were happily splashing themselves and their once shiny gifts as they raced along the sidewalks.

Dani drove the Lexus along Main Street. "It feels okay. I can't imagine that the branch was heavy enough to damage the frame or the suspension." Back at the house, she went right past the spot Clarissa insisted on parking and left the car in the parking lot. To make a point.

She handed Clarissa the keys, "It's fine. You can certainly drive as far as Lorraine's."

Not waiting for Clarissa to respond, Dani headed for her own cottage. Exhausted by the night's drama, she crawled onto her bed without removing her jacket.

When she woke up, it was almost four o'clock. Abby was gone—a note propped against the toaster: *I'm at Drew's.*

Swell. The Christmas Day from hell. She took a very hot shower and found a container of yogurt in the back of the refrigerator. Christmas dinner a la carte. Everyone had someplace to be, someone to be with, and all she had was a damaged house and an angry tenant. She couldn't bear to turn on the TV; all the programs would be warm and fuzzy.

Reruns of *It's a Wonderful Life* and *Miracle on 34th Street*. Christmas carols, happy families. The whole world was wrapped in the warmth of the holiday.

Bundling herself into her jacket and her old Ugg boots, she forced herself to leave the cottage. It was already dark, the Christmas lights on the houses creating kaleidoscopic patterns against the darkness. At least this day was almost over. It was a good thing Spence was having fun in Switzerland. If he'd been here, his day would have been ruined too. Her first Christmas without him. She'd never felt such loneliness.

Lost in her thoughts, she walked the length of Main Street, turned down toward the high school, then back to Main Street, not caring where she went so long as she kept moving. She wasn't aware that Evan's pickup had stopped just ahead of her until she was alongside it, and he was getting out. "Like a ride?"

Dani stopped. Was this a coincidence or had he come looking for her? "I'm not really going anywhere."

"Let me rephrase that," he opened the passenger door, "get in."

Because she did not particularly care where he was taking her, they drove a few blocks before she asked, "Where are we going?"

"To have some Christmas grog and leftovers at my Aunt Joanna's. I'm guessing you haven't eaten since breakfast."

"I'm not dressed for—and she doesn't know me. Are you sure it's okay?"

"My aunt loves a crowd—more is always better. And there's no dress code."

"Oh."

"Sorry I had to take off. I'd made some promises for today."

"You don't have to apologize, not after coming in the middle of the night to cut up a tree. I can never thank you enough."

"How's Mrs. Hamilton holding up?"

"Uh, don't go there. She made me drive her car to prove to her that it's safe. Stood on the steps, hands on her hips, like some snarling elementary school principal."

"And is it all right?"

"Of course. It's just a dent, but she acts as though it's the end of the world. Not a clue that the house has a much bigger dent than her damned car. Selfish old witch!"

He laughed.

Dani didn't.

"Come on, admit that it's a little bit funny."

"Nothing is funny today. Sorry. Maybe you should just take me home. I'm in a black mood."

"Understandable, but not permanent."

As it turned out, Joanna Brunello, her husband Sam Senior, their recently divorced daughter Allison as well as Sam Junior, his wife Monique and their kids were a comfortable distraction. They sang carols, loud and not always on key, devoured thick turkey sandwiches and watched *It's a Wonderful Life*—with most of them, including Evan, delivering the lines right along with the actors. Evidently, it was a Christmas night tradition. Evan stayed by her side all evening, refilling her wine glass, making sure she had plenty to eat.

No one mentioned the tree.

By the time Evan parked his truck in Dani's driveway, she almost felt better. He turned the engine off, but made no move to get out.

To fill the silence. "Thanks for rescuing me again. You have a nice family."

"Loud but, yeah, nice. They've been—a safe haven. Besides your son, do you have family?"

"An aunt in Seattle, who never married. That's it."

"Too bad. My cousins and I have always been close. Aunt Joanna was kind of a substitute mother. My other aunt, Amanda, lives in Pennsylvania now, but when I was growing up, her family lived in Springfield—three more boys. Papa, my grandfather, called us his basketball team."

"Joanna and Amanda. Your grandparents liked names ending in A."

"My mother's name was Brenda."

Dani chuckled, the first time she'd found anything amusing all day. As she opened the truck door, he asked, "May I call you this weekend? We can do something to cheer you up a little." All evening she'd looked so unhappy. He wanted to wrap his arms around her, comfort her. Kiss her. He definitely wanted to kiss her.

"I guess there's nothing I can do about the house until Monday. Yes, please call. I need diversion."

On the porch, he unlocked the door for her, leaned over, restricted himself to kissing her cheek, "Happy Christmas, Dani," and walked back to the truck.

Chapter 12

This time, Dani was pretty sure it was a date. They ended up at the Cinema Triplex in Great Barrington, then ate at a restaurant specializing in sourdough pizza. A fairly decent movie and an incredible pizza on a cloudy Sunday afternoon. Something quietly electric was happening between them but, in the midst of her distress about the house, Dani couldn't wrap her mind around the implications. She was reluctant to look too closely, afraid it was only her imagination. Disappointment she did not need.

In the three years since her divorce, she'd dated a little, seldom seeing the same guy more than two or three times. Dating always involved the same awkward, get-acquainted drill—*I'm divorced, one son, I work at The Sea Breeze Inn, No, I'm not a Chargers fan. Tell me what you do.* Then it was her turn to listen to her date's bio. No chance to be herself because she was too busy trying to say the right things while evaluating him, similar to deciding whether you liked a pair of shoes well enough to buy them. So far, all the shoes had been returned to the shelves fairly quickly.

Evan Murray, however, just might be different. He was easy to be with, didn't try to impress her, accepted who she was, and listened to her. As Drew had suggested, she did the math. Evan was perhaps four or five years younger. That meant he was a senior in high school when she married Ben. A kid she never would have looked at. But on a Sunday afternoon, their ages didn't matter. Just two adults enjoying each other's company.

A little before eight, he parked his truck in the lot behind Clarissa's, and they strolled over to the house to look at what remained of the sunroom.

"Were you able to get in touch with the insurance agent?"

"Yes. I left so many frantic messages, I guess he figured, regardless of the holiday, he should call back just to keep me quiet. I also tracked Jacob down. He and Drew will be here tomorrow afternoon. Hopefully, the insurance adjuster will come too." She sighed. "It looks like hell."

"Fixing it may not take all that long, unless the weather gets in the way."

"If I were superstitious, I'd wonder whether this mess was a sign from the universe that I shouldn't be doing what I'm doing with this house. Maybe Clarissa has supernatural powers we don't know about."

"Are you superstitious?"

"No. Just depressed. I hope I haven't gotten in over my head. What if there are already plenty of B & B's in this area, and I don't get any business?" She stopped. "Don't mind me; I'm just worrying out loud." Back at her cottage, Evan gently took the keys out of her hand and unlocked the door.

"You're just having opening day jitters—and finding a tree in the sunroom hasn't helped. You should be able to work on the rest of the house while the sunroom's being repaired."

"I hope so." She reached around to turn on the switch that controlled the floor lamp. "Thanks for taking my mind off all this. I enjoyed the movie and dinner." *And especially your company.*

"That was one of the goals." Evan's hands closed on her shoulders, gently pulling her closer. It was time to kiss her. His lips brushed hers with a delicious invitation. He drew back slightly to look at her, gauge her reaction. Her eyes were closed. A good sign. The second kiss was more serious, stopping short of searching for her tongue. When this kiss was over, Dani slowly opened her eyes but didn't move.

"Was this one of the goals?"

"Absolutely. Should I apologize?"

The hint of a smile, "Not at all."

"Should I do it again?"

Her translucent eyes were studying him so intently that he decided not to wait for permission. This time tongues were involved, and her arms came up around his neck.

Minutes later, he whispered, "I think I'd better go."

Dani agreed but had mislaid her voice.

"I have to be in Amherst most of tomorrow."

She still couldn't answer.

"Cat got your tongue?"

Now she could. "Some cat."

As she stood in the doorway, watching him get into his truck, she wondered whether Clarissa had been spying on them from her kitchen window. Right now, Dani didn't much care. It had been a very long time since she'd been kissed that way—sexy and tender all at once. She'd forgotten what dissolving felt like.

The next afternoon, she sat on the front steps while Drew, Jacob and Leonard Gustafson, the insurance adjuster, walked around the house, consulting and measuring for what seemed like hours. In truth, only an hour and a half. Leonard took photos, filled in forms, asked Jacob about the quality of the sunroom's construction. Finally, he walked over to the parking lot to look at Clarissa's car.

The torture ended when Leonard had Dani read through the forms to make sure she agreed with the information and then asked her to sign at the bottom. He couldn't give her the exact amount of the settlement today, maybe next week. Having the money in hand would take several weeks.

Weeks! Everything on hold.

The car was simpler. He gave Dani the name of a local body shop where Clarissa could take her car. No need to run all over getting estimates. And they'd provide her with a loaner. That sounded good to Dani, but Clarissa would undoubtedly find something to complain about.

Once the adjuster was gone, she and Jacob and Drew went to her cottage for coffee and conversation about their next step.

Jacob's first question was not what she expected. "Do you really need the sunroom? The living room is plenty large. What are you going to use the sunroom for?"

"Do you mean not rebuild it?"

"Exactly." Like Evan, Jacob always carried a notebook. He tore off a sheet of paper and drew an outline of the house, minus the sunroom.

"This is what it looked like originally. Now the deck is only accessible from the French doors in the dining room." He added new lines. "What if we repair the living room wall but put French doors where the opening into the sunroom was, and extend the deck around that side of the house, about half way along the living room wall. Maybe add flowering shrubs to give the deck privacy from the street."

And from Clarissa's window.

Dani studied the drawing. "Let's go back outside. Show me."

He did.

It was hard to NOT see the sunroom, to see a deck instead, but she was intrigued. Perhaps she didn't need a living room and a sunroom.

"Cheaper?"

"Definitely."

"Will the insurance company expect me to rebuild the sunroom?"

"No."

"The money would be the same?"

"It should be."

"But my insurance rates will go up even before I open for business."

"Undoubtedly. Nothing you do or don't do to the house will change that. Think about the deck idea for a few days before you say yes or no. Either way, we need to demolish the sunroom, so we'll start on that as soon as possible. The money will get here eventually."

That afternoon, she left a message on Abby's phone. "I know you're at work. Call me when you get home. I need counsel."

She wished Evan had called.

It took Dani only one day to accept Jacob's suggestion about extending the deck. She'd brainstormed the possibilities with Abby, who immediately started shopping on-line for more deck furniture. "Maybe you'll need a retractable awning on the side where the sunroom was. It gets more sun than the back of the house."

Evan finally called Tuesday night and stopped by early Wednesday morning. Dani was in the kitchen, unpacking the tablecloths and place mats she'd bought for the five small tables in the dining room.

Before she realized he was in the house, he was beside her. "Sorry I didn't answer your message. I've been staying with a friend in Amherst, interviewing a young sculptor who's going to do some work for me. I'm on my way there again. I'm bidding on a big job that'll take most of next year. A lot of pieces to pull together before I make the final proposal."

She was grateful he'd taken the time to come over. "Let me show you what Jacob has in mind."

He walked around the house, walked it again. Studied Jacob's sketch.

"And?" She was getting nervous. Did he see a flaw she didn't?

"I like it. For one thing, it takes the house back to its original design—now you can safely say New England Colonial in your advertising."

She relaxed. "Thanks. I wasn't sure."

"Glad I could help. I'm late." He kissed her lightly and was gone. Too late, she realized she hadn't asked what the big job was.

In the midst of Jacob's crew tearing down what was left of the sunroom, the winter weather moved in with a vengeance. Some days, they could work only an hour or two. On the plus side, Clarissa's car was quickly repaired, apparently to her satisfaction since Dani hadn't heard from her. However, the morning the workmen began cutting up the sunroom's concrete foundation, Clarissa was on Dani's doorstep, fire in her eyes.

"Why are they cutting up the slab?"

"I'm not rebuilding the sunroom."

If looks could kill, Dani would have been lying at Clarissa's feet. "Why not? My husband built that room on the sunny side of the house so the children would have a bright place to play in winter."

Infuriating woman. It was always about Clarissa, always about HER house. What about *YOU NO LONGER OWN THIS HOUSE* did she not understand?

Dani forgot to count to ten. "There won't be any children living in the house."

"Are you just going to leave this side of the house—empty?"

"The deck will come around to the side."

Clarissa stared at Dani as though she were speaking in tongues, then walked away. "We'll just see about that."

Dani struggled between laughter and anger, and chose laughter; less stressful.

It was Drew who told Dani that, when Jacob applied for the permit to extend the deck, the clerk in the Planning Office mentioned Mrs. Hamilton had already called to complain about the changes to the house—trying to get them to force Dani to rebuild the sunroom.

"She didn't get very far. When he told her that you had the right to change whatever you wanted, so long as Jacob applied for the permits, she hung up on him."

"Surprise, surprise."

"She also told the guy who was installing your new sign in the front yard that what he was doing was illegal. I happened to be out back so I chased her off. Nice looking sign."

"Be sure to tell Abby. She helped design it."

Chapter 13

The drawings for the Veteran's Memorial in Pittsfield were taking up all of Evan's time. He worked right through the New Year's holiday and into January, though he did take time to call Dani on New Year's. He was spending sixteen or seventeen hours a day in his studio—drawing, thinking and drawing some more. At this stage of any job, he could lose himself for days at a time. Interruptions were not welcome. He'd never done a project as large or as complex as this one. The centerpiece of the park was a freestanding sculpture. Getting his vision on paper so the sculptor could transfer it into clay was crucial to the entire project.

By the middle of January, he was finally satisfied with his design. To celebrate, he took Zack for a long walk to make up for all the walks they'd missed while Evan was working. When he unlocked the studio door, he could hear Kanya leaving a voice mail message involving times, places and phone numbers. He grabbed the receiver before she hung up.

"Hey, Kanya. Where are you?"

"New York City."

"Work or play?"

"Work, but I could use some play time. Our delegation is here for a meeting with the World Health Organization."

"Are you translating?"

"No. I'm an assistant to the Director. Much more interesting. Evan, do you have time to come here? I need to talk to you."

He didn't really have the time, but he couldn't refuse. It had been over a year since he'd seen her. "How long will you be there?"

"Until Friday evening."

He was already calculating how he could make this trip work. Get Cathy to feed Zack and pick up the mail. Call Sam so the family wouldn't worry, then deliver the signed contracts for the fishing pier to the County Office on his way out of town. He'd have a day or two to finalize the drawings for the sculpture when he got back. Taking a break would give him time to reconsider some of the details he was still struggling with.

This was Tuesday. "I can be there tomorrow afternoon."

"Perfect. We have a suite of rooms at the Downtown Marriott. One of the delegates couldn't come at the last minute; you can stay in his room."

"Do you have a phone where I can reach you?"

"Try my cell," in her British-accented English, she gave him the number, "or the hotel." She read off more numbers.

It had been getting harder and harder for Dani to ignore the fact that she was seriously attracted to Evan, was preoccupied with him, everything about him. The graceful way his height unfolded when he stood up, the way he looked down into her eyes when he talked to her, giving her his full attention, the way his hands and lips had ignited her insides. She was at once excited and terrified by what she was feeling. She and Ben had failed each other. Failing again might destroy her.

It was Ross who told her that Evan was in New York. Every afternoon after school, Ross had been digging up the garden and spading compost into the soil. "Visiting his girlfriend, I think. He's gone to meet her in New York before. Her name's Kanya. Weird name. He won't be back till Saturday or Sunday."

Girlfriend.

Not surprising. He was young, good looking, charming.

Clearly, she'd been reading more into those kisses than she should have. When he called her on New Year's, he'd told her he was too busy with his drawings to see her, yet he could find the time to run off to New York for several days.

Message received.

She reminded herself that she had a business to run and shouldn't be spending so much time wondering whether he was interested in her, whether she was interested in him. If he really did have a girlfriend, it was better to know now.

When she ran out of rational arguments, she scrubbed the kitchen floor on her hands and knees, then all the bathroom floors. Scrubbing didn't solve the problem, but she was at least tired enough to sleep.

Evan drove back to Lee on Saturday. Kanya and her delegation had taken the 11 p.m. flight to Bangkok Friday night and, since the delegation had reserved the suite through that night, he stayed there by himself. It had been good to see her. Those horrific days after the tsunami had changed both of their lives and would always connect them.

At dinner Wednesday evening, she told him about her engagement to the son of her parents' friends. An arranged marriage. "My family thinks it's time for me to marry, and Thaksin is from a good family. He works in his father's import/export firm. The dowry has already been discussed."

Evan reached across the table to take her hand, tiny in his larger one. "More important than what they think, do you think it's time? I'm sure Stuart wouldn't want you to be alone forever."

"But I don't love Thaksin, not like I loved Stuart." Tears welled up. "Affection maybe. It feels as though I'm settling for—less."

"Perhaps with time?"

She shrugged. With her free hand, she pulled her long black hair into a loose knot at the base of her neck, then let it fall free, a nervous habit he remembered from their days in Chaing Mai. "Family is important in my country. My father would not have approved of my marrying and moving to a foreign country, but I'd have defied him for Stuart." The tears slipped down her cheeks.

Evan wasn't sure what to say. A woman would do this better. "What's good about Thaksin?"

She almost smiled. "You always start with the good. It is one of your nicest characteristics." In a few minutes, "Well, he's nice looking, not much taller than I am, slender, very religious. He takes offerings to the shrines several times a week. Smart. Gentle."

"And the other—things?" Evan was careful not to assume there were bad characteristics. Let her tell him whatever she wanted.

"He's not happy that I have so many Western ways and friends. He doesn't like my traveling or working with men. He was against my coming on this trip. We argued at the airport."

"Does he know about Stuart?"

She nodded slowly. "And about you. He wants me to quit work when we marry."

"Will you?"

"I don't know. Yes, probably. In my country, it's still hard to be an independent woman. I suppose I won't mind not working once I have children."

Evan lifted the hand he still held and kissed it. "I'll miss you."

Thursday afternoon, she had free time so they rode the Staten Island Ferry, buying hot dogs and cokes on the island, then returning to Manhattan, each aware that this might be the last time they'd be alone. They reminisced about working in Northern Thailand, talked about Stuart and Fiona almost without sadness.

She had a formal dinner to attend that night and meetings the next day so Evan went shopping for drafting supplies. Friday night, they ate an early dinner in the hotel dining room. While they were sitting in the lobby, waiting for the rest of the Thai delegation to check out, she put him on the spot. "Is there a woman in your life?"

He hesitated, then decided to confide in her—who better? "Maybe. Maybe not. I haven't known her long, four or five months."

"It didn't take me that much time to fall in love with Stuart."

"She's older than I am, divorced with a teen age son. She came to Lee to open a bed and breakfast."

"Pretty?"

"Mmm—attractive is closer, good facial bones, tall; blue-gray eyes, her hair's not quite blonde, not quite brown, and she has a dimple in her left cheek."

"And?"

"We've spent a few afternoons together. I'm doing some work on her property."

"You like her." Not a question. "I can hear it in your answer. You don't quite want to admit it."

Kanya had caught him out. "I suppose. She's the first one since Fee."

"Four years is a long time. Fiona wouldn't want you to be alone either."

As the Thai delegation headed for the door and a waiting taxi, Evan pulled Kanya into a tight hug that Thaksin wouldn't approve of. "E-mail me. Surely your fiancé can't complain about that. I don't want to lose touch with you."

"Will you come for the wedding?"

Go back to Thailand? Back to where Fiona died. He'd never intended to return.

"I'll see."

There were tears on her cheeks as she left, a graceful wave, her silky midnight hair shifting around her shoulders as she stepped into the revolving door that was slowly separating them.

Though she and Dani had been e-mailing almost every day, Abby hadn't been back in Lee since the day after Christmas. "We're doing inventory—long days, lots of overtime."

At first, Dani didn't question the excuse but, when Abby had missed two weekends, Dani was suspicious and got on the phone. E-mail couldn't take the place of personal conversation. "You can't possibly be doing that much inventory. Did you and Drew have a falling out?"

"Sort of."

"About?"

"His daughter. It happened on Christmas day. You had the whole tree mess to cope with so I didn't tell you. In simple terms, Stephanie wasn't happy that I was intruding on her time with her father. Got really snarky. Actually rude. Maybe her mother put her up to it—who knows. But when I brought her behavior up with Drew later that night, he got all defensive. Took her side, said I just didn't understand teenagers who were dealing with divorce. Somehow, the discussion headed south from there. I didn't expect her to like me, not a requirement. What got to me was that Drew put me in the wrong."

"And so you've retreated to the wilds of Connecticut."

"He hasn't called since then, and I'm damned if I'm going to call."

"How are you?"

"Shitty. How are you?"

"Feeling foolish. According to Ross, Evan's been in New York City visiting his girlfriend."

"Ouch."

"I—I'd begun to hope that—well, I feel foolish."

"I really do need to work this weekend. I'll come as soon as I can."

"We're a sorry pair."

Chapter 14

*J*anuary's weather stayed wet, snowy and windy, slowing and then stopping the repairs on The Maples. Being shut-in by the weather was harder than Dani remembered. Six years in California had stolen her ability to stay inside all day. She longed to walk without being bundled up and drive without fear of sliding into a ditch.

To take her mind off the news about Evan's girlfriend, she called Spence—and of course had to clear her weekend visit with Ben. She drove the toll road to Springfield—at least the Mass Pike was usually ice free—and boarded the train to Baltimore. The Weather Channel claimed Maryland was having milder weather than the Berkshires.

On Saturday, she and Spence drove into D.C. She'd been looking forward to introducing him to what the Smithsonian offered. Ben wasn't much on museums. Perhaps it would give her something special to share with her son. Since Spence had always been interested in airplanes, had wanted to be a pilot when he was in elementary school, they spent the day at the Air and Space Museum.

This Annapolis weekend was definitely better than their first one. The only negative was the news that Ben's child bride was pregnant, due sometime in June. Twenty-something Sherry was having the baby Dani had tried and tried to have after her miscarriage. Add that to the Not Fair list.

Spence was less than thrilled. "I'm sorta old to have a baby sister or brother."

She tried to treat the news lightly. "At least you won't have to share your toys."

He grinned. "Never thought of that. Will it cry a lot?"

"No doubt. You did."

"How come I didn't ever have a brother or sister before?"

A question almost as daunting as where do babies come from. Fortunately, Ben had taken care of that lecture.

"You nearly had a brother, but I miscarried in the fifth month and, from then on, I just never got pregnant again." Probably couldn't.

The good news was that Spence was looking forward to spending Easter week with her.

The Wednesday after she got back from Annapolis, she ran into Evan outside the Post Office. He was wearing a rust-colored parka, his hair longer than usual.

It was too soon. She hadn't had time to figure out what to say about Ross's information—or whether she should say anything at all.

Evan's face lit up when he saw her. "Hey, Dani—I was going to call you again this afternoon, see whether you wanted to have dinner."

Again? There hadn't been a call. The lie came before she could stop it. "I'm busy tonight."

"Tomorrow then?" Though he hadn't touched her, he was filling up all the space around her, interfering with her breathing. How could he so casually ask her out when he'd been in New York, seeing a woman named Kanya? This was exactly why she should forget about having a man in her life. Another pair of shoes to be returned to the shelf.

No sense pursuing the *I'm busy* lie. Time to let him know that she knew where he'd been and with whom. "Ross said you've been in New York." She was daring him to be truthful, waiting to be hurt by the truth. Mad at herself for caring enough to be hurt.

"I called you when I got back Saturday night, but something was wrong with your cell. It wouldn't let me leave a message—and then, well, I got busy with the Pittsfield stuff. I should have tried again, but I've been working 24/7 on the final paperwork for the Memorial project. I just faxed everything off an hour ago." There was an apology in there somewhere.

He was right about her cell phone. She'd forgotten to pack the charger. It wasn't in working order until Monday morning. "I was visiting my son."

"Drew told me."

He had called her, and he'd asked Drew about her. After visiting another woman. "I really need to get going."

He searched her face, asking her eyes what he didn't understand. "Something wrong, Dani? Look, I'm sorry I didn't call before I left. The trip came up unexpectedly. A friend from Thailand was in New York on business."

"Telling me where you're going isn't necessary." *Communication wasn't the issue; the friend was.*

He caught the anger in her voice. "Then why are you angry?"

She hesitated. She'd never been any good at lying. "Ross said you were visiting a girl—your girlfriend."

In the few seconds it had taken her to accuse him of playing fast and loose with her all-too-fragile emotions, it began to snow. The charcoal clouds that had been hovering all morning were dropping soft flakes on her eyelashes and her hair.

Evan had no trouble hearing the hurt in her words. He'd been careless with her feelings, anxious to see Kanya, to keep that connection alive. He'd made arrangements for Zack, called Sam, but he'd forgotten to call Dani. No excuse except that she wasn't yet a fixed point on his radar. The growing attraction between them was a little like dancing—without actually dancing. Briefly coming together, then separating. Hearing the same music but not admitting to what they heard. Moving a few steps apart, watching one another, then coming together again. The tantalizing warmth of hands, the scent of skin, the intensity of their eyes silently sending messages that neither had been brave enough to put into ordinary speech.

"She's a friend, not a girlfriend. A big difference." His eyes willed her to believe him. "Her name's Kanya. She was our translator in Thailand, but now she works for the Thai government. Whenever she comes to the states, we try to get together. She called late last Tuesday, and I left early Wednesday morning."

"Oh." Dani had rushed to judgment, assuming the worst. Not every man was Ben.

"She wanted to tell me she's getting married in a few months." His gloved hand briefly touched Dani's cheek. "I'm glad it bothered you."

In spite of the cold, she felt her face grow warm.

"You're blushing." He leaned forward to kiss her. "I promise to tell you about Kanya, about—everything—if you'll have dinner with me."

The kiss effectively erased whatever her doubts might have been. She wanted to believe him.

Evan chose a small Italian restaurant in Stockbridge. On weekends, it was usually jammed with families but, on a stormy Wednesday night, there were only a few others willing to ignore the threat of snow. At the last minute, Evan had tossed snow chains in the back of the pickup in case the roads got ugly.

On the drive to Stockbridge, their conversation was safely confined to the weather. Evan was already regretting his offer to explain about Kanya, about Thailand. For a guy who regularly made presentations in front government agencies, he was nervous about revisiting the agony of losing Fee. Not even Joanna had asked for details, and he'd never volunteered. But if he was serious about bringing Dani into his life, he needed to tell her.

They were seated at a table in front of an enormous brick fireplace, listening to an old Dean Martin tape of Italian love songs; between them, a carafe of red wine caught the light from the fire. A romantic setting for a decidedly unromantic story. Evan twisted and twisted the stem of his wine glass, not sure he could do this. He never wanted anyone to feel sorry for him, always fought against feeling sorry for himself. A remnant of his childhood. *I don't care that I don't have a father; I have a grandfather.* He'd always believed in his ability to stand alone, to be who he'd taught himself to be.

"Evan, the glass is wearing a hole in the tablecloth. You don't have to tell me."

He forced his hand to stop, focusing on her instead. She was wearing a white wool turtleneck sweater, her hair tucked behind her ears. Tonight, she looked younger than he was. "I want you to know." He paused. "No one but Kanya knows all of it."

The first part of the story was easy. "When I was finishing my graduate degree in Edinburgh, I was awarded one of three places on a team assigned to work in Third World countries under the supervision of UNESCO. We taught small communities how to build and maintain their public open space, like playgrounds and parks. Fiona Dunn and Stuart MacBride were the other two team members. We'd been in a few classes together but, not until we spent two years in the field, relying on one another for everything, did we become close friends. Stuart was a city boy, born and raised in Edinburgh, a master at getting people to do what he wanted them to do, figuring out how to get the supplies we needed and, once we had them, how to keep them from being stolen. He managed the business end of the project. And he was always ready to have fun." Evan finally tasted his wine, remembering Stuart's, *Come on Murray, let's raise some hell.*

The second part was impossibly hard.

"Fiona was from the Borders, where a lot of the ruined Abbeys are. Her family lives a few miles from Jedburgh. She grew up riding horses, loved animals and the outdoors." Whenever his memory saw her, she was running across a field. Fee loved to run. "She specialized in the environmental part." He handed Dani the two photos he'd brought with him, one was a snapshot of the four of them in Phuket, the day before the disaster. Another tourist had taken it with Evan's camera. The other one was of Fiona wearing a tank top and khaki shorts with cargo pockets, her black curls cut short because the humidity made her long hair unmanageable.

Since Evan was using the past tense when he talked about them, Dani realized they must have died. She studied the pictures. "Fiona looks like she had spirit." Sexy, athletic, probably comfortable with who she was, something Dani was still working on.

"Oh yeah." He reached for the picture. The uncharacteristic sadness in his eyes brought tears to Dani's. "She was always outspoken, not intimidated by the difficulties we faced. She loved challenges. It's always been my guess that she dared Stuart to swim out beyond the breakers that morning. Stu could never resist a dare. I wouldn't have let her go, but I was—well, I wasn't there. Should have been there." He'd gone over and over the morning that could never be undone. "I'm getting ahead of myself."

The waitress brought Dani's Shrimp Alfredo and Evan's spaghetti and meatballs. "Black pepper? Grated cheese?"

The formalities of serving the food completed, the waitress left them alone, and Evan slipped back into the story. "Sometime during our time in Nigeria, our first year out, Fee and I—" his voice broke.

Dani finished his sentence, "Fell in love?"

He cleared his throat around the emotion that threatened to overwhelm him and nodded.

"Evan, if it's too hard for you, it really doesn't matter." Dani had already taken several mouthfuls of pasta; he was only picking at his dinner.

"It does matter." He chose his words carefully, "I want you to understand that there hasn't been anyone important in my life since Fee and, even though what happened will always be with me, I want to make room for you in my life."

Such a beautiful speech. Dani reached for his free hand. Now, neither of them was eating.

The crooked smile came. The first time he'd smiled all evening.

He forced himself to continue, afraid he might lose his nerve if he stopped. "Christmas 2004, it was my idea to spend the holidays in Southern Thailand—gorgeous sand, warm water. It would be our last time together for a while. Two couples on a romantic holiday. Kanya and Stuart were planning to marry, so were Fiona and I. Stu was going back for an MBA program, Fee and Kanya needed visas to immigrate— Kanya to Scotland and Fee to come here. Visas like that take months to process, and I had to deal with the farm.

"On Boxing Day morning, I stayed back at the hotel trying to get an internet connection to the states. The others went to the beach. If you remember the news about that day, the tsunami from the earthquake near Sumatra raced across the Indian Ocean, hitting places like Sri Lanka and Phuket. It all happened so fast they never had a chance. The wave I saw was about fifteen or sixteen feet high. From our hotel room, I watched it hit the hotel in front of ours—then slam into ours," he stopped. "I still see it. The nightmares have never entirely gone away."

"I remember seeing pictures on the news." *But you lived those pictures.*

He took a deep breath. "The wave crushed everything in its path, randomly throwing trees, people, cars, and furniture into the streets and onto the beach. An instant trash heap. Afterward—afterward, I tried to find them, Stuart and Fiona and Kanya, but couldn't. Hours later, when I'd given up hope of finding any of them, a waiter from a restaurant near the beach found Kanya on the restaurant's roof and brought her back to the hotel, which was miraculously still standing. She hadn't been in the water when the wave came—but Fee and Stuart—they were already out there. Most of those people were never found because, well, the surge reversed itself, carrying everything—everyone—out to sea. For the next few days, the survivors—we were all looking for someone, calling out names, showing pictures." He studied Fee's picture. "This is the one I showed while Kanya and I searched the hospitals and makeshift morgues." Evan hadn't realized there were tears on his cheeks until Dani reached across the table to hand him her napkin.

It was several minutes before Dani dared to ask, "How did you finally get home?"

"A few days later, I don't remember when exactly, the authorities told me in no uncertain terms that I was flying to Singapore. They wanted foreign tourists out of their way. There were so many others searching like I was. It didn't matter. I hadn't found them. Kanya had already agreed to translate at one of the hospitals.

"It took me a week to get to Boston, four different standby flights. I slept in the airports." He used the napkin to dry his eyes. "Sorry. I didn't think I'd have this much trouble after all this time." He looked at his plate, took a couple of bites, and pushed it aside. He felt full even though he'd eaten almost nothing. "How about some decaf?"

"Sure."

"I'll fast forward to last week. Kanya's family has arranged a marriage for her, but she isn't in love with this man. She feels like she's betraying Stuart. That's why she was so anxious to see me."

Throughout Evan's story, Dani felt her heart breaking for what he'd lived through, realizing that nothing Ben had ever done to her could equal the horror Evan had faced and survived. The strength of this remarkable man, who was beginning to take up more and more space in her life, humbled her.

They drank the coffee in silence. Evan was exhausted. "Maybe we should see what the weather has in store for us." He stood, picked up the check and slipped on his parka. She slid her chair back, retrieving her purse and coat from the empty chair next to her.

Luckily, the weather had held off so the plows could stay ahead of the snow. The roads were safe to drive but, by morning, the temperature would have dropped, leaving black ice. At Dani's door, he gently pulled her into his arms, his cheek resting against her hair.

"Thanks for listening."

"Evan, I'm so—"

He laid his index finger against her lips. "Don't say sorry—please."

She nodded.

"I'd like this—us—to be important. I'd like to show you just how important—but tonight's probably—well not tonight." His kiss was tender. "I'll call. I promise."

Much later, she realized she hadn't said no to the implications in "important." Maybe she was ready to take an emotional risk with this handsome, clever man.

Because Dani had to pick up the set of dishes she'd ordered weeks ago and Evan had an appointment in Pittsfield, they made plans to meet in Lenox on Saturday to choose the new bench for the garden. Teak seat and back, wrought iron legs and armrests, and way more expensive than Dani had anticipated. They lifted it into the bed of his truck—this was getting to be a habit—and she followed his truck back to The Maples. Together, they carried the bench into the garden. Ross had finished reworking the soil, and Jacob's crew had laid the forms for the paths so the colored concrete could be poured, weather permitting. As soon as spring showed up, the planting would begin but, since the daytime temperatures usually hovered around 40 degrees, it would be a while yet.

"Once everything's finished, it'll be a perfect spot." She sat on the bench, imagining the flowers spilling onto the walkways, with the pond and the bridge as the centerpiece. "I'm glad you suggested a bench."

"Ask one of Jacob's men to bolt it down after the concrete cures."

"Good idea. Clarissa undoubtedly won't want to pay me back."

"We'll see. I can be very persuasive."

"You do manage her rather well."

"Don't tell her. She likes to think she's managing me."

He sat beside Dani, putting his arm around her shoulders, but she couldn't let herself relax into him. "Clarissa is probably watching us."

His arm tightened around her. "She's not the boss of me—or you." With his other hand, he turned her face so he could look into her eyes just before he kissed her. When the kiss ended, they walked hand-in-hand into Dani's cottage, locking the door behind them. No words were necessary. They each knew what was going to happen.

When she was first married, Ben always took charge of their sex life. He made the moves, she followed; when he was satisfied, he assumed she was and she seldom told him otherwise. On a scale of one to ten, she'd have rated their sex life a solid six, seven on a good day. Not entirely his fault. After she miscarried, she'd so wanted to have another child that conceiving dominated her thought—instead of mutual pleasure. In the last years of their marriage, she was consumed with charting her ovulation cycles and taking her temperature. Her obsession with getting pregnant didn't help their relationship, and Ben eventually looked elsewhere. Hard as it was to admit, her hesitation about being involved with someone else, with Evan, wasn't so much fear of being hurt again, as fear of failing again. After Ben left, she'd been angry at his rejection, about him wanting Sherry instead of her.

It took another year before she saw that she shared the blame.

Now, lying beneath Evan, Dani knew she had never before come close to experiencing the soaring ecstasy he awakened in her. Slowly, deftly, he'd undressed her, pulling her sweater over her head, sliding her slacks down over her hips. Eventually, all her clothing—and his— was on the floor. His hands and his lips caressing her—at first softly, then so urgently that she couldn't lie still, wanting him more than she'd ever imagined she could want someone.

"Please—Evan—now." She'd never asked Ben like that—hadn't known she could ask.

He entered her quickly, setting off explosion after explosion in her body, melting even her bones.

An eleven, no question about it.

Later, lying on his side, Evan pushed a pillow beneath his head so he was looking down at her face, flushed and warm from passion, a little drowsy.

The intensity of his eyes made her ask, "What?"

"You are beautiful."

She felt beautiful.

He made her feel beautiful again and again.

The next day, the real world intruded on the magical place they'd created for themselves. Staying in that warm cocoon, wrapped in wrinkled sheets, wasn't possible. There was work to be done. Evan spent the morning staring at the preliminary drawings for the picnic area adjacent to the fishing pier—a mundane project after the excitement of designing the sculpture. Nevertheless, the drawings had to be finished in a few days. A fresh pot of coffee and an extra long walk with Zack were no help. He simply couldn't focus.

Was she having the same problem? He called in the middle of the afternoon. She sounded tired. Jacob's crew was painting the siding on the new living room wall, and she was putting the final touches on one of the bedrooms.

"Dinner tonight? Here at the farm." Maybe seeing her would pull him out of the limbo he'd been in all day—or make it worse. He needed to touch her, talk to her.

She wanted to be there, beside him, right now. But she had work to do. "I'll pick up something from the grocery store."

What had worried Dani was that he might not call, might have thought better about being—involved with her. Involved. An unromantic word, but a safe one. But he had called.

Having dinner would be good.

Followed by more sex.

It all seemed too fast yet, if she examined what had been happening in the weeks leading up to last night, it wasn't.

Chapter 15

$\mathcal{B}$ecause Abby needed one or two historical pictures of The Maples for the web page and was also thinking of framing a few to hang in the entry hall, Dani resigned herself to asking Clarissa whether she had early photos of the house. Dani liked the idea of decorating with the house's history; she'd already obtained current photos of Lee's Main Street, as well as a few showing what Lee looked like in the 1930's and '70's.

If only she didn't need to ask Clarissa for help.

After Dani left four phone messages, Clarissa finally replied. There were, indeed, some photos of the house, and Clarissa would show them to her at two o'clock on Friday. She didn't ask whether that time was convenient for Dani.

Polly and Dani spent Friday morning unpacking and storing the new linens. Polly was proving to be good at understanding what the day-to-day operation of the house would require, and she was a hard worker. It was Polly who suggested Dani buy the environmental alert signs to put in the bathrooms, encouraging guests to use their towels more than once—cutting down on the laundry. "My instructor says all the big hotels are using this system."

Dani let Polly finish up and was at Clarissa's door promptly at two.

"Good, you're on time."

And good afternoon to you too.

A large cardboard box of photos was in the center of the coffee table. Clarissa motioned Dani toward the couch, seating herself in the wing back chair. As usual, no offer of coffee or tea, one of which Dani could have used, since she'd skipped lunch. "I don't know exactly what you are looking for, so you can choose for yourself. I do want the originals back."

With Clarissa watching her every move, Dani began searching for pictures of the house, ignoring those with people. Abby had said that size wasn't an issue. Any picture could be scanned into Photo Shop and, from there, Abby could crop or enlarge the images to suit herself.

"We didn't take many photos in those days," Clarissa explained, "not like people do today. Film was expensive."

Dani nodded, concentrating on the task at hand. In the first half hour, she found three good photos of the front of the house. One taken before the sunroom had been built. "That was the day we moved in, in 1948." In another photo, the sunroom had been added and the maples were newly planted, their spindly trunks supported by tall stakes. "That was in the late fifties." The third had been taken after a heavy snowstorm, whipped cream drifts piled high against the porch, icicles hanging from the edge of the roof.

"What year was this?" Dani handed the picture to Clarissa.

"The year JT died—1970."

"Your son?"

"My younger son." Clarissa reached into the stack of people photos that Dani had discarded and pulled out one of a young man, more boy than man, wearing an army uniform, smiling at the camera. He was fair, like Clarissa.

"JT was very proud of his uniform." Clarissa looked tenderly at the picture of her son and, for the first time, Dani saw real emotion in this woman who had gone out of her way to make Dani's life difficult. Clarissa Hamilton had a human side.

A few moments later, Clarissa pulled out another photo. "This is my other son, Matthew." A handsome teenager in a tuxedo stood beside a girl wearing what was probably a prom dress.

"Beautiful girl. His girlfriend?"

"A farm girl from over toward Stockbridge. I don't remember her name. I never understood what he saw in her. Fortunately he married someone more suitable. Matt died in a plane crash when he was just thirty-three." She was quiet for a few moments. "Both of my boys."

Dani couldn't imagine what it would feel like to lose Spence; the pain would be intolerable. Yet Clarissa had lost two sons. Surviving those blows took a special kind of strength. Dani surprised herself by feeling sorry for the woman sitting across from her. "It must be hard to lose a child, two children." Strange to be saying something kind to Clarissa. So often the words they exchanged were sharp.

Clarissa didn't reply.

Dani studied Matt's picture. Something about him was familiar. The hair, maybe the shape of his face.

By the time Dani left an hour later, she had also chosen some early pictures of the garden and a colored photo taken when the maples were more mature, wearing their bright red foliage. Clarissa's voice followed her out the door, "Be sure you bring them back." Gone was the mother who had lost her sons.

Abby was delighted with Dani's choices but suggested they should also have a picture of the Hamilton family. Since Mr. Hamilton had been a local selectman and a state senator, a group photo would humanize the house's history. Asking Clarissa for another photograph was too much to face this week—what with the furniture being moved up from the basement and the shutters being installed—so Dani called Lorraine. Two days later, a brown envelope was pushed through the new mail slot next to the front door. Photo for Dani. On the inside was a 5" x 7" colored snapshot of the Hamilton family lined up in front of the house. On the back was a yellow post-it: *Summer 1968. Front row, l to r, my brothers JT and Matt, Aileen and me. My parents are behind us.* Without giving it a closer look, Dani put the envelope in the For Abby box next to the computer.

As she had with the other pictures, Abby scanned these into the computer, made whatever adjustments seemed necessary, and eventually printed all of them out on photographic paper. She was still shopping for a good framing deal on the eleven pictures she'd selected.

The metamorphosis of the Hamilton house was almost complete. Dani had mixed her own oak furniture with Clarissa's more traditional walnut and mahogany pieces. She chose bright golds, oranges and reds for accents, coarsely woven fabrics, patterned baskets to hold magazines and armloads of silk flowers. She scoured the secondhand and antique stores for lamps, some with brass bases, others with pewter, though she was having trouble finding shades she liked. For the most part, she was happy with the eclectic style she was creating. The local B & B's typically emphasized historical periods. The Maples, by comparison, was a young house, not even ninety yet. It could wear brighter colors.

For nearly two years, Brenda Murray had been lying to almost everyone, except Matthew of course. She surprised herself by being rather good at deceit. She let her college friends think she was dating a variety of eligible young men, enjoying the glamour of living in Washington while putting her Political Science degree to good use working as a lobbyist for an environmental group. Her Washington colleagues knew she had a live-in boyfriend but, since Brenda didn't socialize with them very often, they hadn't met Matthew, didn't even know his name. Whenever one of her sisters or her mother asked if she was seeing someone, she deflected their questions, reminding them that she was working twelve-hour days and was too busy for socializing.

Without being told, however, Liz Murray instinctively knew there was someone important in her daughter's life, but was wise enough to keep her suspicions to herself. Raising three daughters had taught her that parental interrogations never produced good results, certainly not with her youngest, who would simply retreat into defensive silence. Better to wait for Brenda to come to her. Not until Brenda called from D.C., asking Liz to take care of "my son Evan" while she made a business trip to Florida, did Liz realize how little she knew about her youngest daughter's life. Three months before, Brenda had flown to Albany and driven over to the farm for the weekend, never mentioning a child.

After Brenda's phone call, Liz had sent Ross to look for the crib they'd stored in the barn, burying her anger with her daughter by cleaning the crib and and borrowing some bedding from Amanda.

This time, when Brenda arrived at Murray Farms, young Evan was sleeping contentedly in his car seat, unaware he was meeting his maternal grandmother for the first time. Brenda carried the car seat into the kitchen while Liz brought the bags filled with bottles, toys and clothes.

At a loss about how to begin a conversation that didn't include *Why didn't you tell me about him?* Liz took the non-confrontational road, "Do you want some iced tea?"

"No thanks. I have an afternoon flight back to D.C." She handed Liz a manila folder. "I've written down the name of the hotel, the flight numbers, and the date I'm returning. I'll be in Miami for a week." When Liz didn't respond, "He's a really good baby, sleeps through the night, isn't afraid of strangers, and doesn't seem to have any food allergies." Brenda hesitated, "You're sure this is okay with you— Dad too?" Perhaps she'd suddenly realized that presenting her parents with a grandson they'd known nothing about could be something of a shock.

"It's okay, but it's a strange way to meet my grandson." Liz changed the topic. "Dad wanted to be here to see you, but he's making deliveries today."

"That's right, Fridays. Have you had good crops this summer?"

"Average. But now that we have the new hothouses and can raise produce year round, winters are actually better for us." As if Brenda actually cared. She'd hated the farm, couldn't wait to go to college, and had seldom come home, even for holidays. "How old is Evan?"

"Seven months. He was born on January 25. His middle name is Andrew and, before you ask, no, I'm not married."

Evan Andrew Murray. Dark auburn hair curled around his sleeping face. Had Brenda been truthful about Evan's father, Liz would have remembered Matthew Hamilton. Brenda had dated him in high school, but they'd gone their separate ways after graduation. A few years later, one of Brenda's high school friends had written to tell her that Matt had married someone named Suzanne Petteys, a girl he'd met while attending law school. A daughter, Rose, was born shortly after the wedding and, two years later another daughter, Cynthia, completed the family. Occasionally, Matt brought his young family to visit, but very few of the locals had met Suzanne or the girls.

When Matt and Suzanne separated, he accepted a partnership with a high profile law firm in Washington and, three months later, he ran into Brenda at a cocktail party. It didn't take long for him to be spending more time at her apartment than his, keeping his small studio apartment so he had a valid mailing address and telephone. Until the divorce was final and the financial and custody issues were settled, it was wiser to keep his new living arrangements, and his son, a secret.

"Thanks for not asking questions." Brenda kissed her mother goodbye, something she'd rarely done as a child or an adult. "When I get back, we'll talk."

The day Brenda was due to return to Washington, Ross Murray saw the special bulletin on the evening news. A Miami to Washington flight had crashed during a violent thunderstorm near Atlanta. "What airline was Brenda on?"

Liz hunted for the folder Brenda had left, flipping the pages with one hand because she was holding a freshly diapered Evan on her hip. "Eastern, 344." She noted that the reservation was listed for Brenda Duncan, not Murray. Duncan was her middle name.

Ross quickly changed the channel, looking for a report on another station, then, "My God, Lizzie, it's the same plane that crashed. They're saying no one survived."

The business of identifying bodies and notifying relatives took the airline several days. Convincing the airline that Brenda Duncan and Brenda Murray were one and the same took much longer and ultimately required submitting her dental records. When her body was finally released to her parents, the crash was old news, her family's grieving made harder by the bureaucratic morass they were forced to cope with. During those difficult weeks, the one bright spot was Evan. Thank God Brenda hadn't taken him with her.

Only a few of the Murrays' closest friends attended the family's private graveside service two months later. There was no obituary in *The Berkshire Eagle*. Liz didn't want to answer any more questions from friends and neighbors than she'd already had. Those who might have been interested in the coincidence of Matthew Hamilton and Brenda Murray dying on the same plane missed the scandal—and Suzanne was spared knowing who her husband had been living with and that he had a son. The weekend after Brenda's burial, Liz and her daughter Joanna drove to D.C. to clean out Brenda's apartment, keeping all of Evan's things, as well as photographs and Brenda's important papers—

especially Evan's birth certificate, *father unknown*—and getting rid of everything else, including what were probably the personal effects of Evan's father. Expensive clothing and golf clubs. The only thing Liz saved for Evan was a Rolex watch. She found no clues to solve the mystery. It was her best guess that he'd been on the same plane; otherwise, he would have come looking for his son.

So many unknowns.

Liz didn't really want to know the truth about the father, didn't want anyone else to have a claim on Evan. She and Ross intended to apply for legal guardianship and eventually adopt him. What was over was over. Her other daughters' families closed ranks around Evan, and no one in town seemed to care how he'd ended up in Lee. Whatever whispers there were eventually went underground.

It took nearly two years for the adoption to be finalized and, once all the paperwork had been recorded and Evan was safely theirs, Liz spent a couple of days in the Springfield City Library, looking at the microfiche records of *The Washington Post's* account of the Atlanta plane crash—particularly the list of victims. When she came to Matthew Andrew Hamilton, Washington and Boston, survived by a wife and two daughters, Liz had the answer, but she never told anyone else, not even Ross, what she'd found. The secret would be safer with her. Liz had learned long ago, when the Murray and Hamilton children were in high school, to give Matt's family, especially his mother, a wide berth. Evan was better off being a Murray.

By that time, Evan was a contented three year old who followed his Papa everywhere on the farm and could already tell when the tomatoes were ripe and help Ross put them in the baskets for the roadside stand.

Although initially Clarissa was pleased that Matthew had chosen Suzanne as his wife, Clarissa never thought she was good enough for him, despite being a Boston debutante and the daughter of one of that city's top lawyers. But then no woman would have measured up. During the marriage, Matthew's mother and wife tolerated one another by avoiding all but the most necessary encounters at weddings, christenings and funerals.

Matthew's sudden death, however, put Suzanne and Clarissa on a collision course. There was no longer a need to keep the peace. Clarissa wanted the funeral to be in Lee and the burial to be in the Hamilton family crypt in Springfield. "You are practically not married to him"— the divorce would have been final in two months—"so his parents should make these decisions."

Suzanne, the only child of a defense attorney known for his toughness in the courtroom, stood her ground. Now there was no reason to pull her punches when dealing with her mother-in-law. "He's still legally my husband and my daughters' father. The funeral will be in Boston. His colleagues, my family, our friends, my children's friends are all here. It's been years since he lived in Lee. You can inter him in Springfield. I don't care about that—but the funeral will be here at St. Joseph's. It's where we were married and the girls were christened."

Because Judd's friends in The General Court were also in Boston, he took Suzanne's side. Clarissa was outnumbered. Lorraine drove herself and Clarissa's mother to Boston on the morning of the funeral. Clarissa had been staying in the Boston condo since they'd heard the news. Aileen was somewhere in Europe; Judd hadn't been able to contact her.

The obituary notices appeared in *The Boston Globe* and *The Washington Post*. Suzanne carefully avoided putting one in *The Berkshire Eagle*, mostly to spite Clarissa.

Though Suzanne was understandably upset by Matt's death, she was also upset by the loss of her temporary spousal support. After Cynthia was born, she and Matt had bought a historic Back Bay house with a very large mortgage. When he died, the only savings they had was his $50,000 life insurance policy. Though he'd been making good money, there wasn't much in reserve. Maintaining separate households had put a strain on their finances. It wouldn't be long until Suzanne would be out of money. Judd offered to make the child support payments for a while, not bothering to consult Clarissa.

No one was particularly surprised when, less than a year later, Suzanne married one of the partners in her father's firm, sold the Back Bay house, and moved to Brookline. Rose and Cynthia seldom saw their paternal grandparents, though Clarissa and Judd sent birthday presents and attended graduations.

Four children and only Lorraine paid attention to her parents. It wasn't supposed to turn out that way.

Chapter 16

Clarissa was bored. Winter did that to her and, now that she was living in a workshop that was barely a thousand square feet, she often had nothing to do. At some point she got tired of reading, and she'd never liked watching soaps all afternoon. When she still owned her house, there was always something to clean or rearrange, friends to invite for lunch, but the guesthouse was much too small for entertaining more than one other person. Quilting filled some of her time, but that too became tedious. Many days, going outside was risky. The ice on the sidewalks and streets made walking and driving hazardous.

She spent every other Monday morning at The Sewing Basket. Since her newest class was quite large, it might be time to offer an advanced class, perhaps on alternate Mondays. She needed to discuss the possibility with Phoebe, who was always looking for ways to attract customers. Nowadays, not as many women had time to sew. The quilting class and the Thursday night knitting class, which Phoebe taught, brought in women who might not otherwise have patronized the shop.

But teaching classes didn't fill enough of her time either. Lunching with friends, usually at restaurants, was pleasant but cost money, which Lorraine kept telling her she didn't have. She played bridge every other Saturday evening and occasionally entered local tournaments.

Minding other people's business did, however, provide a certain amount of entertainment, though she didn't have many opportunities to share her information anymore. Judd had always claimed he wasn't interested in the local gossip she passed on, but he at least appeared to listen. Lately, she'd been keeping track of the number of nights Evan Murray spent at the other guesthouse with that woman. Once or twice a week, his truck was parked in the lot when she went to bed and was still there when she got up in the morning. Not that Clarissa was a prude. Plenty of people had affairs, plenty of people lived together without ever marrying. But she liked Evan, expected better of him. Whatever did he see in her? He needed to find someone who was younger. Not a divorced mother.

When Natalie met Clarissa at Sullivan Station for their biweekly lunch, Natalie became the third person in two days to compliment The Maples, unaware that Clarissa did not enjoy hearing praise about the changes in her house. The first person to mention it had been one of her quilting students; the second was the cashier at the Co-op.

Natalie was close to gushing. "It's charming. I rather like it without the sunroom, and the darker color is quite stylish. When the lawn comes back in the spring and the roses along the porch are blooming, the house will look wonderful."

Not ready to let her irritation show, Clarissa simply answered, "I suppose." She was tired of others expecting her to be flattered because they liked the way the house—that was no longer her house—looked. The Maples had nothing to do with her, and she wanted nothing to do with it. Natalie had never said the house looked wonderful when Clarissa owned it.

The difficult part was, of course, that the house did look good. Fresh paint, albeit a different color, the new deck, the rebuilt front porch and, as soon as the weather warmed up, the garden would start to bloom. This year, it would look better than it had the last couple of years. She was glad she'd asked Evan to work on it. He and that redheaded boy had begun lining the pond with broken glass, creating a mosaic of flowers. The bench was a nice touch too, though she didn't intend to pay for it.

Natalie was not about to drop the subject. "Have you been inside?"

"No."

"Aren't you curious about what it's like without the sunroom? I bet she wouldn't mind if you asked to go inside. She seems rather pleasant."

"When did you meet her?"

"She and Evan Murray were at the dedication of the new playground he designed for Stockbridge."

"Oh." Clarissa had no idea Evan designed playgrounds or, for that matter, why Natalie would be at its dedication.

"Are they a couple?"

"I haven't the foggiest." *But he certainly spends plenty of nights at her place.*

"He was quite attentive."

Clarissa redirected the conversation. "So how's your daughter Nina doing since her husband left her?"

A day at a time, a night at a time, Dani and Evan were finding their way through the early stages of their relationship. Both were busy. Because the sculptor had suggested that the base of the sculpture needed more reinforcement, Evan was reworking some of the specifications. Construction on the park itself wouldn't begin until summer; construction on the fishing pier would start as soon as the ground dried out.

Dani was almost done decorating the upstairs rooms, putting the finishing touches on everything, trying not to be obsessive but being obsessive in spite of herself. She and Evan tried to save time for each other on weekends, sometimes a night or two during the week. She wasn't sure where their affair was going; however, relationships, like dances, didn't always "go" anywhere.

Twice she'd spent the weekend at Evan's, the two of them squirreled into his loft, eating, making love, sleeping, making love. She was discovering that she sometimes enjoyed seducing him. Was this love or lust masquerading as love? There certainly was tenderness and passion and conversation. With no plan.

A plan might interfere with the dance steps.

Suddenly it was February. Dani still hadn't set a date for the The Maples' opening. Something else might go wrong. Nevertheless, she needed to commit to a date so Abby could begin advertising. The extension on the deck was finally finished, though it had only one coat of waterproofing stain. Every time Jacob planned to add the final coat, it snowed. At least the wood was protected from winter's punishment. With some of the insurance money, Dani had bought additional wicker porch furniture which she was storing in the basement until the weather improved.

The new kitchen was outfitted with pots and pans, dishes and silverware. She was gradually stocking the pantry with non-perishables and was practicing with the new stove, trying out various muffin mixes for the breakfast buffet, seasoning the griddle so the pancakes wouldn't stick. A few times, she invited Evan and Drew to join her and Polly for breakfast at dinnertime, setting up one of the small tables in the dining room, arranging the buffet, and serving them as though they were paying guests. Test driving the logistics.

When she no longer had an excuse for not setting an opening date, she crossed her fingers and chose the first full weekend in March. Grateful Dani had finally made up her mind, Abby immediately began printing and mailing fliers, formally launching the website, then notifying the B & B organizations that would be listing The Maples. Twice Dani ran a half page ad in *The Berkshire Eagle*, and Abby asked Drew to make a small wooden sign that could be temporarily attached to the top of the sign in the front yard: **Grand Opening March 5th**

Grand might be overstating the case.

To Dani's amazement, a reservation for the second Friday and Saturday in March came through a week later. A couple from New York City. Booking one room was not going to make her rich, but she felt rich. People wanted to stay in her house. A day later, another reservation came in for the same weekend.

Having researched the prices of the other establishments in and around Lee, she'd kept her prices at the low end to be competitive. Perhaps that explained the quick responses.

Ready or not, The Maples was in business.

The trouble with obsessions is that you can't tell that you're obsessed until your brain and body hit the wall. Before the moment of impact, obsession passes itself off as necessity or doing a good job or proving yourself. Dani's obsession with making The Maples a success took up residence in her life while she wasn't looking.

After her first guests checked out on Monday, she made herself two lists: one for what hadn't gone well, one for what had.

The first thing she learned was that she needed to pay closer attention to special dietary requirements. Though the check-in form asked about special needs, Dani didn't notice that one couple hadn't filled that part in. It turned out the woman was a strict vegan and he was diabetic. Their first breakfast was a disaster. It hadn't occurred to Dani that powdered eggs were in the muffin mixes, and there was sugar in the brand of flavored creams she'd purchased. Ultimately, the woman had toast with jam, juice and black coffee. He had bacon, eggs, potatoes and coffee without flavored cream. On the second morning, Dani found a recipe for vegan breakfast burritos that the woman loved, and her husband had another artery-clogging breakfast with a different brand of vanilla creamer in his coffee.

On the positive side, they loved the room—they'd been in the one with a view over the woods.

The other couple didn't have food issues but asked endless questions about the local tourist sights. After eight or nine attractions were thoroughly discussed, Dani ran out of ideas. She needed to learn more about the area. In the end, however, the couple drove to Stockbridge on both Saturday and Sunday, never going to the other places Dani had told them about. Was it her bad advice or their inability to experiment with different places? Hard to get everything right.

The biggest life lesson was the amount of time and energy it took to run The Maples.

When Spence was five or six, he had a hamster—Hammy—who was addicted to running and running and running in the wheel attached to the side of his cage. He barely took time out to eat. Then, one morning, the wheel wasn't moving and Hammy's tiny body was lying at the bottom. Spence was devastated and tearfully refused the replacement hamster Ben offered to buy him. "It'll just die too."

The Maples had only been open two weeks and already Dani felt like Hammy, running and running and running without enough time to eat properly or take a deep breath. No time to read the newspaper or give herself a manicure. She'd expected the start up would be tough, that she'd be overdoing everything until she found out just how much effort and time were really required to keep the house—running. She was simultaneously wired and exhausted. Whenever she sat down, she thought of a dozen things she should be doing and, after few minutes, she'd be doing them. She'd quickly learned that she wasn't especially good at delegating. Even though Polly's primary job was to make up the rooms, Dani couldn't keep herself from helping change sheets or putting out clean towels, fretting over where to place the complimentary soaps or how many muffins would be needed the next morning. One thing was certain—she and Polly spent way too much time lugging the vacuum up and down the stairs. They needed a second vacuum.

She recognized the frantic pace she'd set for herself was fueled by fear, fear that she'd offend a guest, that there wouldn't be enough business, that she'd fail. This project, this house, was now her life. Failure wasn't an option.

Her days began early. She was in the kitchen by six, preparing for breakfast. Baking muffins, frying bacon or sausage, making pancakes or dipping French toast. A short order cook. The buffet had coffee, tea and juice, fresh fruit, cold cereal, along with 2% milk, flavored coffee creams, half-and-half, sugar, artificial sweetners—covering all the bases. In between cooking full breakfasts, she packed up muffins and coffee for guests who didn't have time for breakfast at the house. While Dani was taking orders and then serving, she could take a few minutes to answer questions guests had. If she had time, she'd pour herself a cup of coffee while she explained how to get to Tanglewood or what the Shaker Village outside of Pittsfield offered. Abby had made sure there were plenty of brochures for all the local attractions.

Polly cleaned up after breakfast and started on the rooms as soon as they were empty. Her classes were between one and four, Monday through Thursday. On Monday and Tuesday—Polly's days off—Dani did everything. Already she'd begun to dread those two days.

She'd called the Quills to ask whether they kept postage stamps on hand and which taxi companies were the most reliable. Louise promised to visit The Maples after Easter. She was too busy now. Dani had learned the hard way to get guests to clarify exactly what they meant by *through*. If they said they were booking Tuesday through Thursday, did they mean they were staying Thursday night or that they would check out Thursday morning. Twice she'd fallen into that trap.

Every morning, guests had to be checked out; afternoons, new guests checked in. She spent a lot of time recommending restaurants and local attractions, occasionally making calls about tickets to local events. Incredible how many phone numbers she needed. While Polly was cleaning the rooms, Dani paid bills, answered e-mails, went grocery shopping, and picked up goodies from the bakery. The afternoon tea/coffee buffet was another opportunity to talk with her guests because she didn't have to do anything more than keep the coffee coming and the tea water hot. Guest-bonding. Louise had reminded Dani that the guests not only needed to like the house and the service, they also needed to feel comfortable with her, since repeat customers would be a major part of her business. She'd begun keeping a record of guests' food preferences, their jobs, their children's names. Having the information on file would give her a quick refresher when guests made second and third visits. If they did.

Most days, she barely had time to open a carton of yogurt and fix a couple slices of toast for lunch. Dinner was frozen fish and vegetables, maybe scrambled eggs—usually eaten around eight or nine after she'd prepared the dining room tables for breakfast. Doing laundry was catch as catch can. If she or Polly hadn't finished it during the day, like as not she was doing it at ten or eleven when she locked up. Those guests who would be returning later than that were given the front door's security code, which changed daily. Fortunately, Jacob had installed an intercom system between Dani's cottage, the office, and all the rooms so, if someone had a problem after hours, they could contact her.

She'd also learned that a guest's definition of an emergency was not always hers. Such as the woman in the yellow bedroom who—at 11:15 p.m.—wanted to know what the temperature was supposed to be the next day. Only once had there been a real emergency. The man in the blue room called to ask about the closest ER because his wife was having an asthma attack. Afraid he might not find Fairview Hospital on his own, Dani drove them to Great Barrington. A night's sleep lost.

She was already worried about how to handle Spence's Easter Week visit. Where would she find the time for him? Twice she'd had to cancel plans with Evan so, when he called the Thursday before Spence's arrival, suggesting they have dinner, she said yes. "It's been a crazy week."

"Is Chinese takeout okay?"

As luck would have it, in the middle of their dinner, she received a call from a B & B outside of Lenox, asking if she had a vacant room since that establishment was full. She did and, while Evan kept eating, she checked them in. By the time she got back to her place, Evan was asleep on her couch. He'd been working long hours too. Without waking him, she tossed out the remaining food—which had reached the cold, slimy stage—took a shower, laid a comforter over him, and went to bed.

When her alarm went off at 5:30 a.m., she was dreaming of fried chicken.

Oh Lord—Evan.

She checked the living room. He was gone. If these last weeks were any measure of what her life was going to be like for the next few months or years—she wouldn't have any personal life left. She brushed her teeth, slipped into clean slacks and a sweater, ran a comb through her hair, pulled it into a pony tail—she desperately needed a haircut— and headed for the main house. It was time to start breakfast.

She owed Evan an apology.

Chapter 17

During Easter Week, The Maples was completely booked. Good news financially. Bad news for Spence's visit.

Luckily, the college was also on break, so Polly was willing to work more hours. "I can use the extra money; my friends and I are planning a trip to California. I'll be gone most of June and July. I hope you don't mind." While Polly was waxing rhapsodic about the trip, Dani was panicking. She'd have to find someone to fill in. No way could she do everything herself for two months. That much she knew. How had she overlooked that fact when she was making her original pro/con list: *Why I should and shouldn't own a B & B.* To be fair, she'd known it would be hard, just not this hard. Little by little, The Maples was succeeding, but she was exhausted all the time. Why was it that what you wanted had hidden traps? Maybe Margo could recommend another young woman to take Polly's place.

As it turned out, she needn't have worried that Spence might be bored spending a week in Lee. He was gone most of every day. Soccer games with Ross and a collection of local teenagers—some Spence's age, some older—occupied every morning. Twice, he and Ross showed up at Dani's for lunch; on the other days, they ate at Ross's. None of his new friends had their driver's licenses yet, so bicycles and skateboards were the vehicles of choice. Spence had checked his skateboard through as luggage; his California bike had been shipped to Lee with Dani's furniture and stored in the basement because Ben had bought him an expensive mountain bike for his fourteenth birthday. She hadn't noticed any mountains in Annapolis. Ben was either becoming more generous or was currying favor with his son.

One night, they went to the movies with Evan, a couple of evenings, she and Spence ate popcorn and watched TV and, though Spence hated shopping, he was more than willing to go to the Converse store at the outlet because he needed soccer shoes again. All in all, he seemed to enjoy himself.

It wasn't until they were at the airport Saturday afternoon that he casually mentioned the poker games.

"Poker! You've been gambling?" The teenage years had arrived.

"Not gambling exactly. Learning to play poker, that's all."

"Where?"

"The back room at The Sewing Basket."

Not the answer she expected. "At the fabric store!" Hardly a den of iniquity.

"Yeah, well, Ross and a couple other guys have been learning to play, and they let me come along. We weren't playing for money or anything. Just practicing."

Dani was trying to keep her composure. Flying apart might make poker seem more intriguing.

"Who's teaching you?"

"That old lady in the other cottage."

"Mrs. Hamilton?"

"Yeah."

"She plays poker?"

"Her father taught her to play. I guess the lessons for the guys started when the lady at the store asked Mrs. H to teach her grandson, Mickey. His older cousins were sort of taking advantage of him. Anyhow, Dad plays."

"It's practically a requirement in the Navy."

"We don't play for money. She gives all of us the same number of chips and a cheat sheet that shows what beats what. I think she likes showing us; maybe it gives her something to do. And she's really good at bluffing."

"No doubt."

"You aren't mad are you?"

"You should've asked, and I think she should have checked with me; after all, you're under age. Of course that would have required talking to me and we don't talk much."

"I promise to stay away from the local casinos."

"They wouldn't let you in."

"Too bad." He grinned, enjoying her frustration.

"Please tell your father that you've been playing." So she wouldn't have to.

He grinned again and kissed her goodbye. "I bet I can beat him."

Probably could. Ben had never been much good at poker.

As soon as she got back to Lee, she called Evan for Monique's phone number. Better to find out how the other mothers felt about the poker lessons before she confronted Clarissa.

Because Evan's phone had caller ID, he answered with "Coast clear?"

The sound of his voice improved her day. "As a matter of fact it is. Tomorrow might be better, though. Everyone will be checking out, and no one else is scheduled in until Tuesday afternoon."

"Sounds like a plan. I'll pick you up."

"I need Monique's phone number. I only have Sam's business number."

He read it to her. "What's up?"

"I discovered Clarissa has been teaching Spence and Ross and a couple other kids to play poker."

As usual, when it came to Clarissa's antics, Evan laughed.

And as usual, Dani wasn't seeing the humor in the situation. "Not funny yet."

"It's just poker. She's not teaching them to roll joints. Picture her wearing an eyeshade. I love it."

Monique's reaction was close to Evan's.

"There's nothing to worry about. Phoebe's grandson Mickey was regularly losing his allowance to his older cousins. That's how it got started. The odds of Clarissa Hamilton corrupting the youth of Lee are low. Ross was complaining that she wouldn't let them swear in her presence and, amazingly, he's stopped swearing around the house. I doubt he's given it up when he's with his friends, but I'll take what I can get."

Despite Monique's reassurance, Dani was still annoyed, but then she'd been annoyed at Clarissa since October. It had become a way of life.

After Clarissa's meltdown about the sunroom, they'd been successfully avoiding one another. But when the Lexus pulled into the lot while Dani was unloading groceries, Dani decided to get the poker issue off her mind.

"Mrs. Hamilton."

Clarissa pushed the remote to lock her car, carefully avoiding eye contact with Dani.

"I'd like to talk to you about the poker lessons you were giving my son. I wish you'd asked me about teaching him. Spence's only fourteen."

Clarissa finally looked at her. "He told me you wouldn't care, so I saw no need to get your permission. The lessons were harmless."

"You should've asked me first."

Clarissa's chin came up slightly, her eyes narrowed. "I can't help it if you haven't taught your son to tell you about his activities."

Dani knew she shouldn't respond; but she did. "Don't question my parenting."

"Would you prefer I question your morality? Carrying on with Evan Murray while your son is in the same house."

Absolutely not true.

"Evan was not at the house last week." Dani emphasized every word. "And my social life is none of your business."

"Social life." Clarissa almost sniffed. "Interesting choice of words for an affair with a man younger than you are."

Dani's face warmed with embarrassment and fury. For weeks, she'd been pretty sure that Clarissa was watching their exits and entrances, but to accuse her of being with Evan while Spence was visiting was a bald-faced lie. Before considering the consequences of saying what had been on her mind for months, she blurted out the truth. "I should never have agreed to let you live on my property. You've been a pain in the butt since day one."

Not waiting for a response, Dani retreated to her own cottage, too shaken to trust herself to say anything else. She and Evan hadn't made a secret of the fact that they were sleeping together. Didn't think it was necessary in the current cultural climate. They'd spent a couple of Sunday afternoons with the Brunellos, had drinks at The Locker Room with Drew and Abby, shopped for groceries together, and attended the dedication for the Stockbridge park.

But Clarissa made it sound dirty. Victorian mores in the Twenty-First century.

Dani was still upset when Evan picked her up on Sunday night. Before he helped her into the truck, he kissed her. Dani could almost feel Clarissa's eyes on them.

He pulled back, "Kissing's better when both people participate."

"Sorry."

As they drove toward the farm, "So what's interfering with your kissing technique? Up to now it's been excellent." He was trying to make her smile.

"Clarissa. She accused me of taking advantage of your youth and exposing Spence to my sordid love life. My morality has been brought into question. It got ugly. And for once, don't side with her and laugh."

"Is there more?"

"I told her she was a pain in the butt and that I was sorry I'd let her stay in the cottage."

"Wish I'd been a fly on the wall."

"We were outside."

"You know what I mean."

"I hate arguments. I do them badly. I always end up saying things I shouldn't. She was getting back at me for my questions about the poker games, and I took the bait."

"Do you think we're doing something immoral?"

"Of course not."

"Do you care what she thinks?"

"No, but—"

"Dani. I am 31 years old—a grown up. It's a bit late for anyone to worry about corrupting me. Do you think the difference in our ages is a problem?"

"No. But others—"

"Don't matter. I've been talked about all my life. It started in kindergarten. I learned really early not to care about those kinds of attitudes."

"In the Navy, everyone had something to say about everyone's business. When Ben walked out on our marriage, the whole naval base knew within twenty-four hours. It was hideous, like being stripped naked in public."

Evan was quiet the rest of the way to the farm. When he shut off the engine, they sat in the truck for a few moments. Then he turned to her, placing his hands on each side of her face so she had to look at him. "Dani, I don't give my heart away easily. I enjoy your company, I enjoy having sex with you, and I'm pretty sure I'm falling in love with you. I don't think either of us wants to hurry the process, but we don't have to hide from the world."

Such simple tenderness—wisdom—in his words. The feel of his hands on her face brought tears to her eyes. She wasn't sure she was in love with him, but she enjoyed the sex, enjoyed his company. Was beginning to let herself hope that she could love him. Still, there was so much they didn't know about one another, one very important thing he didn't know about her.

"I probably can't have any more children." She hadn't intended to say that so bluntly and certainly not tonight. He'd told her—so beautifully—that he cared for her; then she'd broad jumped to the possibility she couldn't give him a family.

"Whoa—that's from left field."

"Well, you told me about Fiona. This is something about me you need to know. I lost a baby when Spence was two and then tried and tried to have another child. If you do want kids, if you found someone younger who could, I mean—" Too late, she wished she hadn't brought it up.

He leaned over and kissed her, effectively silencing whatever else she was going to say and saving himself from saying he didn't care about having children. That would have been a lie. He didn't want to lie to her. He and Fiona had discussed starting a family. He wanted to be the father he'd never had. But Fiona was gone. This relationship was entirely different—special in its own way. He needed to think this information through before he answered her.

Clarissa was of two minds about her conversation with *that woman* over the poker lessons. On the one hand, she hadn't known that Spence was so young. The other three boys were fifteen, so she hadn't thought much about the age issue. If it had been JT or Matt, she might have felt the same way, but she had no intention of telling *her* that. At the same time, there was no harm in the lessons—more informational than dangerous. Judd had always bragged about her ability at cards, sometimes had let her sit in on poker games with him and his friends— and there were times when she won. Though Lorraine and Aileen hadn't been keen about the game, occasionally, the whole family played for salted peanuts or navy beans, inexpensive entertainment on snowy nights. So long ago.

Mentioning the affair with Evan was ill-timed. She'd been caught out about the poker lessons and couldn't find any other weapon. There was something not right about Evan sleeping with *her*. He was always sweetly polite to Clarissa, smiling, paying attention to her. She liked that—liked him. No one had treated her so well in a long time. And now he was shacked up with *the enemy*, and *the enemy* had admitted *she* was sorry that Clarissa had the right to live in Judd's workshop. Did *she* mean *she* would revoke that part of the sale contract? Could *she*?

Clarissa didn't feel fear very often—so much had disappeared from her life that there wasn't much to be afraid of anymore. But not being allowed to live here—that was frightening. Lorraine might make her move to the assisted living *prison*.

Nevertheless, apologizing was not an option.

Chapter 18

The week after Easter, Abby came across The Maples' first guest review on *The New England Bed and Breakfast* website. On a scale of one to five, five being the highest, someone had given The Maples twos in every category: Rooms, Service, Cleanliness, Food.

Twos for God's sake!

When she contacted the website, she got a canned response: *The names and e-mail addresses of the reviewers are confidential.* A phone call didn't get her any farther. She searched two or three other ranking services, but so far The Maples had received no other reviews at all. Understandable. It had been open only two months.

From the beginning, either Dani or Abby had made follow-up phone calls a week after the guests returned home to get first hand feedback. A few people brushed off their questions with "Everything was fine," not wanting to be bothered, but most were helpful and generally positive. Based on some of the suggestions, Dani had bought a CD player for the living room, broadened the number and type of magazines she subscribed to, and kept a better variety of snacks in the refrigerator for late night raids.

Twos!

Abby didn't tell Dani about the review. It could be an anomaly but, when the second one appeared a week later on the *Berkshire Mountains* website, she showed both of them to Dani. This one, in spite of another series of Twos, included a glowing comment about the cottage garden.

Puzzled, Dani went through all the reservation records, trying to remember who would have been that dissatisfied. She was stumped and worried. Was it just one person or two different people? Bad reviews could kill her fledgling business. The Maples was still in the red, but at least some cash was coming in. She didn't have to draw on her back-up funds as often—but she needed to reach break-even status pretty soon. And if those two websites decided to remove the listing for The Maples because of the negative ratings, then what? Though The Maples would also be listed in two B & B handbooks, those new editions wouldn't be out for another six months. In the electronic age, the websites were undoubtedly more important for generating business. This was a disaster in the making.

Needing counsel, she called Louise Quill, asking if she had time to meet for coffee. "I need your advice."

Once they were seated in a booth at The Brown Bean, Dani handed Louise the two reviews Abby had printed out. "Have you ever had reviews like that?"

Louise hunted for her glasses in her oversize purse, then read the pages. "Actually, no. When we first started, it took a while before our reviews showed up, but most of them were four and five star rankings."

Not the answer Dani needed. She'd been hoping this kind of thing was normal in the start up process.

Louise handed the pages back, "Is the verbal feedback you get from guests good?"

"Almost all of it is. Knowing that I'm new at this, most people take the time to make thoughtful suggestions. No one has seemed particularly upset. I mean, I didn't expect to be perfect right out of the box, but these worry me."

"They'd worry us too. It's hard to know how much potential customers rely on these kinds of things. How's your vacancy factor?"

"I have four rooms. Most of the time at least one room is rented. On weekends, I'm usually full. Midweek averages two rooms a night. I figured it would take time to build a reputation. I didn't expect a full house instantly."

"Those are reasonable occupancy rates."

"I thought so, given that I don't have a Victorian mansion or a George-Washington-slept-here house. It's just an ordinary, early Twentieth Century colonial. No historical pedigree to trade on. But it cleaned up rather well, despite a tree falling on the sunroom."

When Louise asked whether Dani would like her to come over the next day, Dani didn't hesitate. "Would you? I'd really appreciate it. I could use another pair of eyes."

"I've been wanting to see what you've done with the house, but I keep getting sidetracked. Our daughter had another baby this winter, so I've been trying to help her. I'll be sure to come tomorrow afternoon about tea time. Is that okay?"

"Perfect. Who handles tea at your place?"

"George. He's the garrulous one, loves talking to the guests. I prefer staying in the background."

Having Louise do a walk-though helped in a variety of ways. Whenever she saw something that she thought Dani should change, she mentioned it—and Dani took careful notes—a kind of master class in B & B management. But overall, the changes Louise suggested were minor.

"Right now, just keep doing the best you can. Don't second guess yourself too much or you'll stop being who you are, and that's part of what makes each B & B unique. Most people will like you, but not everyone."

Night after night, Dani lay awake, going over and over what someone would find to criticize. Each morning, she promised herself she would stay positive but, by noon, she was doing exactly what Louise told her not to do—second-guessing everything she said and did.

A week later, without telling Dani, Abby called the *New England B & B* website again, trying a different approach. She asked whether they ever did follow-ups on the people who had used their website. After getting nowhere with the first three assistants, who were skilled in stonewalling such inquiries, Abby asked to talk to the supervisor, who was at least willing to listen. She explained that the site only did random checks of those who responded, inquiring how they had first found the website, whether it was easy to use, and if they had any suggestions about its layout. The company also asked whether the reviewers had revisited the B & B's they'd evaluated and whether they had additional information they'd like to share.

Abby pushed for more. "I don't want you to violate the respondent's privacy, but did you follow up on the person who reviewed The Maples?" She gave the supervisor the date.

"Let me check." The line was silent for almost ten minutes.

"No, we didn't, but it's a bit odd, so perhaps we should."

"What's odd?"

"The review originated at an e-mail address in Lee."

"We've never had anyone local stay at The Maples."

"As I said, it's odd. I'll let you know if I find out anything." Abby left her cell number and Dani's.

The Berkshire site wouldn't let Abby get past the voice menu.

When Abby explained the Lee connection, Dani was relieved. "Since no one local has stayed here, let's assume whoever gave the review made a mistake. Got the wrong name or something. Easy enough to do on-line."

When no other negative reviews showed up and two positive ones were entered on the Berkshire site, Abby put the issue aside.

Sam's truck was parked beside the barn when Evan returned from walking Zack. He'd spent most of the day bringing his books up to date. The nuts and bolts of managing his business weren't nearly as much fun as the designing. "Hey Cousin, haven't seen much of you."

"Planting season. The yards of Lee are waking up. Profitably busy." Sam handed him a brown envelope through the truck window.

"What's this?"

"I think it's the answer to a family mystery. I want you to look at these without any prompting from me." He started the engine, "Call me when you're finished," and left.

Inside the envelope were two 4" x 6" color snapshots, a framed 5" x 7" color photo, and a faded photocopy of a newspaper obituary. Intrigued, Evan laid them out on his drafting table and switched on the fluorescent lights. Something strange was going on. Sam was not given to enigmatic messages.

He recognized the framed picture; it was usually hanging in The Maples' front hall. The Hamilton family. He'd glanced at it when the row of historical photographs first appeared, but he hadn't looked at it closely. Four children, a younger Clarissa and her husband, who had died not long after Evan returned from Thailand. One of the smaller snapshots was a picture of his mother. She was wearing what must have been a prom dress—her date was in a tuxedo. He turned it over. Someone had written Matt and Brenda 1964. That would have been his mother's junior or senior year. The second snapshot was of Evan and Sarah Fletcher, his prom date when he was a junior.

This photo mystery probably had nothing to do with the girls, so he covered each of them with pieces of blank paper. Using one of the magnifying glasses he kept for deciphering blueprints and topo maps, he studied the two tuxedo-clad teens. There was no doubt about what Sam wanted him to see.

Evan was looking at two pictures of himself.

As teenagers, he and this Matt looked almost identical: both tall, Evan was 6'3", dark auburn hair with a tendency to curl, straight noses, the same slightly crooked smiles. Only their eyes were different. Matt's were blue.

As Evan began reading the obituary notice, his hands were unsteady, and he was unintentionally holding his breath. His life was about to change. He'd always said that he didn't care who his father was, insisted that his rather unusual childhood had been okay. Whenever the who? question tried to surface, he effectively beat it back—sure that he was comfortable not knowing.

The obituary was dated September 7, 1979. Matthew Andrew Hamilton, 1946-1979. The face in the grainy newsprint picture was the same face Evan saw in the mirror every morning, the same vertical furrow between his eyes. He skimmed the article, then read it more carefully, noting the date and location of the plane crash. The same crash that killed his mother.

They'd died together. Space and time collided.

He was Matthew Hamilton's son. Illegitimate son. According to the obit, Evan had two half sisters, two additional aunts.

And Clarissa Hamilton was his grandmother.

Slowly, he refolded the obituary and returned everything to the envelope without looking at the framed photo.

Undoubtedly, the tuxedo pictures and the obituary had come from Aunt Joanna. He resisted the temptation to call her; he couldn't coherently talk to anyone right now. It would take time to digest the peculiar turn his life had just taken. There were now more pages in his biography, the missing pages he always believed hadn't mattered.

Not knowing had been easy. Knowing what he thought he didn't need to know was already tampering with the internal mechanism that regulated his view of himself. In the time it had taken to look at the contents of the envelope, he'd morphed into another person.

Until he was eleven or twelve, Evan had dreamed that his father would, one day, miraculously appear at the farmhouse. *Hi Evan, I'm your father. I've been looking and looking for you. I didn't know your mother was dead.* Then his father would hug him hard. Evan could almost feel his father's arms. In those years, he'd needed to know that his father wanted to find him.

Now, standing in his studio, Evan felt the sharp futility of that childish fantasy. Instead of his father finding him, Sam had found his dead father. Not the scenario Evan had wished for.

Nervous energy surged through him. He needed to go somewhere, do something, but he didn't want to see anyone, talk to anyone. Physical exercise had always been his escape valve, effective therapy in times of crisis. After Fee died, he had walked and walked, never quite able to walk far enough. This felt similar. It was of course too late to walk now. In lieu of stumbling over rough ground in the dark, he found what remained of the bottle of scotch he kept in the kitchen cupboard for Sam, who preferred scotch to beer. He poured the amber liquid into a coffee mug, sipped at it, then quickly downed all of it. The raw heat burned his throat. He poured himself a second drink. This one was strangely soothing. After the third one, he fell asleep on top of his bed. Sometime during the night, Zack settled himself on the bed along Evan's back.

He almost woke up when he heard someone moving around his tiny kitchen but didn't come fully awake until he smelled the coffee. With effort, he pushed himself to a sitting position—his head screaming in protest—and saw Sam pouring coffee into a mug. Hopefully not the one Evan had used for the scotch.

"Skip the cream and sugar; black will help your hangover."

Evan clutched the mug with both hands, neither of which was steady. He considered arguing that he didn't have a hangover, but the empty Scotch bottle on the counter gave him away.

Sam sat on the foot of the bed, drinking his own cup of coffee. "I was worried. You didn't call. Maybe I should have been here when you looked at the pictures and the obit."

"Wouldn't have mattered." His mouth tasted like he'd eaten something rotten. "Where'd you get them?"

"Mom had the two prom pictures and the article. I borrowed the framed one from Dani, who originally got it from Lorraine Sessions. When I showed Mom the framed one, she went looking for the other two in Grandma's stash of photos."

"How'd you get started on this?"

"I noticed the framed one in Dani's hallway one day. I was waiting outside her office while she was checking a guest in. Let's face it—you're his clone; there's a resemblance to Senator Hamilton too. I figured someone besides me might notice, and I'd rather be the one to show you."

"Your mom knew?"

"I didn't grill her, but I don't think she was exactly surprised. Better that she tell you what she knows."

"Anyone else know?"

Sam shrugged. "Mrs. Hamilton may know but prefer not to claim you." When Evan didn't respond, "That's meant to be funny."

"It may be truer than you know."

"You might not want to claim her either. The grandmother from hell."

Evan drank more of the coffee, willing it to clear the fog in his head. "Thanks for checking on me."

"That's what we do in the Murray family—of course now that you're also a Hamilton—"

Evan finally smiled. "You may be older than I am, but I'm still bigger."

"Okay. I can leave now. You don't seem in danger of slashing your wrists."

"Too messy. Strange to finally have the answer to—some of it."

"No doubt. But you're still you."

"Profound. Go water your flowers or something. And take Dani's picture back to her."

When she hadn't heard from Evan in nearly a week, Dani left a message on his cell phone. Two days later, she left another.

It wasn't like Evan to ignore a message—not for this long, certainly not since they'd been sleeping together. The fishing pier was almost finished, no reason for him to be too busy to call her.

Saturday afternoon, since there were only two rooms occupied and Polly could handle whatever came up, Dani drove to Murray Farms. Evan hadn't mentioned leaving town. After his New York City visit with Kanya, he'd been careful to let her know his whereabouts.

His pickup was gone, so she took a chance that Cathy might be at the farmhouse.

"He hasn't been here all week. When he finishes a job, he often takes off with Zack. But this time, he didn't tell me to get the mail. He just left with Zack."

"He's not quite done with the fishing pier."

"Sorry, Dani. I really don't know. Sam's usually at the greenhouses on the weekend. Maybe he knows."

But Sam was gone.

And so she went home. Not exactly worried. Uneasy.

The one person who could have helped her was Joanna, though she would have been guessing at his destination.

When Evan finally confronted her about Matthew Hamilton, she'd told him as much as she knew, which wasn't much, and gave him the Rolex watch she and her mother had found at Brenda's apartment. "I'm assuming it was—his."

Evan turned it over in his hands, "Expensive."

"Mom saved it for you."

"How did she find the obituary?"

"After your adoption was final, she made a couple of trips to the library in Springfield, ostensibly doing research for some new strain of tomatoes Papa was interested in. I suppose she found something in those records that gave her a clue to his identity."

"Like the plane's manifest?"

"Possibly. Your grandmother could keep her counsel. She didn't confide in me and I doubt that Papa knew. He was no good at keeping secrets. Best guess, she didn't want to be involved with the Hamiltons, to run the risk of sharing you if someone contested the adoption. In those days, the Hamiltons could have caused trouble if they wanted to. Mrs. Hamilton always acted like Matt was slumming because he was dating Brenda, conveniently ignoring the fact that her own parents had come from what once was called shanty Irish. Marrying Judd Hamilton made Clarissa think she was better than everyone else, even her own family. I'm sure Mom only meant to protect you."

Before he left, Joanna located the address of Brenda's D.C. apartment. The obit had provided him with the name of Matthew Hamilton's law firm. Back at the studio, Evan packed his duffle bag, loaded Zack and his food and water bowls into the truck, and headed for Washington, checking into a motel outside the beltway around one in the morning. In many ways, the trip was stupid. He'd just be looking at buildings, walking the surrounding streets. For all he knew, the buildings he was interested in were gone. After thirty years, there might not be anything to find. Nevertheless, he needed to start somewhere.

Brenda's apartment was on a two block street near DuPont circle. The five-story building, probably built in the sixties, was modern then, unremarkable now—within walking distance of the government buildings. This was perhaps where he'd spent the first seven months of his life. If the plane hadn't crashed, he might have spent many more years in this city. He and Zack walked the streets, stopped for a late lunch at a restaurant with outside seating and an affection for dogs. Later that afternoon, leaving Zack in the truck with the window cracked, he found the building housing Willard and Isaacson, Attorneys at Law. Their suite occupied the top two floors, a view of the city spread out beneath the floor-to-ceiling windows. Dark wall paneling, thick rugs. Sitting at an elaborate desk, a fashionably dressed receptionist was talking into a tiny headset. When her conversation ended, she turned to Evan. "May I help you?" Her eyes took note of his Levi's and turtleneck sweater, obviously not what their typical clients wore.

"I'm looking for information about an attorney who worked with this firm in the late 1970's. Matthew Hamilton."

"That's a long time ago." Longer than she'd been alive and, thus, ancient history.

"Is there someone still working here who might remember him?" Evan wasn't sure what he was after.

"The oldest member of the firm is Mr. Isaacson. He founded it in 1974."

"Is he in?"

"He never comes in on Wednesday," she smiled for the first time, "golf day. He'll be in tomorrow."

Evan handed her his business card. "Would you ask him to call my cell number tomorrow. I'm staying locally for a day or two. I need to ask him some questions about Matthew Hamilton."

She studied his card, circling the cell number. "Are you a relative Mr. Murray?"

"Yes. I'm his son." He'd never before referred to himself as anyone's son, only grandson, though—like everyone in the Murray clan—he'd called his grandfather Papa.

"Your last name isn't—"

"Murray is my mother's name."

The conversation with Frank Isaacson didn't offer much insight into Matthew Hamilton. Isaacson remembered hiring him, remembered his death and attending the funeral in Boston. "Hamilton and his wife, I don't remember her name, were in the process of divorcing, but it wasn't final. The daughters were quite young. His father was a senator at The Massachusetts General Court. A well-known family."

"What kind of law did he practice?"

"This firm specializes in corporate law, especially firms with government contracts."

"Did you like him?"

"I admired his legal abilities. He didn't socialize with members of the firm. Stayed to himself."

Stayed with his mistress.

"Our receptionist said you're his son."

"So I'm told." Evan thanked him for his time and hung up.

Not much to go on.

Chapter 19

From D.C., Evan drove north, following the Hudson River into the Catskills where he'd often hiked, renting a rustic cabin outside the resort town of Pine Hill. He wasn't ready to go home and face questions from Sam or Joanna. Or Dani. He'd never been able to share pain with anyone, except Fiona. He hadn't yet learned to share those kinds of feelings with Dani, though he had found the strength to tell her about Fiona.

Having this new identity had sucker-punched him.

Evan Hamilton.

It didn't sound right, never would. He needed time to absorb the information. Right now, he didn't want to inflict the anger that had taken up residence in his gut on anyone else. Didn't want to hurt them. Hiking the local trails for three or four hours a day helped him sleep at night, but the angry questions continued to gnaw at him. He was struggling to come to terms with his grandmother's motive for not telling him, or anyone. The reasons had been hers alone and, as Joanna had said, not intended to harm. In spite of the rational arguments he laid out for himself, he was lost—and bitter. He couldn't understand why discovering who his father was hurt so much. All the years he'd casually claimed he'd had a good childhood, he'd been lying to himself without knowing it.

Never before had he been bitter. Not about having no parents and, except for the first few months after her death, not even about losing Fee. Now an unreasonable bitterness burned his heart. How could his grandmother have let him believe she knew nothing? She who had demanded honesty from everyone. When he left for Scotland, he'd been twenty-two, an adult. Surely, he should have been given what little information there was.

When Evan was a child, family meant cousins, aunts, uncles and of course grandparents—all from the Murray side. Though he knew he didn't have parents like Sam and his sisters did, no one made an issue about that difference, and so he was okay with the arrangement. However, his second week in kindergarten, a five year old girl with green eyes informed him that everyone had to know who his father was.

"I don't."

"That's terrible. Maybe you did something wrong." Her green eyes had brimmed with tears for him.

Evan didn't think his life was terrible, certainly never imagined that he might have caused his father's disappearance from his life. When he confronted Liz Murray with the little girl's news, Liz had carefully explained that, on paper at least, she and Papa were his parents, and they loved him. That was enough for him—then.

Except for the green-eyed girl, none of his school friends made fun of him or asked questions, but the sense of being different shadowed him. Papa might play catch with him—but not one-on-one basketball. On the other hand, Papa taught him about plants and soil and geology, took him on camping trips and hiking. "I'm too old to carry one of those backpacks. You'll have to get Sam Senior to take you backpacking."

After raising three girls, Ross Murray enjoyed teaching Evan about tools, how to build things. All those lessons encouraged Evan's interest in landscaping and architecture. Liz occasionally talked about Brenda, so did Joanna, and showed him pictures of her. But his mother was never quite real to him. And of course there were no pictures of his father.

Now the name Hamilton had been added to his genealogy. Unfortunately, the people who had all the pieces of the story were conveniently dead. No way to resolve anything. He was angriest with his grandmother and, secondarily, with Joanna. On his first day back in Lee, he dumped his pent up fury on her, exploding in the middle of her attempt to explain what little she knew and slamming out the door.

Joanna was stunned. Evan had never behaved this way before. Never. Seriously worried, she sent her husband after him, to no avail.

When Evan had been gone two weeks, Dani again went in search of Sam, who referred her to Joanna. "My mother has a better handle on the story though, I confess, I'm the one who opened Pandora's box."

When she first met Joanna Brunello on Christmas night, Dani had instantly liked the tall, dark-haired woman, but she wasn't sure Joanna would want to explain what was going on within her family to someone who was almost a stranger. Nevertheless, she made the call.

Joanna was gracious, yet all she would say was that it was Evan's story to tell.

What story? Something about Fiona? Perhaps she had been found. Until now, Evan's absence hadn't really frightened Dani, but the possibility of his beloved Fiona returning forced Dani to admit to herself she did not want to lose him.

In the three weeks he'd been gone, she had missed him in countless ways. She'd gotten used to seeing him working in her garden, having him come into the kitchen at the main house to sit while she cooked breakfast or prepared afternoon tea. They went out for pizza and sometimes a movie, or he brought Chinese take-out. Simple, comfortable markers in her life. And most important, she missed the nights at her place or his—work schedules permitting—learning to love each other.

Two days after Evan returned to the farm, Sam called Dani. "He's been back for a couple of days. Chewed my mother out—not like him at all—and since then, he's been hiding out in the barn, not taking calls from anyone. I just thought you'd like to know."

"Do you think I should go over there?"

"No idea. My parents didn't have much luck talking to him, and he gave me short shrift. He's not in a good mood."

Dani couldn't let another day go by without seeing him. Once again, she left Polly in charge of the house and drove to the farm, too nervous to appreciate the soft spring twilight all around her.

She found him in the barnyard, throwing a ball for Zack. He was thinner. His hair was longer than usual, touching his collar. When he saw her, for just a moment she was afraid he'd go inside, but he stood very still, the ball that Zack wanted him to throw clutched in his hand.

She walked uncertainly toward him. How quickly she'd become tentative with him.

His eyes were darker than usual, his smile buried behind the tightness of his mouth. The easygoing Evan who could gentle Clarissa had disappeared into this rigid, distant Evan. Her heart felt the difference.

Reaching down to pet Zack, she kept it simple, "Hi."

"Hi."

"You've been gone for a while." *God, I've missed you.*

He didn't look at her; instead, he threw the ball and watched intently as Zack sped after it and raced back. When Zack dropped it at his feet, Evan retrieved it and threw it again. Still not looking at her.

She tried again. "Where've you been?"

"The Catskills." Another throw for Zack.

"Hiking?"

"Yeah."

"I wondered."

"Do you need something?"

An explanation for all this. But she was damned if she'd ask for one.

"I just wanted to see that you were okay." This conversation was going nowhere. He was freezing her out.

After a few more moments of his silence, she walked slowly back to her car, hoping he'd call after her, stop her, but he didn't. As she turned the car around, he threw the ball again, not looking in her direction.

When she found a safe place to park alongside the highway, she turned the engine off and let the tears come, unsure whether she was crying for herself—or Evan. All these months she'd gradually been letting him into her life, experimenting with caring for a man again, experimenting with falling in love. Now that she was ready to love him, he'd turned away, letting the pain of whatever had invaded his life hold her at arm's length.

When her vision was clear enough that she could drive, she went home. Polly had a dinner date at five, and Dani had promised to be back to handle afternoon tea. Trying not to think about Evan, she set up the three tables for breakfast; one room was empty tonight. Then she paid a few bills, confirmed a couple of reservations—one for three couples over the Memorial Day weekend. The Maples had been recommended to them by a former guest. Repeat customers and word-of-mouth reviews were beginning to fill the reservation book, and there had been no more negative reviews. She should be happy. But tonight, the success or failure of The Maples didn't seem important.

She'd taken her shower and was watching the late news when the doorbell rang. Evan was standing on the porch, hunched forward, his hands in his pockets, as though expecting to be turned away.

"I came to apologize."

She pulled the door wider. At least he'd come looking for her, knew at some level he'd hurt her.

"Can I get you something, coffee?"

"Nothing, thanks."

She curled herself into the corner of the couch, hoping he'd sit beside her, but he continued standing.

"Evan, sit down, you're making me nervous."

"It's just that I've been, well, thoughtless. I should at least have called. Cathy told me you'd been out to the farm looking for me."

"It's okay." *Liar*

"No, not really. Nothing's okay right now, but I can't, well, I just wanted you to know it's not you. It's—something else."

His face was so sad. The usual amusement that backlit his eyes and the crooked, mischievous smile were gone. He reminded her of Spence when he was upset, not admitting he needed her to comfort him, wanting to be tough, but really needing her arms around him. It was that look that made her brave enough to stand up and slip her arms around him. At first, he stood stiffly in her embrace, then, ever-so-slightly, he relaxed.

Against her ear, almost a whisper. "Dani, I need to work this out for myself."

"Is it about Fiona?"

He shook his head, kissed her cheek and stepped away. "Be patient with me."

A kiss on the cheek. This from the man she'd been sharing her bed with.

"Please don't shut me out." She placed her hands on either side of his face, forcing him to look at her. "Please."

"I have to do this alone. I can't talk about it yet—with anyone, not even you." This time he kissed her lips, but there was no warmth in his touch.

He was standing in front of her without being there.

"I need your patience."

"I don't seem to have a choice." Her voice couldn't hide the sarcasm.

"Sometimes, we don't get choices."

Tell me about it.

She stood in the doorway long after his truck was gone, willing him to come back.

Dani hadn't wanted this romantic journey with Evan to have an itinerary, hadn't been daydreaming about commitment or happy-ever-after, but she hadn't expected his *I have to do this alone* speech, hadn't expected him to casually kiss her and disappear from her life.

From no plan to no Evan.

A couple of times, she saw Ross and Sam in the garden, adding plants, pulling weeds. She was tempted to ask Sam how Evan was, but didn't want to admit Evan had so easily pushed her aside without telling her why. The *it isn't about you* was no comfort either. He was essentially saying, "I have a problem but I'm not sharing." Too much like Ben and his precious Navy with all of its secrets. Obviously she didn't have a high enough clearance for Evan either.

She'd believed he was different. Charming, gentle. Easy laughter that made her want to laugh with him. The way he looked into her eyes as though he knew exactly what she was thinking.

One week. Two. Closing in on three.

The first week of June, he called her cell; his voice was soft in her ear. "Hi, Dani."

She was instantly short of breath. "Hi" was all she could manage.

"Are you okay?"

"Yes." *If you discount being really pissed off at you—and lonely.*

"Good—I—well—I wanted to tell you that I'm going to Thailand day after tomorrow—for Kanya's wedding."

"How long will you be gone?" *Not that it makes any difference since I don't have the pleasure of your company any more.*

"I'll be there four days. Then I'm going to Edinburgh. One of my professors at the University wants me to conduct a week of workshops built around the projects Stuart and Fee and I were part of."

"That's nice."

"I'll be staying with Stu's folks in Edinburgh. When the workshops are over, I'll drive down to see Fee's family."

You're going halfway around the world to be with your past, but you don't have the time or don't want to stop by here to say goodbye to me. "Have a safe trip." Before she said what was really on her mind, she hung up.

The change in him was so—maddening. If she wasn't the issue then why was he avoiding her? Where was the man who wanted her to know he had room for her in his life? Clearly that "room" was no longer available.

Tempting as it was, she would not ask Joanna or Sam again. Their loyalty lay with Evan, not with her and, anyway, she didn't want them to explain. She wanted him to explain. The tears came quietly and stayed until morning. She vowed these were the last tears she would shed over him.

The next day, she looked and felt like hell. Abby finally pried the story from her but couldn't offer much comfort except to listen and agree that men weren't worth the mental agony they created. Abby and Drew were neither going forward or backward, and Abby was almost ready to return to the world of match.com.

Houses, however, didn't ask you to wait until they felt better. Dani was beginning to see why Clarissa had sunk most of her emotional energy into the house. It wasn't a perfect answer, but right now it was an answer.

And in three days, Spence would come for his six week summer vacation with her.

Evan couldn't seem to pull himself out of the pit he'd fallen into, not even long enough to be nicer to Dani. He wasn't surprised she'd hung up. He deserved that, and more. It had taken him two days to work up the courage to call her, but he knew that, if he left town without telling her, their relationship would certainly be over. By the tone of her voice, it might already be over.

He should tell her what the problem was. Though he'd walled himself off from her, his feelings hadn't changed. If anything, they'd strengthened. He missed talking to her, missed the comfort and excitement of her body. However, he simply couldn't talk about Matthew Hamilton until he'd talked to the other Hamiltons.

He was toying with the idea of going to his father's widow, asking what Matthew had been like, but doing that would remind her that Matthew had been an adulterer. Even worse, maybe she'd never known about Brenda, and Evan would be the first to tell her, hurting her and her daughters just to satisfy his own craving for a postmortem on this newly discovered father.

What right did he have to disrupt three other lives, six if he factored in Clarissa and her two daughters? He'd already disrupted his relationship with Dani.

And once he'd asked his questions, what difference would the answers make in his life? Would he change his profession? Move away from Lee? Doubtful.

He couldn't figure out why knowing about Matthew Hamilton had thrown such a huge monkey wrench into his life. He'd never believed in identity crises, yet he was having one of his own.

Spending time abroad—putting space between himself and his father—might clear the cobwebs so that, when he returned, he'd be better able to decide what his next steps should be.

Chapter 20

Spence's visit was off to a good start. His plane was on time, and he was genuinely glad to see her. Sherry's baby was due any day. "Dad's a basket case and Sherry's really crabby."

By the time they stopped at the grocery store and the bakery, it was nearly 12:30 when they got to The Maples. Spence pulled his skateboard and the two duffle bags he'd brought out of the trunk and hurried to his room. A week ago, Ross had e-mailed an invitation to join soccer practice at one o'clock. The junior varsity team was getting in shape for the fall semester and, since some of the team members were on vacation, Spence could fill in. He didn't have to be asked twice.

Dani found Victoria putting a load of laundry in the dryer. "Everything quiet?"

"Pretty much. The Longmans just left and the couple registered in the yellow room aren't here yet. No phone calls." She pulled the scrunchy off her pony tail, smoothed her long dark blonde hair, rewound the scrunchy, and checked her watch. "I'm finished with the laundry. The rooms are ready. Anything else?"

"No. Thanks for staying late so I could go to the airport."

"No problem. I'll be in at eight on Monday." With that, she scooped up the small purple backpack that doubled as her purse and headed for the door. "I'm meeting friends." Although she was only sixteen, Victoria was working out better than Dani expected, but she'd be glad when Polly returned.

A few minutes later, Spence dashed through the kitchen. "I'm off. Be back for dinner." He snatched an apple from the bowl and let the back screen slam.

With the younger generation out of the house, Dani could use the afternoon to catch up on paperwork, then fix a nice dinner for Spence. She'd have to pay more attention to cooking full meals while he was here.

She was still putting the groceries away when Abby arrived. She and Drew were attending his niece's wedding in Pittsfield. Abby had called ahead to ask if she could stay in Polly's room since Spence was using his and Drew's daughter was at her father's.

"A whole afternoon and evening with Stephanie. I can hardly wait."

"Drew really should sort her out. It's not fair to you."

"We've agreed not to discuss it. The last time I dug my heels in, we didn't speak to one another for nearly a month. Right now, making a point about Stephanie isn't worth wrecking the rest of our relationship. It's impossible for him to see her as anything but the sweet three year old who loved to sit on his lap. Thank God she'll be going to boarding school this fall. I can survive until then. Maybe she'll have a miraculous attitude adjustment."

While Abby was changing her clothes, Dani set up the cart for afternoon tea and folded the towels Victoria had put in the dryer, reminding herself to order more of them. She was always running low. Having another dozen would help. Her arms full of towels, she climbed the stairs, thinking more about ordering towels than where she was putting her feet.

And then all her plans for the afternoon changed.

Whenever she tried to explain exactly what happened, Dani had no clear recollection of how she'd tripped on the top step, but she did remember trying to catch herself without dropping the clean laundry. In the struggle to regain her balance, her ankle twisted awkwardly, all of her weight coming down on it the wrong way, the towels tumbling onto the steps. As she fell, she heard a cracking sound, felt a sharp pain zigzag up her leg.

That was when she yelled for Abby.

While Abby was helping her sit up, the last guests arrived. "Great timing. Can you sit here?" Dani nodded, leaning against the railing. "You're not going to pass out or anything? I don't need you in a heap at the bottom of the stairs."

Her teeth clenched against the pain, Dani could only shake her head.

It seemed like hours, though it couldn't possibly have been more than fifteen or twenty minutes until Abby and the guests reached the top of the stairs where Dani was sitting. They were concerned about her ankle, asking whether there was anything they could do, carefully maneuvering their luggage around her. Abby assured them everything was under control, which of course it wasn't, and took them to the yellow room.

Instead of waiting for Abby's help, Dani slowly inched herself down the stairs on her butt, one agonizing step at a time, trying not to let her left ankle touch anything. It was throbbing now, already swelling. Probably broken. How could she have been so careless! All for some stupid towels. Since she'd owned this house, she'd carried hundreds of things up and down those stairs. Now, she wouldn't be able to take care of her house. Polly wouldn't be back until the middle of next month, and Victoria only worked until noon.

When Abby called Drew to explain their predicament, he suggested she call Joanna to stay at the house while Abby drove Dani to the ER. Luckily, Joanna was at home and pulled into the driveway within fifteen minutes. It took both Joanna and Abby—with Dani hopping on her good leg—to get her to the car.

"You'll miss the wedding," Dani protested.

"Stephanie will be thrilled about that, and I'm spared her sulking."

"I've ruined everything. Your day, Spence's visit, and maybe my business." Her tears had nothing to do with the physical pain.

An afternoon of waiting to have her ankle x-rayed, then more waiting for the x-rays to be read. Eventually, her left leg had a fiberglass cast that began at the ball of her foot and ended mid calf. At least she'd been given something for the pain. The process had been exhausting. The doctor insisted she stay in the hospital overnight so he could take more x-rays in the morning to make sure the cast was holding the broken bone in place. Tomorrow, the rehab facility would send someone over to teach her how to cope with the cast and how to use the crutches. Maybe she could go home late tomorrow, maybe not. Along with all the other problems her clumsiness had created, it was going to cost a fortune. Though Ben paid for her medical insurance, there was a deductible, and he probably wouldn't pay for that.

As soon as the cast was on and Dani was settled in a room with a man whose leg was in traction, Abby picked up her purse and car keys. "Try not to worry."

"Like that's possible."

"Get them to give you a sleeping pill. After the day you've had, you need to sleep."

"What about Spence?"

"What about *don't worry* didn't you understand?"

The next morning, the doctor re x-rayed her ankle and told her she could go home the following day. Was that Sunday or Monday? She was already losing track of time.

Practicing with the crutches was even more exhausting than having the cast put on. Despite two hours of following instructions about their placement and how to distribute her weight, she wasn't very good at using them. After lunch, she fell asleep as soon as she managed to get herself from the chair into bed. The simplest tasks took incredible energy and time. Going to the bathroom was a major project. At home, she'd need a higher toilet seat, as well as something to help her balance herself in the shower and cover the cast since she wasn't supposed to get it wet. One stupid move and she'd become helpless.

When she woke up an hour or so later, Spence was sitting in a chair by the window, playing a video game. She was so glad to see him. "Hi, honey."

Instantly, he was beside her. "Hey, you're awake." He looked worried. "How do you feel?"

"Been better. How'd you get here?"

"Abby brought me as soon as everyone checked in today." He pointed at a shopping bag on the foot of her bed. "Since you'll be here one more night, Abby sent personal stuff for you."

"Thank heavens for Abby. What've you been up to?"

"This morning she let me help cook breakfast, and we did all the rooms." He seemed rather pleased with himself. Who would have guessed that changing sheets and cleaning bathrooms would qualify as an adventure of sorts. "Joanna's going to come after me in a little while."

"If Abby drove you, who's at the house? Joanna?"

"Nope. Mrs. Hamilton."

Good Lord!

Dani pushed the button that raised the bed to a sitting position. Letting Clarissa take care of The Maples was akin to letting the fox into the hen house. Dani could only imagine Clarissa's glee at having full run of HER house once again. No telling what she'd say to the guests.

Reading her expression, "It's kinda my fault. I just needed to see you, see that you were okay."

Months ago, those words would have squashed all Dani's doubts about her relationship with Spence, would have sent her heart soaring. Today, all she could think of was Clarissa taking care of The Maples. Give her an inch, she'd want a mile, undoubtedly gloating because Dani needed her help.

"Don't worry Mom. Abby and I will be fine, but I sure wish I could drive."

Dani produced a wobbly smile. "Fat chance." One thing she didn't have to worry about yet.

When the tall blonde with the sports car asked if Clarissa would mind keeping an eye on things at the house for an hour or so, Clarissa's first inclination was to tell her *No*. Why should she help out? It hadn't been her idea to turn the house into a business that needed someone on call all the time. What had any of this done for her? An ugly asphalt parking lot with people coming and going at all hours. However, in the midst of her mental diatribe, it occurred to her this was the perfect opportunity to finally get into the house—without sneaking in—and have a look around. Even better, *that woman* would have to be grateful for Clarissa's help.

So she said yes.

The blonde left her cell phone number and a list of instructions—in case of an emergency. There were five registered guests, all of whom had already gone out to enjoy the day. The only thing Clarissa had to do was answer the phone. The blonde would be home in time to serve tea. Easy. She and Judd had often had people staying in both guesthouses and, when he was running for office, she hosted large receptions for constituents. She knew how to work a crowd. Paying guests couldn't be much different. Might actually be interesting.

She hadn't been inside the house since the sunroom had been torn down. In the living room, the first thing she noticed was the Hamilton family's writing desk with a vase of fresh flowers on top. At least *she* hadn't gotten rid of that. She opened the French doors and stepped onto the new deck, following it to the back where it overlooked the garden. Evan had done a superb job. She had to admit the flowers hadn't looked this good in years. The warm weather, on the heels of a wet spring, had produced a lush tangle of blooms. She settled herself into one of the wicker chairs with the bright yellow cushions. She'd always liked having her morning coffee out here. If Judd was home, he'd sometimes join her. One of the few occasions in their marriage when they took time to talk—the younger generation would say connect. He was always busy with his business or with politics, assuming—as most men of his generation did—that his wife had no interest in either one. Clarissa was expected to content herself with the children and the house. Separate worlds joined at first by love, later by affection, finally by habit. After he died, she'd been surprised how little difference his permanent absence made in her day-to-day life. He'd been absent so often.

On her way back to the house, Abby stopped at the bakery in Lee to pick up the pastries and cookies for afternoon tea. By the time she walked into The Maples' kitchen, it was almost 4:30. Clarissa already had the tea water boiling and the coffee, both decaf and caffeinated, ready to be transferred to the thermos containers. The pitcher of iced tea Abby had left in the refrigerator was also on the cart.

The colorful crockery plates Dani had picked up at a local yard sale were waiting for the contents of the boxes Abby was carrying. Dani would have been annoyed that her tenant had made herself at home in the kitchen, but Abby was relieved Clarissa had taken the initiative, since two guests were already sitting in the living room, reading magazines.

"I didn't know when you'd get back, so I started the hot drinks." Clarissa was already opening the boxes, setting out the chocolate-covered eclairs, mini cupcakes, and a selection of cookies. "If you have other things to do, I'll be glad to take these in. The Conrads and I have been having the most interesting conversation." Clarissa poured the hot water into the oversize china teapot and placed it in the center of the tea cart.

Abby was quick to accept the offer. She'd had a long day. "If you wouldn't mind—thank you."

Leaving Clarissa in charge gave Abby time to take a shower and change her clothes. She still had to feed Spence, set up for breakfast, and check for new reservations. No wonder Dani had been running on the edge since The Maples opened. Tomorrow would be even harder since all the rooms were booked. Drew had volunteered to pick Dani up at the hospital in the morning, help get her settled into the cottage, and install a safety railing in the shower. Monday afternoon, Abby would have to drive to Enfield to talk to her boss about an extended leave, then pick up clothes and her laptop, and make arrangements to have her mail forwarded. In truth, she was rather looking forward to a hiatus from her job, which had recently been stressing her out. Dani's crisis was, ironically, doing Abby a favor.

She made a mental note to see if The Maples could afford to pay Clarissa for her services. Abby was fairly certain Dani was going to be horrified that her tenant was helping out but, right now, there wasn't another solution. The Maples would need Clarissa's help with afternoon tea for at least a day or two, maybe longer if Clarissa was willing.

When Clarissa returned to her guesthouse, it was after six o'clock. She heated the tomato soup she'd made the day before, added broccoli, then grated a little cheddar cheese on top. She couldn't remember when she'd enjoyed an afternoon so much, so much in fact that, when the blonde asked her whether she could repeat today's performance for a few more days—"Just until I get used to this"—Clarissa accepted readily. The guests were pleasant, so appreciative of her help. She'd answered questions about the area, suggested one or two excursions that weren't usually in the guidebooks, and gave them a synopsis of Lee's history. Tea time flew by.

Before she went to bed, she sorted through her collection of linen doilies, more attractive than the woven mats *that woman* was using on the cart. As she drifted off to sleep, she was planning what she would wear tomorrow.

Drew picked Dani up at nine. She felt like she'd been locked in that hospital room for weeks. The outside world was beautiful. It took her nearly ten minutes to negotiate the path from the parking lot to her cottage. Normally, it took her just seconds. Her forearms already ached, her armpits were sore, and keeping her foot off the ground sapped every ounce of her energy. Having Spence and Abby hovering over her didn't help. No doubt they were expecting her to fall. At some level, she knew they meant well, but the attention was irritating.

"This just takes time. Don't you two have something more constructive to do? Drew's working in the bathroom. I'll yell for him if I need help."

The look they exchanged said *humor her*. She knew she was bitchy. Mad at the world—and especially at herself. All she wanted to do was lie down—preferably in a tub of bubble bath. But then how would she get herself out? She managed the three steps leading from her living room to the bedroom. Thank goodness they were wide enough for the crutches—and headed for her bed. Drew had certainly heard her come in but wisely kept working. No hovering from him. Just the way she wanted it right now.

Since The Maples had been open, she'd lost nearly six pounds running up and down the stairs. Using the crutches should take off another five pounds. Strange sort of weight reduction program. Pretty soon her clothes wouldn't fit.

The pain pills had left her groggy. Half asleep, she heard Drew leave, but she couldn't rouse herself enough to thank him. Later.

Carrying a tray with a sandwich and a cold can of Pepsi, Abby woke her just before noon. "I have an appointment with my boss, and I need to sign some papers at HR, then stop at my place. If I break all speed records, I'll be back here around seven. Spence is on desk duty in the house. He can call you on the intercom if he needs anything. Clarissa will take care of today's tea, and Drew promised to come back around six to keep Spence company. There's lasagna defrosting on the kitchen counter. Spence has the cooking instructions."

This mess was asking a lot of Abby's friendship. "Do you really want to do this? Can you afford to miss work?"

"Yup, and I don't want any arguments from you. I'm rather looking forward to the change of lifestyle. Besides, I'll get to see more of Drew."

"In my current position, I'd be a fool to argue. Maybe tomorrow I can be useful."

Chapter 21

When Spence tapped hesitantly on her bedroom door the next morning, Dani had been awake for almost an hour, grateful to be in her own bed but, at the same time, fretting about all the things she needed to do and couldn't. It wasn't only her life that was upside down. Spence was spending his summer holiday making beds, and Abby had taken emergency leave.

"They don't call it emergency any more. Personal necessity. That way, I don't have to explain what I'm doing. Useful if I'm in the Bahamas with one of the Vice Presidents."

"But you don't get paid."

"True. However, my health insurance is still in effect in case I trip on the stairs."

"Very funny."

"I thought so."

Spence came in, carrying a tray with coffee, juice, scrambled eggs and toast. When had he learned to carry a tray without spilling everything? So sweet.

"Abby made the coffee, but I did the rest, even the eggs."

She pushed herself up so he could place the tray across her legs. "Is everything okay at the house?"

"Sure. It's a lot easier with Victoria here. Today, I'm cleaning the kitchen and the downstairs bathroom while Abby does the shopping." Spence knew how to clean a bathroom! Amazing.

"What about soccer practice? I hope you don't have to miss that."

"It's not until one o'clock."

"Honey, I'm really sorry about wrecking your holiday."

He grinned, "It's sorta cool, especially the cooking. Tomorrow, I get to do bacon. And the guests are really nice to me. I have to get back to the kitchen. Do you need anything?"

He was so grown up.

"I'm fine. Tell Abby I'll be over when I figure out how to get dressed."

After two days in the hospital, food cooked in her own kitchen by her son tasted wonderful. She devoured everything. Spence's eggs were seasoned with something she couldn't identify. She'd have to ask.

With Abby's help, she'd showered last night, wrapping the cast in plastic. The railing Drew had installed was a godsend. Balancing on her good leg, holding onto the rail with one hand, she'd awkwardly washed herself and her hair with the other hand. Putting her clothes on wasn't as tough as taking a shower because she could sit on the edge of the bed, maneuver her underpants and walking shorts part way, then, leaning on the crutches, tug both up the rest of the way. The bra and blouse were easier. Though she usually didn't wear her running shoes at work, she was wearing the right one to give herself better stability. Then there was brushing her teeth—more leaning on the crutches—and running a comb through her hair. Finally, she pulled the duvet up far enough so it looked like she had made her bed. An hour and ten minutes to do what typically took her ten minutes, and she still needed to walk—not the right word for lurching with the crutches—to the house. This whole process needed to get easier and faster.

On her way across the yard, she stopped alongside the garden to rest her arms, enjoying the riot of color. All the flowers seemed to be blooming at once. It was so good to be home, even with crutches and a pain pill prescription.

The kitchen was empty—the dishwasher running, the counter immaculate. She headed for the office.

When Abby returned from shopping, Dani was still trying to find something to rest the cast on under the computer desk. Abby handed her a can of lemonade. "Congratulations. You're wearing clothes and you've walked over here."

"Yeah, Yeah. The incredible Dani Springer."

"A shade cranky, eh?"

"Damn straight. I'm clumsy, slow and worn out because I'm clumsy and slow. Keep the lemonade. It'll just increase my trips to the bathroom."

"You don't need to add dehydration to your list of woes. Drink."

"I thought I'd try to do some office work since I can't get up the stairs and serving food is out. Once they replace this cast with something I can walk on, I'll be able to move around better."

"The office is yours."

"I sure ruined Spence's holiday. Both times he visits, he has to fend for himself. Easter I was swamped with the house and now—"

"Stop it, Dani. You didn't do this on purpose. He's fine, and I think he already has a crush on Victoria."

"Not necessarily good news."

"Don't worry. She has a boyfriend. She's treating Spence like a little brother."

"And Clarissa is doing the tea?" Saying it was scary.

"I didn't have any other options. She's actually an asset. Requires no oversight, which is a nicer way of saying she brooks no interference."

"That's what I'm afraid of."

Dani worked through lunch, eating a ham sandwich while she was paying the bills. The office chair had rollers so she could maneuver over to the copy machine and the fax, and pull herself up to lean on the counter to check in the new arrivals, Mr. and Mrs. Fredrich from Michigan. Once they saw her cast, they were genuinely sympathetic, waiting patiently until Abby came to show them to their room.

By two o'clock, Dani was deeply tired, her ankle protesting being jostled about, so she made her way back to her cottage, intending only to lie down for an hour but, when she woke up, it was nearly five o'clock. She'd planned to be at the house during tea, to see what Clarissa was up to. Dani was afraid that, having established a foothold in The Maples' daily routine, Clarissa would be hard to evict.

As soon as Dani left her cottage, she heard Clarissa's voice. "Yes, I planned the garden and my husband built the pond and bridge as a gift for me. I've always loved working with flowers." No mention that this bridge was actually Evan's and that Clarissa was no longer taking care of the flowers.

A fifty-something couple and a younger woman were sitting in the wicker chairs on the deck; Clarissa was standing at the deck railing pointing out the various flowers.

"What are the white ones, there to the left?" the older woman asked.

"Foxglove, always one of my favorites. It does well in a cottage garden like this. Would you like more tea, Mrs. Cox?"

As Clarissa moved to the cart, Dani's eyes fell on the unfamiliar cups, saucers and plates— fine china, small blue flowers on a white background—and a matching teapot. Where had those come from? Where were the woven mats and the multicolored crockery Dani had bought?

"No thank you."

It was then that Clarissa noticed Dani standing on the walkway below the deck.

"Ah, Ms. Springer, I didn't see you down there. Folks, this is the owner of The Maples." Clarissa sounded like a smarmy tour guide. "She broke her ankle last Saturday. How are you doing?" Clearly making nice in front of the guests.

"I'm slow, but I'll get faster." *And then you'll be out of here.*

"May I present Mr. and Mrs. Cox and their niece, Janis Holiday. The Coxes are in the master suite and Miss Holiday and her sister are in the blue room. Her sister has a headache and went to lie down. They arrived yesterday."

Dani remembered making the reservations for them last month. "So glad you're staying with us."

"Hey, Mom!" Spence was at the back door. "Dad just called. Sherry finally had the baby last night." He hurried toward her, the four people on the deck, watching and listening. "Her name's Emma. Six pounds even."

Hooray for Sherry.

Spence turned to the guests. "Sorry to interrupt but she's my half sister." He turned back to Dani, "Dad says they're both fine and will be home tomorrow." Barely taking a breath, "Can I have dinner at Ross's? His dad will bring me home."

"Be sure to thank them."

He rolled his eyes and was gone.

"Does your son live with his father?" This from Mrs. Cox.

"For the last year, yes." Resisting the temptation to explain that she was not a bad mother, "It's been good for him."

Making a dignified exit on crutches was impossible.

That evening, when she and Abby went over the reservations for July and August, and checked May's income and expenses, Abby suggested that Dani offer Clarissa minimum wage—two hours a day, seven days a week—until Dani was, literally, back on her feet. "With Clarissa helping, there's one less job to worry about. I'm not nearly as efficient as you are, and Victoria is still new to the job, so things take longer than if you and Polly were on duty."

"I should be paying you too."

"I'm doing this because I want to."

That brought tears to Dani's eyes. "Thank you."

"Don't get sloppy or I just might submit a bill, and I don't work cheap."

Dani laughed. "Okay, but I owe you big time."

"And you should probably thank Clarissa for stepping in. One or two well-placed strokes can't hurt."

"That's asking a lot. After everything she's done to interfere with me, now she's actually in my house, telling people her husband built that bridge. Calling it *The Tea Hour!* Come on. Way too cutesy. And she's giving garden lectures. The inch and mile rule."

"Look at the half-full rule instead. Now that she's part of the process, maybe she'll stay off your case."

"When it comes to Mrs.—*My husband was a Senator*—Hamilton, the glass is always half empty."

"Does your ankle hurt?"

Abby could read her too well. "Yes, dammit."

"Where are your pills?"

"In my bathroom."

"I'll be right back and, after they've taken effect, perhaps we can talk about some of the new ideas I have for the website."

Though Dani knew she was going to have to tolerate Clarissa for a few weeks, she waited two days before discussing *The Tea Hour* with her. The guests had gone out for dinner, and Clarissa was in the kitchen, washing what was undoubtedly her personal china by hand. "If you'd use my crockery, everything could go straight into the dishwasher."

"Those kinds of dishes are for breakfast, not for tea."

Dani stopped herself. *Do not say what you're thinking. You need her for a while. Say what you came to say before you're entangled in an argument you cannot win. She only wants to be right about something that has no right or wrong.*

"Until I can walk better, Abby and I have decided to pay you for the two hours a day that you're handling the afternoon tea." It was so hard to be civil.

Without looking at Dani, "Yes, I should be paid."

"I can only give you the minimum wage."

Clarissa dried her hands on a tea towel, as though contemplating whether she would accept the offer, then met Dani's eyes. "I'm worth more, you know, but that is acceptable for the time being. Retroactive to last Sunday."

"Of course. You'll have a check on Friday—that's when Victoria gets paid." She adjusted the crutches, readying herself to escape. *For the time being.* What did that mean?

"By the way, I'd also like to make arrangements with the bakery about the pastries we buy."

We!

Dani felt her face flush with fury, glad she hadn't thanked her for helping. Clarissa did not need strokes; she gave them to herself.

"You'll have to do that on your own time, and I can't afford to spend any more money than I'm already spending at the bakery. Lucilla knows what my budget is. Please do not exceed it."

"I just want to make sure we don't serve the same things every day. Guests appreciate variety."

On the surface, it looked like Clarissa was being helpful. Why did Dani feel as though she'd lost this round?

In the few days she'd been managing *The Tea Hour*, Clarissa had decided she should have a say in what The Maples bought from the bakery. The tall blonde generally brought back brownies, ordinary cookies and tea breads because, by the time she did the daily shopping, the best of Lucilla's pastries were already gone. Lucilla was known for her lemon scones, pastry wraps with fruit filling, tea biscuits flavored with lavender, and a variety of other specialties. Clarissa didn't want to serve ordinary cookies or brownies; she wanted the special items. The morning after her conversation with Dani, Clarissa was at the bakery an hour after it opened. Late enough so that the day's baking was finished and the shelves were full, early enough to beat out the other customers.

When the young woman behind the counter had boxed Clarissa's choices and charged everything to The Maples' account, Clarissa asked to see Lucilla.

Lucilla Yost was amply built, her blue apron white with flour, her hands stained with the blueberries that had gone into that day's wraps. She was not happy about this interruption because she was in the middle of frosting a wedding cake that would be picked up at ten.

"Mrs. Hamilton, what do you need that Sharon cannot get for you? I'm very busy."

Clarissa smiled her best smile. "I'll be doing the ordering for The Maples from now on. Please set aside a selection of each day's specials for me. Perhaps a total of ten each day. I'll be in to pick them up by eleven o'clock."

"I don't set things aside. First come, first serve." Lucilla planted her hands on her hips and narrowed her eyes. "Ms. Springer isn't that fussy."

"But I am, and I'm doing the teas. If you'll accommodate me, you can put a display card on the tea cart, giving your establishment credit for the pastries—with your address, in case our guests would like to purchase something else on their way home. If you have business cards, I can put those out too. Your signature pastries are unique in this area, and it can't hurt to do some extra advertising." Clarissa made it sound like the wisest of arrangements and that she was doing Lucilla a favor.

Lucilla told her she'd think about it and returned to the kitchen. The frosting was getting warm.

Two days later, business cards and a 4" x 6" laminated display card were delivered to The Maples. Dani didn't ask about the new tea cart advertising. She was fairly certain Clarissa would explain, so very patiently, that it was only right to give Lucilla the credit for her unique baked goods. Clarissa had a knack for putting herself in the position of being the only one who knew the right way to do things, implying that the other person—in this case Dani—was somehow remiss. A trick that was almost impossible to defend against. Better to pick battles that could be won. And besides, as soon as the cast was gone, so was Clarissa.

Chapter 22

When Lorraine expressed surprise that her mother was working for Dani, Clarissa was quick to brush her daughter off with "I enjoy meeting people who are interested in hearing about Lee's history." Lorraine wasn't fooled. Clarissa liked being the center of attention. Always had. *The Tea Hour* was the perfect stage.

Lorraine decided there was probably nothing to be gained by reminding her mother that, when she'd discovered the house would become a B & B, she'd tried to kill the sale, acting as though sacred land was being desecrated by Saracen invaders. Now, Clarissa was happily making shopping lists, checking the room register in the The Maples' office for the guests' names and home towns, then running off to the bakery. The Senator's wife was back in the game.

But what was the game? That was what worried Lorraine. If it was just to be in the house once again, not a big problem. Hard, though, to imagine Clarissa sharing the house with Dani under any circumstances. Lorraine suspected Dani wasn't fond of the arrangement either. Hopefully, she was watching her back.

Every afternoon, Clarissa picked a small bouquet from the garden, arranging the flowers in a delicate cut glass vase she'd received as a wedding present from Judd's aunt. The vase was a perfect fit for the tea cart and, when guests admired the flowers, she could launch into a discussion about her garden. If it wasn't too hot or raining and she was serving tea on the deck, she could point out where that day's flowers were growing.

The last time the garden had looked this good was the day of Judd's funeral nearly four years ago. In the days following his sudden death, all she'd heard from people was "I'm so sorry for your loss." Such a stupid word. Judd wasn't lost; he was dead. There was no chance of finding him, not in Clarissa's lifetime anyway.

Back at the house, after the graveside ceremony, it was refreshing to hear something else: "What beautiful flowers. I've heard about this garden."

Instead of standing by the front door to greet Judd's friends and colleagues, she'd stayed on the deck, letting Lorraine say all the right things. For once, Clarissa didn't care what others thought about her. Her grief was providing an acceptable time out. If she behaved badly, she had the excuse of excuses. When JT died and she'd wanted to bury herself in her bed, Judd had made her face the world, would not let her hide. "We still have Matt and the girls. They're grieving too. This isn't just about us." At some level she knew he was right, but she punished him for weeks with her silence.

It was a shock that Judd too was actually gone. For fifty plus years, he'd indulged her, put up with her nagging, allowed her to move back to Lee without chastising her. Truth be told, she'd probably needed chastising sometimes. Marriage hadn't been easy—for either of them. Judd loved working with his hands, loved people, and they in turn loved him. Look at the crowd attending his funeral. Standing room only. If Clarissa were to drop dead tomorrow, only a handful would mourn her. Instead of drawing people to her, she often drove them away because, if she let them get too close, they might find out she wasn't what she seemed to be. Hidden inside the Senator's wife was just Clari Malone, fourth of five children, always in hand-me-downs. Pretty but, otherwise, nothing special. She'd struggled all her life to leave Clari behind. Her mother had once accused her of putting on airs because she insisted on being called Clarissa. Neve Malone never had time to put on airs. She had to work too hard just to keep the household running.

Aileen hadn't come back to the house after the funeral. Had barely spoken to her mother at the church. Thirty years without her youngest.

What was the use of having children if they died or ran away? So much put into them and so little in return.

The months after Judd's death passed in a kind of semi-darkness— as though the world were lit with only a 15 watt bulb. Even when Judd was in Boston and she was in Lee, he was her anchor, a fixed point that she could always turn to. Admittedly, she hadn't always treated him well. And he'd let her. That was as much honesty as Clarissa allowed herself.

A few months before his death, Judd had noticed Evan Murray's resemblance to Matt. Once Judd retired from The Court and vacated the condo overlooking the Charles River, he'd been appointed to Lee's local Planning Board. Something to keep him occupied. Clarissa was glad he wasn't underfoot all day.

Evan had appeared before the Board to present his proposal for redesigning the gazebo on The Green, his first major job since he'd set up his design business.

"Evan Murray, you know, Liz and Ross Murray's grandson. The one they adopted. Matt dated one of their daughters."

"I don't know who he is." She did, however, remember the Murrays. They worked a farm south of town. Three girls.

"This guy—probably 27 or so—is a dead ringer for Matt at that age—same voice. Until a year or so ago, he was out of the country, has a graduate degree from a Scottish university, worked for UNESCO. Impressive CV and an impressive design for the gazebo. We voted to give him the contract."

She'd been horrified that Judd would suggest their son might have an illegitimate child. Their son. "You're imagining the resemblance."

Not until Sam Brunello stopped taking care of her yard—*You'll be happier with someone else. My cousin has agreed to fill in for me until you find a more suitable gardener*— did she meet the young man Judd had mentioned. The Saturday after Sam quit, Evan Murray appeared on her doorstep. If she hadn't been warned about the resemblance, she might have fainted dead away. She was looking at Matthew in Levi's and a t-shirt—clothing he'd never actually worn because Clarissa believed denim was only for men who did manual labor.

"Mrs. Hamilton, I'm Sam's cousin, Evan Murray. I'll help out for a few weeks. But you need to find someone permanently. I am not a gardener." Then he smiled at her, and she knew Judd had been right— this young man was her grandson.

She'd stumbled over her explanation about the yard, what she expected, pretending she wasn't unnerved.

Each Saturday, she waited for him, as though Matt were coming to visit. She often wondered whether Evan knew about his relationship to her. Probably not. If Liz Murray had known, she would not have been anxious to tell him. Liz had not liked her. And Clarissa was no fan of Liz. A woman working on her hands and knees in the fields. Liz had refused to keep Brenda away from Matt, and Clarissa had had no luck getting Matt to date other girls.

Judd would be pleased that this grandson had rebuilt the bridge. Several times, she'd been on the verge of telling Evan that she might be his grandmother but decided to keep her counsel.

Clarissa hadn't seen Evan's truck at The Maples since May. Hopefully, he and *that woman* had broken up. She was all wrong for him.

When the inquiry from *The New England Bed and Breakfast* website appeared in The Sewing Basket's e-mail, Phoebe almost deleted it until she noticed the subject line read *The Maples*. The query was about a review with Phoebe's website address. Had it truly come from her website? Phoebe responded *No one at this address wrote such a review.* And promptly forgot about it.

The next day, however, the website sent another message, showing the date and time of the entry they'd received, asking her to check her records. Because Phoebe did most of her buying and bill paying on-line, she regularly backed up all her outgoing e-mails, at least until tax season was over. With the date and time information, she searched the sent file for May, and there was the Sent designation for *The New England* website. The e-mail that followed it was an order for Fat Quarters that Clarissa had sent to a fabric wholesaler in Fall River on the same day. Two and two added up to four very quickly.

Phoebe's answer to the website was that someone had used The Sewing Basket's site without her authorization, and she was absolutely certain that person had never stayed at The Maples. She apologized and suggested the website remove the review.

They responded promptly. "We removed that review. Thank you for your help."

What should she do with what she suspected—knew? The dilemma chased her around for several days. Phoebe wasn't eager to accuse Clarissa because her quilting classes brought necessary business into the shop. At the same time, she didn't want Dani Springer's business to suffer. Of course now that Phoebe knew what Clarissa had used her computer for, she would review the sent folder more regularly and also remind Clarissa that she could only use the computer for class-related business.

Phoebe finally decided to tell Dani and let her do whatever she wanted with the information. It was well-known that there was little love lost between the two women, that Clarissa had been gunning for Dani from the beginning.

When Phoebe finished showing Dani and Abby the evidence against Clarissa and, with Abby's help, located the record of the review Clarissa had sent to the *Berkshire* site—Dani was speechless. Such a terrible thing to do. The ugliness of it went beyond anything else Clarissa had done. The fake reviews were obviously payback for Dani saying she was sorry she'd let Clarissa live in the cottage. The dates lined up.

On their way back to The Maples, Abby asked "What do you want to do?"

"Kill her, but it probably wouldn't do any good. She'd just haunt the place. There's no way to win with her. If I confront her, she'll try something else."

"I suppose you're right. But it doesn't seem fair that she can get away with something like this."

"Technically, she hasn't gotten away with it. Phoebe knows, we know, and the website removed her review. I feel so much better knowing that the reviews didn't come from one of our guests."

"So that's it? You're going to let it slide?"

"For now. I like the idea of having a secret weapon. There may be another time I'll need information like this. Assuming Clarissa has a conscience, she may be a little uncomfortable wondering whether Phoebe knows."

"Tossing her out of the cottage would be my vote, but I have a mean streak."

Chapter 23

After Matthew died, Lorraine erased the word *family* from her vocabulary. JT had already been gone nine years and Aileen was still in Europe, pretending she didn't have a family. There were dozens of Malone relatives sprinkled in and around Massachusetts and New York, though Lorraine had never had much contact with them, thanks to her mother's determination to rise above what she saw as her humble beginnings. When Lorraine and Aileen were in elementary school, Grandma Malone had taught them how to knit and do satin stitch embroidery, while the boys went fishing with Grandpa. Days away from their mother's oversight. But Lorraine could remember only a handful of times, other than major holidays, when the Malone grandparents had been invited to their house.

For most of Lorraine's childhood, the Hamilton grandparents lived in Springfield, where her grandfather was a municipal court judge. They visited Lee a few times a year, their impending visits necessitating days of house cleaning and new outfits for everyone. Proving—over and over—that Judd's family was a picture perfect family in a picture perfect house. It had long been Lorraine's belief that her mother was always trying to impress her in-laws and ignoring her own parents.

Lorraine's best childhood memories were of playing with her siblings. They'd entertained themselves, relied on each other, and had the run of the town. Much of their fun involved making end runs around the lists of chores their mother left for them each day, bonding in their attempts to prevent their mother from having total control over their lives. By the time Lorraine and Aileen were in high school, the boys had left home, and that sibling closeness disappeared.

As an adult, Lorraine had gotten used to being an only child.

By marrying Grant in a rural chapel near Bennington, Vermont—with her best friend Sophia and Grant's brother Ernest as witnesses—Lorraine had successfully avoided involving her mother in the wedding plans. She didn't need the kind of drama that her mother would have brought to the occasion. An enormous end run that her mother would probably never forgive. Lorraine did, however, regret not having her father give her away. Since her father's death, she and her mother had been stuck with each other.

Then Evan Murray called to ask if he could talk to her, and *family* reentered her vocabulary.

Evan had spent hours debating just how to introduce himself as her nephew. If only there were a script he could follow. He'd been agonizing over how to address her. He didn't know her well enough to call her Lorraine. And in case they weren't related, Aunt Lorraine wouldn't do either. When he was taking care of her mother's yard, they'd occasionally exchanged innocuous comments about the weather or the roses. Nothing substantial.

When she opened her front door, he chose formality. "Mrs. Sessions, thank you for seeing me."

She led him into the living room, three of its white walls covered with bookshelves. On the fourth wall were two large Ansel Adams prints hanging side by side. Grant had chosen the photographs, as well as the gray leather sofa, ebony-stained end tables, and Swedish style pewter lamps. If furnishing the house had been left to Lorraine, he'd once quipped to friends, they'd be sitting on folding chairs and eating off apple crates. She seemed to have no desire or ability to decorate their surroundings. Thus, the Sessions' living area had a distinctly masculine feel—the only splashes of color provided by the dust jackets on the books.

Evan sat on the couch; Lorraine settled into a black leather chair. "How can I help you?" Her tone of voice was the one she used when parents of her students came to talk about report cards. It was hard to turn off teacher-speak, even in the summer.

"I'm interested in talking to your brother's widow and her daughters." In the thirty years since Matt's death, Suzanne had not kept in touch with Matthew's family. The result, no doubt, of the argument over where to hold his funeral. Too bad. Lorraine had rather liked Suzanne. Since then, she and Grant made a point of seeing Rose and Cindy occasionally, had attended their weddings and the christenings of Cindy's children.

"Why?"

He took a deep breath and hoped for the best. "I have reason to believe Matthew Hamilton was—is—my father."

A deceptively simple statement filled with a thousand complications. Stunned, Lorraine carefully examined each of the eleven words, making sure she'd heard him correctly. After what seemed like minutes but were really seconds, she asked, "My brother, Matthew?"

"Yes."

She searched her memory for Evan's mother's name but couldn't find it. The best she could do was "Liz Murray was your grandmother?"

"Yes. My mother was Brenda. Her youngest. Brenda and Matthew dated in high school. My Aunt Joanna has a picture, probably taken at their Senior Prom." His other aunt, the aunt he'd always had. Now this woman was probably his aunt too.

Lorraine remembered the pretty, dark-haired cheerleader her mother always referred to as *that farm girl*. Matt had been badly smitten; then he and Brenda went off to different colleges, and eventually Suzanne entered the picture. Initially, her mother had been delighted with Suzanne. *Her father heads an important law firm in Boston.*

Lorraine studied Evan's face. She'd never properly looked at him, never really given him more than a cursory glance, the way you do with people who are just passing by. Seeing without seeing.

His hair was the same color as Matthew's, and his eyes were almost the color of his hair. Copper or maybe rust. She never knew the proper names of colors. All the Hamilton children had inherited Clarissa's blue eyes. Evan was tall, with Matt's lanky looseness that fooled you into thinking he was moving slowly.

"What makes you think so?"

"Several things," Evan smiled nervously.

And—while he was telling her about Sam bringing him the pictures, about the obituary and the watch his grandmother had saved—Lorraine heard nothing. Instead, she was mesmerized by suddenly recognizing her brother in this young man's smile. How had she missed it? How had her mother missed it—or maybe she hadn't.

She interrupted his story. "You look like him, especially your smile, the way it comes in stages, from right to left." Matt's had done that, making it seem a bit crooked.

They both fell silent, startled by her quick acknowledgment of the resemblance, uncertain how to proceed.

"It's been over thirty years since his death."

"I'm thirty-one."

"What is it you want?" Her question was more abrupt than she intended, her usual steadiness threatened by the tightness in her throat.

Evan heard Clarissa's voice in the question but, then, Lorraine was Clarissa's daughter. "I don't mean to cause any trouble. I'd simply like to verify the relationship, probably with DNA from one of his daughters. I'm not sure how it's done." He should have checked on that before coming. "And I'd like to know more about him, what he was like." He leaned forward, his elbows resting on his knees, trying to convert feelings he didn't understand into words he knew were inadequate. "I honestly don't know what I want. Having a father, even a dead one, is new to me. Until now, I had no clue who my father was and believed I didn't care. Now I find that I do care, and it's been—difficult." Difficult in ways he'd never expected and still couldn't put into words. "If Matthew's wife didn't know about my mother, perhaps my turning up would be upsetting." Evan's weeks of uncertainty spilled into the room.

Lorraine doubted Suzanne would be upset. She'd moved on quite quickly after Matt's death. "Actually, my DNA might serve to verify Matthew's paternity. Surely, there's a lab somewhere locally that would do the work."

"I hadn't thought of that. Of course. That would be simpler." His relief was palpable. "Would you mind?"

"Not at all," she smiled across the coffee table. "I've never had a nephew. Neither my sister nor I had children and my other brother died in Viet Nam when he was barely twenty. Given JT's way with the girls, however, I could have other nieces and nephews I don't know about. The girls started chasing him in eighth grade."

Evan relaxed. She was handling the situation better than he'd expected. "I'd like to talk to you about—him, Matthew. Sometime."

"I'd love to talk about him." She'd been closer to Matt than she was to either JT or Aileen. Even after all these years, she still missed having Matt to confide in—Grant didn't much like being her confidant. Warming to the project, "Would you like me to contact Rose and Cynthia, pave the way a bit? Let them tell their mother."

"Yes, absolutely. I've made myself a nervous wreck, wondering how to broach the subject with you, with everyone."

"And my mother?"

Evan laughed softly. "Facing German tanks in the Ardennes would be easier."

Lorraine joined his laughter. "Great metaphor. She is given to running over everything in her path."

"Except Dani."

"Not that she hasn't tried."

"How do you think your mother will react?"

"No idea. Should I come hold your hand?"

"I suppose I'll have to go it on my own, but not yet. I'll wait for the DNA results—and then plot a course."

"She may already have guessed."

"Then why wouldn't she have said something to me?"

"I gave up speculating about what my mother will or will not do when I was in high school. Occasionally I feel that I know her, sometimes even understand her; other times, she's an enigma. Did you know she's playing hostess for the afternoon teas at The Maples?"

"Hell has truly frozen over. How did that happen?"

He hadn't had the nerve to call Dani yet. Once again, he'd neglected her, turned away from her when he probably should have gone to her for support, talked to her about all the bits and pieces of his new identity. What it felt like to be rearranged.

"Dani broke her ankle a few weeks ago—her friend from Connecticut has been running The Maples for her. Mom filled in for tea the day after the accident and was an overnight sensation—her words, not mine. She can be quite charming when it serves her purpose. I know she really loves doing the teas because it's all she talks about, acts like the guests have become her friends. I suspect she believes The Maples might go out of business without her services."

Before he left Lorraine's, they chose a lab from the yellow pages and made an appointment. When they met at the lab outside Pittsfield two days later, Lorraine had already called Rose. "She's excited about meeting you." She handed him a yellow post-it. "I've written her e-mail address and her phone number down for you. She promised to tell Cynthia."

Twenty-four hours later, the DNA results were delivered by priority mail. Lorraine Hamilton Sessions and Evan Murray did, indeed, share the Hamilton DNA.

As soon as the first cast came off and the walking cast went on, Dani began driving, doing the errands that didn't require a lot of walking. At least some of her life was returning to normal. A few days later, she felt confident enough to cook breakfast for the guests since Spence could take the orders and do the serving. She wasn't ready to risk carrying a tray just yet. Because she didn't like using the cane the physical therapist had given her, she needed to watch her balance.

Today, Abby was sleeping in. She deserved time off and, as soon as this new cast was removed, she'd be able to go back to Enfield.

"Mom, Evan Murray's out on the deck. He wants to talk to you."

At the mention of Evan's name, Dani's heart took an extra beat. He'd finally come to see her. A week ago, she'd asked Sam if he'd heard from him. He hadn't. Evidently she wasn't the only one he was ignoring.

She paused to make sure her voice was calm. "Tell him I'll be out in a few minutes. How are things in the dining room?"

"Everyone's done. The Koenigs said they'll check out in an hour or so."

"Let me know when they come down." She was constantly amazed at Spence's poise, his sense of responsibility. Was that her influence or Ben's? Maybe he was simply growing up. "If you'll clear the tables, I'll wash up later."

She wished she had a comb and lipstick in the kitchen, but she didn't. Evan would just have to take her without make up, in her cropped denims and the dark green polo shirt with The Maples' logo on the left. Abby had ordered the shirts for summer—a uniform of sorts. Clarissa, of course, had immediately declared she would not be caught dead in one of them. "I don't wear t-shirts."

Before stepping onto the deck, Dani stood in the doorway, enjoying the sight of him. It felt so natural to see him sitting in a wicker chair, his feet propped on the deck railing, studying the garden. He was wearing twill khaki slacks, a white short-sleeved linen shirt that hung loose, and leather sandals. She'd never seen him in summer clothes. They suited him, accentuated his lean frame. It had been a month, maybe longer, since his phone call telling her he was going to Thailand. Even longer since she'd actually seen him, touched him, since he'd inexplicably moved away from her. First Ben, then Spence, now Evan. Was there something about her that sent men fleeing from her presence?

She walked—more like hobbling—to the deck railing and turned to face him. "You're back." Absurdly stating the obvious.

He smiled that tantalizing smile, unfolded himself from the chair and folded her in his arms. His lips brushed her hair. "I just heard about your ankle."

In the comfort of his arms, it was easy to forget the hurt and anger, as if they had never been. Though she wanted him to keep holding her, she stepped back so she could see his eyes. Would they resume the intimate conversation they'd once had with hers.

"Do you have a few minutes to spare?" He pulled another chair close to the one he'd been sitting in, so they were almost facing one another.

"Yes. One couple will be checking out soon. Spence is watching the front desk for me."

"How have you managed everything?" He reached down and placed his hand lightly on the boot-like cast.

"Abby's been a saint, Spence too. She's going home soon, but Spence will be here for another two or three weeks. Now that I'm off crutches, I'm hoping he doesn't need to help me as much, and he can spend more time with Ross and the soccer team. I fell on the day he arrived, so he hasn't had much fun."

Evan counted back. *A day or two after I left. I didn't know.*

Instead of apologizing, "I heard a rumor that Clarissa has been doing your afternoon teas."

"True."

"And both of you are still alive?" Though his eyes weren't talking, they were laughing. A start.

"So far. As soon as my ankle is back to normal, I'll be able to do the teas myself. She thinks she owns *The Tea Hour,* as she's renamed it. Uses her own china—my dishes aren't proper—and her linen doilies. God I hate doilies. She's also conned Lucilla, at the bakery, into setting aside some of the best pastries each day in return for advertising the bakery on the tea cart. Clarissa always has some sort of agenda. Loves telling the guests the bakery makes all the pastries at her request. The really annoying part is that the guests like her. I saw one couple stop at her cottage the other morning to tell her goodbye, and several women have told me I should hire her to give quilting demonstrations."

Evan considered laughing but thought better of it. Soon he would have to tell Clarissa about Matthew and, once she knew, he too might be in danger of her taking a proprietary interest in his life. That would not be funny.

"And," Dani continued, "she tells everyone that the bridge in the garden is the one her husband built. Makes me furious. She lies so smoothly you'd think she'd been the one in politics instead of her husband." Dani leaned back in the chair. "Sorry, I'm rattling, but she is completely impossible." It felt so good to be telling him her problems.

Now Evan did laugh, couldn't help himself.

"When did you get home?"

"Several days ago. Been sleeping a lot. I forget that jet lag sneaks back even on the second and third day. And I had some appointments."

"I'm glad you're back." *I've missed you, but I wish you'd called. Despite the fact that we were—note the past tense—sleeping together, somehow, I've never made it onto your calling list.*

"Me too." *And I know I should have called as soon as I got back, but I needed to think about how to approach Lorraine. Probably not a good enough excuse.*

"Are things—you—better?" *And will you ever tell me what's going on? Will we get back to where we were?*

"Yes and no."

"Not an acceptable answer." She was suddenly tired of being shut out.

He leaned forward and took one of her hands in both of his. "I want to tell you part of the story—but I can't tell you all of it yet because I still have—things to take care of."

And so she was still on the outside looking in. He certainly was a private person. She couldn't bring herself to use the word secretive—but it might be more appropriate. A few months ago, he'd claimed he wanted her to be in his space—in his life—but he didn't seem able to completely share that space with her. When they were beginning to care about one another—love one another—Evan had seemed so open, so easy to talk to, but that openness had vanished. Was it because she'd told him she probably couldn't have children?

"I'm going to Boston tomorrow. Can you have dinner with me tonight?"

"Yes." She was so glad he'd asked.

"About six?"

"I'll be ready."

She pushed herself out of the chair, the awkwardness of the cast interfering with the simplest of moves. They were standing close—close enough to kiss.

"Mom, the Koenigs are in the office."

The moment was lost.

Evan had made a reservation at the same restaurant where he'd told her about the tsunami several days before they slept together for the first time. A century or two ago. Because it was high season in the Berkshires and the restaurant's parking lot was full, they parked a couple blocks away. Getting in and out of Evan's pickup, with its high step, took Dani extra time and he had to steady her for a moment when she reached the ground.

As she hobbled beside him, he pulled her arm through his, adjusting his long stride to fit her shortened one. Each time he touched her, smiled at her, her heart lifted. Perhaps they might find their way back to those weeks last winter.

This time Dani ordered a salad. The weather was too warm for anything heavier. Evan studied the menu through reading glasses—she'd never seen him wear glasses before— and finally chose pizza. "You can have some of it too. I can't eat all of it. Do you want wine or a beer?" He removed the glasses and slid them in his shirt pocket.

"I'm still on pain pills, so I'll stick to iced tea."

He gave the waiter the order. "How did you fall?"

"Ungracefully." She tried to make the story funny—now that the ordeal was almost over, she could see the funny parts. "All to save unbreakable towels."

"Lucky that Abby was there."

"If I'd had to call Clarissa, she might just have finished the job by kicking me down the stairs."

"When does this cast come off?"

"Next week. I've promised myself I'll never again complain about working long hours. Having to watch others do what I should be doing is humbling."

"When I get back, we'll celebrate. I don't know exactly how long I'll be gone."

She didn't want to talk about celebrating; she wanted him to talk about himself. "What's in Boston?"

The iced tea and his beer arrived. He held his glass against hers. "To better days."

She wasn't about to be put off. "Boston?"

"Let me tell you the most important part. I know—have found out—who my father is." He set his glass down without tasting the beer. From his expression, Dani couldn't decide if he was happy or sad. "It happened a few weeks before I left for Thailand."

That coincided with his *I need to work this out by myself* speech.

"The information has had a strange effect on me. Sort of set me adrift. I always thought knowing would make me feel complete. That I'd be happy. Instead, I feel—well—betrayed. For most of my life, my grandmother knew who he was, but she died without telling me. So much—so many feelings I didn't know that I had have been bubbling to the surface. Getting in the way of—everything."

Dani watched his eyes. They weren't laughing.

"The information has changed me—is maybe still changing me. I haven't completely come to terms with it."

"Can I help?"

He reached across the table to take her hand. "Yesterday, I received the DNA verification. That's part of what I've been doing since I got home and now, well, now there are some people I need to talk to before I finish the story for you. I promise I'll tell you everything."

"Is he still alive?"

"No."

"Oh Evan." Her voice broke. He knew who the man was but would never meet him.

"Yeah, well that's part of my frustration. I'll only know him through others. Not the same as actually having a conversation with him."

"And these others are in Boston?"

"Some of them."

Chapter 24

To save herself a second trip to the Medical Center, Dani scheduled her ob-gyn visit for the same day the cast was due to come off. In the ten months she'd been in Lee, she hadn't taken the time to find a doctor. Now she needed to take the time. She could no longer just assume she wasn't going to conceive again. She needed verification. The answer would perhaps determine whether her relationship with Evan was heading somewhere permanent—or ending.

The first day without the boot cast, her leg felt so light that she couldn't quite control it. She kept lifting it too far when she went up steps. Someone watching her might think she was slightly drunk. When she and Abby finished work that night, they celebrated her freedom by having a large, three-topping pizza delivered and devouring the whole thing.

Needing to get back to her job and a regular paycheck, Abby packed up her car on Friday afternoon. "If you discover you can't manage yet, let me know before I go back to work on Monday."

"Yes ma'am." Dani knew full well she wouldn't have the nerve to ask her to come back. She'd figure out how to cope. Abby'd already given up enough of her time and money.

The answer from the ob-gyn was what she expected—not what she wanted. There would be no more children.

Perhaps, then, there would be no more Evan.

He wanted a family, deserved one. Loving her might not be enough, but nothing she could do or say would change the fact that her fallopian tubes weren't going to cooperate.

She might be back to square one.

Alone. With a house and the beginnings of a business. A year ago, she'd believed this new life—this house—would be enough.

Now it wasn't.

Loving Evan had changed everything.

She wanted him in her life far more than she wanted this house or this job. The irony of the change in her priorities wasn't lost on her.

Before they resumed their relationship—if they did—he must be told. Of course, there was always the possibility that he didn't intend to continue the relationship, and so fallopian tubes would not be important.

Polly returned from California the last week in July, tanned and broke, ready to go to work. Victoria, having spent two months at The Maples, was anxious to join her family for their annual trek to Cape Cod before she began her senior year.

Now that Polly was working and Dani's ankle was 90%, The Maples was almost back to what passed for normal. Time to end Clarissa's reign over the tea cart. Even before the cast came off, Dani had been dithering over how and when to break the news to her tenant. But the day she received Lucilla's monthly bill, she switched from dithering to action. The bakery bill was twice what Dani had been spending. Add on Clarissa's salary and *The Tea Hour* was definitely over budget. No question that The Maples had needed Clarissa while Dani was hobbling around, but Clarissa's services were no longer necessary. Time to face her.

As Dani walked into the kitchen Friday evening, her heart was pounding. What was there about this woman that was simultaneously annoying and terrifying? Dani held out Clarissa's paycheck. Clarissa dried her hands on a tea towel, took the check and carefully studied it, as she did every Friday.

Dani plunged in. "Mrs. Hamilton, since my cast is off and Polly is back, well, I appreciate your stepping in to help with afternoon tea, but I won't be needing you any longer."

Clarissa's expression gave nothing away. Then, "You're firing me?"

It didn't seem like firing to Dani. "This job was temporary; you knew that. My ankle is okay now, so I don't need the extra help." How many ways did she need to say it.

"Well, you are certainly going to be sorry you've fired me." There was that fired word again. The bully was back. "Your guests will expect me to be here."

How did she manage to twist everything? Against all wisdom, Dani went on offense. "Impossible as it may seem, they aren't coming just for you." But what if some of them did? "And the bill you've run up at the bakery is double what it should be. I specifically asked you not to go over what I had been spending."

Clarissa's eyes were icy. "I remember no such thing. You told me I could select the pastries."

"You remember only what you want to remember. I did not tell you to bankrupt me."

"I do not lie." Though she was only about 5'4", Clarissa drew herself up—squaring her shoulders—and, for a moment, Dani imagined her becoming taller.

"Neither do I."

Standoff. Time to exit.

Dani didn't stop at the office but went straight to her cottage. She didn't want to argue any more. Things would only go from ugly to uglier.

When she locked the house up for the night, she checked the kitchen. Clarissa had already removed all of her china and, thank goodness, the doilies. Dani didn't question the rightness of telling Clarissa that her services were no longer needed. Dani and Polly could handle most things, just as they had before Dani's accident. And Abby was still doing the web page. The "job" had only been temporary—Clarissa had known that up front.

The next day, the Lexus didn't leave the parking lot and there was no sign of Clarissa. Dani dreaded running into her, uneasy about what the fallout was going to be. With Clarissa, there was always fallout. Maybe there'd be more negative reviews—though Phoebe was carefully monitoring the e-mail account.

Two days later, the Lexus left the parking lot.

The news that Dani Springer had unceremoniously fired Clarissa Hamilton had been circulating Lee for several days before Dani heard it from Joanna, who called to tell Dani that Evan would be back in two days. His trip to Boston had turned into two weeks. "He asked me to call you."

As usual, he couldn't manage to call her himself. *Don't go there. It isn't Joanna's fault.*

"Firing is an exaggeration. The job was temporary. My ankle is healed, and I don't need the extra help. End of scandal."

"She's claiming you accused her of running up a bill at Lucilla's."

"She did. Perhaps I should take out an ad in the *The Eagle* and print the evidence. Damn."

"Don't shoot the messenger, Dani."

"Sorry. You're not the one I want to shoot. Well, she can tell the story any way she likes. At least she's out from under foot—though still too close for comfort."

"And you wish she'd disappear."

"Every day. So where has Evan been all this time?"

"I'm not entirely sure, but he called from Florida. That surprised me. How much did he tell you?"

"Just that he knew who his father was and that he'd tell me the details when he'd seen other people."

"Be patient."

"I'm tired of being patient and tired of being at the bottom of his information food chain. Somehow it seems I should be higher." She hadn't meant to confess her hurt.

"I suspect you're higher than all the rest of us. But Evan's had a lifetime of being something of a loner, not confiding in any of us. He doesn't have the knack of sharing, especially painful things. I still know very little about what happened in Thailand. I only know it took him a long time to heal emotionally. Men don't share those kinds of things well."

"My ex didn't either. Thanks for warning me about Clarissa. My best guess is that people know her method of operation and will blow the story off. No sense running all over town trying to sell my version." Better to lie low and let it become old news.

The day Evan was due back in town, Dani received a phone call from a guest who had stayed at The Maples four weeks earlier. Ruth Schmidt wanted to reserve two rooms, one for herself and one for a friend who was an avid quilter and anxious to meet Mrs. Hamilton. When Dani explained that Mrs. Hamilton had only been filling in during Dani's absence and was no longer hostessing the afternoon tea, Ms. Schmidt asked for Clarissa's phone number.

And did not book the rooms.

Clarissa's curse, *You'll be sorry*, replayed itself in Dani's memory. The ultimate punishment: The Maples was going to lose bookings because Clarissa had been sent away.

Evan's journey from Boston to Philadelphia and then to Florida provided facts about Matthew through others' memories, but hadn't really given him the father he was searching for. Too late for that.

He spent an evening in Boston with Rose, who worked for a prominent auditing firm. She was a petite blonde, fashionably dressed, very much the sophisticated career woman. She and her husband Justin were leaving for Europe in two days, so that evening was the only time she was available.

Because Rose had just turned eight when her father left Boston for D.C., her recollections of Matthew were primarily filtered through what others had told her. "I mostly remember the fighting. Mother always complained that Dad worked too much, but he told her she was the daughter of a lawyer so she should have known he'd work long hours. I'm not sure they were a good match. Mother was only twenty-two and pregnant with me when they married. Maybe too young. I think that's why I waited until I was in my thirties to get married."

"Any good memories?"

"Oh sure. He taught Cindy and me how to ride our bikes. On weekends, the four of us would go for walks. He loved ice cream cones, loved trying new flavors. I don't remember him punishing us for anything. Mother usually did the disciplining. I'm sorry I don't have a clearer picture of him. I mostly remember what our stepfather did with us."

Although she didn't have many memories to share, Rose seemed delighted to have a half-brother. She hugged him hard as they parted, "Welcome to the family, such as it is."

The next afternoon, he drove out to Brookline to talk to Suzanne. Easy to see where Rose got her looks. Suzanne was beautiful, well-dressed, definitely accustomed to having money. They spent two afternoons looking at family pictures and talking about Matthew. The second afternoon, he felt confident enough to ask, "Did you know there was someone else?"

"There wasn't anyone when we separated. I'm sure of that. But once he was in Washington, I got the feeling he'd found someone. No matter what time I called his apartment, he wasn't there. I could only catch him at his office. He preferred coming here to see the girls rather than having them visit him. Little things that began to add up."

Suzanne was easy to like. His father had good taste in women.

"Have you told his mother about yourself?"

"I'm saving that pleasure for last."

"Like cake frosting?"

"More like brussel sprouts."

"You know her then?"

He explained about the garden and the bridge. "At the time, I had no idea I was rebuilding my grandfather's bridge."

"Judd could build anything. Maybe you get some of your abilities from him. Matt, however, could hardly change a light bulb. I always suspected it was because whatever anyone did around the Hamilton house had to pass her inspection, so he simply opted out."

"Not a fan I take it."

"Only until Matt and I were married, and then everything between me and Clarissa went south. She's very competitive. I wasn't in the mood to compete with her for my husband. Do you like her?"

"Not sure. I do know you have to be tough with her sometimes." He told her about Clarissa's ongoing war with Dani.

"I think I'd like Dani. I could never beat Clarissa at her game without putting Matthew in the middle, so she usually got her way. Judd gave in to her too, anything to keep the peace. She's probably never forgiven me for having your father's funeral in Boston. It was the only time I stood up to her."

Evan thanked her for her time and the stack of pictures she gave him.

"Matt would have been proud to have a son like you."

"I hope so."

His time with Cindy was brief and noisy. Her twin sons were seven, her daughter three and so the conversation was interrupted every few minutes. She was taller than Rose and looked a little like Lorraine. Cindy had been six when her father left. "He always smelled of shaving lotion. He and my mother fought a lot and the fights were always followed by long silences." She grinned. "Please note there is never any silence in our house. My husband, Patrick, likes it that way."

Evan's decision to visit Aileen in Florida was made on the spur of the moment, yet when he called her from Cindy's, she wasn't surprised by his request. "My sister called. She said this news was too good to keep to herself."

Aileen and Bart's house—actually a small Italian-style villa—was warm and inviting, colorful fabrics, deep cushions, and enormous windows. Everything Lorraine's house was not. He had very different half-sisters and very different Hamilton aunts.

Aileen spent long hours with him, reminiscing about her childhood, recounting the pranks she and her siblings played on each other, describing what Clarissa and Judd had been like in those days.

"You'd have liked your grandfather. He loved building things and working with people. When he built something, it lasted. Everyone trusted him even after he went into politics. He was the one who stayed in touch with me, sent me money when I was in Europe, occasionally flew down here after I returned from abroad."

"And your mother didn't know?"

"The family mantra has always been *what Mom doesn't know doesn't hurt us.*"

"I'll remember that."

Evan flew back to Boston, picked up his car from the Long Term parking lot, and arrived at the farm after midnight. The trip had drained him, yet he was calmer. Happier than when he'd begun the journey.

Shortly before noon, he called Joanna, "Just checking in. I'm at the farm."

"Stay put. I'm coming over."

Though he was accustomed to Joanna's penchant for cutting to the chase, her tone carried a sharper edge than usual.

With a cup of coffee in one hand and Zack's ball in the other, he went outside to wait for her and give the dog some much-needed attention. It felt good to be home. For the last two months, he'd been going and coming and going and coming. He was ready to settle in. Fortunately, there was an additional design job waiting for him, and the Pittsfield sculpture was ready for his inspection before it was sent to be cast.

He hadn't decided how to approach Clarissa. He was tempted to ask Lorraine to do what she'd done with Rose. Taking the coward's way out.

Fifteen minutes later, Joanna's SUV swung into the barnyard. The older she got, the more she looked like his grandmother, gray beginning to appear at her temples. She was in her sixties, though he never thought of her being that old.

She kissed his cheek. "Any coffee left?"

"Half a pot."

"That might be enough."

He had the distinct impression he was in trouble. After she'd poured coffee for herself and added a substantial amount of sugar, he tried to lighten the mood, "What am I being arrested for, officer? What have I done?"

"It's not so much what you've done as what you haven't."

He was lost. "Do I have to guess? I hate guessing."

"You asked me to call Dani for you. Why in the hell didn't you call her yourself?"

"Well, it seemed—" He had no answer that made sense.

"Do you want to keep your relationship with her? Because if you do, you need to stop leaving her on the sidelines."

He was about to say something in his own defense, but she cut him off. "You leave and don't tell her; you make her come looking for you. Ross gave her the wrong information about Kanya because you hadn't told her why you were in New York. Ross felt awful. You expect her to be patient while you're trying to get your head on straight, but it's got to stop or you're going to lose her."

"But I—"

"You've played the lone-wolf long enough. Pull her into the loop, let her help, talk to her. This morning you called me first. I don't have to be first." She took a breath. "Do you love her?"

"Very much."

"Then, dammit, go see her before you do anything else. Matthew Hamilton has been dead for thirty years. No hurry about him or his family. You've had a family all your life. Maybe not exactly like other people's, but you've been loved and taken care of, probably better than the Hamilton children were. I'm not pitting Murrays against Hamiltons; I just want you to remember that what you think you've missed out on may not be a big deal."

She swallowed the last of her coffee, set the cup on the counter, and left.

Chapter 25

$\mathcal{J}$oanna's fish-or-cut-bait lecture was spot on.
He'd come to the same conclusion in Florida.

Enough of chasing the past. Matthew wasn't going anywhere. Dani was the present and, hopefully, the future. She mattered more than a dead father who was out of reach.

Get over it, Murray.

Get on with your life.

He called Dani just after six. Instead of beginning with an apology that would litter the atmosphere with guilt, he opted for behaving as though they were still a couple—then maybe they might still be a couple.

"Have you eaten?"

"No. I'm just cleaning up after tea."

"Can I interest you in Chinese takeout?"

"Sweet and sour pork?"

"Always."

A beginning. God, he'd missed her, missed everything they'd shared. What had possessed him to go running after someone who had been dead thirty years? Matthew Hamilton could not help Evan live his life or love this woman.

And he did love this woman. He was lightheaded with that certainty.

Besides the sweet and sour pork, he bought three other entrees, an order of spring rolls and both white and brown rice. He was hungry.

Dani changed into clean white cotton slacks—coffee had splashed on her others—and found a bright yellow and orange blouse. California colors. She was barefoot; wearing shoes all day made her ankle ache by evening.

Evan had sounded like Evan on the phone. Should she hope for an apology or just move on, assuming there wouldn't be one? Men generally didn't apologize well or revisit the rights and wrongs of a situation. Picking over emotional debris was a female preoccupation.

Although he had a key to her cottage, he rang the doorbell. Wise. Not presuming too much. He had such lovely manners. Along with the oversize shopping bag from Nouvelle China, he carried a bouquet of long-stemmed red roses, probably from Sam's greenhouses.

Instead of throwing herself into his arms, she simply smiled. "Chinese food and roses. Must be a special occasion."

He leaned over and kissed her. "When my hands aren't full, I'll do better."

She hoped he would. "Let me put the flowers in water. Thank you."

"You're welcome."

"You know where the dishes are." A night in. Familiar and comfortable, both of them intent on picking up where they'd left off. As though there had been no gap.

He laid out the forks, plates and napkins.

"There's wine if you want some—or beer. I'll have wine."

"So you're off the pain pills?"

"Except for an occasional Aleve. A dozen trips up and down the stairs remind me that I broke my ankle."

During dinner they talked about everything that wasn't important.

The weather.

The chances of good fall color this year.

Cathy and her family moving. The repair work and painting that the farmhouse needed.

The new design job at the golf club.

Spence's soccer camp.

Dani being appointed to the membership committee at the Chamber of Commerce.

When they finished eating, they took their wine to the living room and sat on the couch—almost touching. Evan laid a fat brown envelope on the coffee table.

"And this is?"

"My obsession for the last few months." Dani reached for it, but he stopped her, turning on the couch so he was facing her.

"Dani Springer—"

So formal. "Yes, Evan Murray."

"I love you. Will you marry me?"

No preamble.

No hesitancy.

Just like that. Exquisite words suspended between them. Simple, profound, life-changing words that declared his love.

After the divorce, Dani had been afraid there would never again be love in her life, afraid that a second failure could prove life-threatening. Tonight, love's reappearance didn't feel at all threatening. It felt right and worth waiting for. But she needed to explain about her infertility before she lost her courage. She set her wine glass down. As he was about to say something else, she laid her index finger against his lips.

"Me first. I need to tell you this." *Inhale.* "Well, I—just to be sure, I had some tests done because, even though you love me—perhaps that won't be enough." *Exhale.*

He gently removed her finger so he could speak. "Dani, it doesn't matter whether you can have children or not."

"I can't, so perhaps you—"

This time he touched his finger to her lips. "Shhh. It's not important."

"But you deserve a family of your own."

"Did you hear me? It's not important. Do you love me?" The intensity of his eyes held her, the sienna darker than she remembered.

"Yes." A whisper.

This kiss stole her breath, his hands tangled in her hair.

When the kiss ended, "This is what's important."

"But—"

"Dani, you do remember that I'm adopted, don't you?"

She nodded.

"And I turned out rather well if I do say so." He was teasing her.

"They were your grandparents; it's different."

"Doesn't matter. Do you have an objection to adopting?"

"No, but wouldn't you want—"

"I want you."

A sweet, simple answer. All Dani's uncertainty evaporated and she let herself rest against him. "Doesn't adopting take a long time? People wait years."

"It might not take as long if we adopt a baby or two from another country, like China or Korea, maybe an African child."

Dani sat up. "Two?"

"Saves on paper work." He grinned.

"Poor Spence."

"Why?"

"So many babies all at once."

"Should I ask his permission to marry you, that is, if you say yes."

"A thousand times yes. He'll love being consulted."

"I want him to feel comfortable coming here, staying with us."

At eleven, they walked hand-in-hand to the main house to lock up for the evening, their heads full of plans for their future.

Back in Dani's cottage, they ignored the envelope on the coffee table, standing in the dark, slowly undressing each other—remembering the scent of skin, the curve of hip, the way they fit together. Delicious anticipation, held at arm's length until the final race to climax.

When she woke during the night, she was curled against his back. Snug. Loved. At that moment, she didn't need to understand why he'd been out tilting at windmills—seeming to ignore her. She just needed his back against her. She wondered briefly what was in the envelope, then drifted off to sleep.

When her alarm went off at 5:30, Evan was gone, a note on the pillow next to her. "Same time tonight?" with a heart drawn below. He'd taken the brown envelope with him.

She floated through the day. Her ankle was healing, Clarissa was out of the house, and Evan was back in her life.

The only flaw was the heat. The temperature was in the nineties, the humidity not far behind. Even with a/c, she was hot and sticky. Cooking and cleaning were not cool jobs. At midmorning, she mixed two pitchers of Crystal Light tea, added plenty of ice cubes, took one pitcher upstairs to Polly, and left the other in the office. She'd have to serve afternoon tea in the living room. Too hot to use the deck. A cram course in just how ugly New England summers could be. If they were lucky, it would rain later, but she wasn't counting on it.

Just before afternoon tea, she went to her cottage, took a quick shower—her second of the day— and put on the coolest outfit she owned.

At exactly six, Evan called. "How about dinner in a refrigerator someplace?"

"Hot at your place too?"

"Barns don't have air conditioning or insulation. The best I've got is fans. Anyhow, I'm thinking of The Cactus Garden. Since you spent a lot of time in California, I assume you like Mexican food. Is seven okay?"

Any time or place or cuisine he suggested would be okay. "Yes and yes."

"I've missed you today." His voice was softer.

"That's what you get for sneaking off this morning."

"I forgot I'd left Zack inside. Seemed wise to get back and let him out. I was too late, by the way. Since Cathy's not here to dogsit anymore, I need to take the time to put in a doggy door. See you soon."

He carried the mysterious envelope into the restaurant. As soon as they finished ordering, he undid the clasp and pulled out photographs of all sizes.

She leaned toward him. "Tell me."

Evan chose the two prom pictures, turning them so they were right side up for Dani. "The one on your left is my junior prom picture."

She studied them, looked up at him as though verifying what he looked like, then looked back at the pictures. "What's his name?"

"Matthew Hamilton."

Dani wasn't sure she'd heard correctly. "Matthew Hamilton?"

"Yes."

"As in—"

"The Hamilton Hamiltons. Yes."

"She's your grandmother?"

"Afraid so."

"Of all the coincidences possible. She's your grandmother. Oh God, Evan, she hates my guts. She's been telling everyone I fired her. I didn't—exactly. But who's going to believe me? And now I'm going to be related to her. Could this be more awkward?"

"If you go with me when I talk to her, that could be awkward."

Dani wanted to laugh at the absurdity of this turn of events, needed to laugh. It was such a relief to have Evan tell her why he'd been behaving strangely—to have Evan. Clarissa was really a minor issue. Dani could hardly wait to tell Abby. "Do you mind if I laugh?"

"Go right ahead. I've laughed at your problems with her. I owe you."

And so she laughed; eventually they both did.

"Do you think she knows?"

"I asked Lorraine the same question. She says Clarissa might but probably wouldn't be eager to let on. Lorraine's been a big help. Put me in touch with Matthew's other family and with Lorraine's sister, Aileen."

"You've been visiting Hamiltons." The reasons for his absences were falling into place; it truly hadn't been about her.

"I have, and they've all been very kind. Clarissa is my last stop. I'm wondering whether I should make out my will before I talk to her."

"After all the battles she and I have fought this year, imagine her response to our getting married."

"Perhaps this is a deal breaker for you?"

"I'll think about it." She hoped he knew she was kidding.

Their meals came. Sizzling beef fajitas, the rich smell of warm corn tortillas, rice and black beans. She would have preferred fish tacos, but they hadn't found their way onto The Cactus Garden's menu.

He showed her the rest of the pictures, told her about the Hamiltons he'd met, brought her back into his life.

"She's always seemed to like you. You're one of the few people she smiles at."

"Given her reputation, I'm not sure I want that on my resume. *Clarissa Hamilton likes him.* Might be bad for business."

She told him about losing Ruth Schmidt's business.

"You could rehire her."

"And let her win? Not on your life. Anyhow, I can't afford her. Once the fall color is gone, business will slow down and I'm still not in the black. She was costing me about five hundred dollars a month."

"So how am I going to tell her I'm related to her?"

"You might ask Lorraine to go with you. She's had lots of experience handling her mother."

"To her credit, Lorraine offered."

"Take her up on it."

"Clarissa can probably smell fear. As you so accurately put it, it's not wise to let her win."

"Do you want her to welcome you into the family or just know that you are family?"

"She doesn't need to welcome me. Aunt Joanna reminded me I've always had a loving family. I don't need the Hamiltons. For the first time in my adult life, I think Aunt Joanna was truly pissed off at me and my preoccupation with this father thing. Very bottom line, my aunt."

He didn't tell Dani that she'd been the real reason for the dressing down Joanna had administered.

Clarissa was at loose ends. The next quilting class wouldn't start for another week, and the bridge group was on hiatus until after Labor Day. She missed *The Tea Hour*, having people to talk to.

On top of everything else, Evan Murray's truck was again parked in the lot behind her house. Every night. She was disappointed. She rather hoped the affair was over.

For lack of anything better to do, she began a thorough house cleaning, one room at a time. Because of the heat, she got up at six and quit working around ten or eleven. Several times, she lunched with Lorraine, a few times with Natalie.

"Mrs. Hamilton?"

She was emptying her trash when Evan walked over from her guesthouse. "Hello Evan."

"Do you have some time to talk?" There was that smile. She'd never been able to resist it in Matt either.

"Yes."

Evan took the trash basket from her and carried it inside.

"Can I get you coffee or is it too warm?"

"I'd like some—please." Holding onto the cup would steady his hands and his nerves. "Just black."

She must have already had some made because, in a few minutes, she brought him a cup and saucer, then went back to the kitchen for hers.

When she had seated herself across from him, he began his story, closely watching her reaction. The abridged version took about fifteen minutes and ended with him handing her the one page DNA report from the lab.

"I want you to read this so you know everything I've said is true."

She read it carefully, though she really didn't need the proof. She only had to look at him to know he was Matt's son. When he began working for her, she'd decided that feigning ignorance of their relationship was the best way to handle what could be a potential scandal. By pretending what he was telling her was new information, she didn't have to admit she'd known she was his grandmother but said nothing. Her reasons for hiding what she knew were, admittedly, old-fashioned. This grandson was illegitimate. Separated or not, Matt had been an adulterer. In the Twenty-First century, people weren't as shocked by such moral issues. In Clarissa's century, children born outside of marriage tarnished a family.

Evan waited patiently for her to say something. When she didn't, "I just wanted you to know."

"Why?"

"Because now I know. I'm not planning to hang a banner across Main Street, if that's what worries you. Very few people know, and I really don't want anything from you, from anyone."

"Who else knows?"

"Besides your family, my Aunt Joanna and Sam—and Dani."

That hit hard. "You told *her*?"

"Of course. She's going to be my wife."

"You're marrying *her*!" Illegitimacy immediately took a back seat to that woman being her granddaughter-in-law. First, she'd usurped the house, then fired her, and now—had insinuated herself into the Hamilton family. Clarissa stood up. "You should leave now."

"I'm sorry if I upset you."

She looked away.

213

Evan retrieved the DNA report and did as she requested.

Upset didn't begin to describe her emotions. Removing her shoes, she lay on top of the quilted bedspread she'd finished last week and stared at the ceiling. She needed a strategy.

Chapter 26

$\mathcal{E}$van was working sixteen hour days. The sculpture he'd designed for the Veteran's Memorial had been cast and, as soon as the site was ready, it would be installed. The golf course job was on schedule, so long as the weather held. He'd broken his one job at a time rule because he needed money to repair the farmhouse and, if he and Dani were serious about starting a family, they needed savings and life insurance, things the single Evan had never worried about. Adoption agencies would look closely at finances.

Most of the time, he was living at Dani's—unless work kept him at the studio after midnight; then he slept in the loft rather than drive when he was exhausted. Since his conversation with Clarissa, he hadn't crossed her path. Just as well. He'd reported their meeting to Lorraine, who wasn't surprised that her mother was avoiding him and Dani. "She's ignoring my phone calls too. When things happen that she can't control, she goes to ground. After JT was killed, we couldn't coax her out of the house for weeks. She deals with disaster by not dealing with it."

"I'm a disaster?"

"Maybe. Best guess is that you marrying Dani is the real disaster. From the beginning, she's blamed Dani for the loss of the house. Easier to blame a stranger than to admit the house had to be sold. My father didn't leave much of an estate, and the house was getting to be more than she could physically manage; her knees bothered her all the time, and her bank account was running on empty. Clarissa Hamilton, however, doesn't like reality. Dani not only owns Mom's house but is about to be part of the family. Mom's always had a them/us mentality."

The Saturday before Spence's fifteenth birthday, Dani and Evan drove to Annapolis. Abby was staying at The Maples overnight to help Polly. Besides celebrating Spence's birthday, Evan wanted to ask him for Dani's hand. Joanna had given Evan Liz's engagement ring, which he'd had reset—consulting with Abby about its style and Dani's ring size. He was carrying the box in the duffle bag he used as his weekend suitcase.

For several days, he'd been uneasy about telling Spence that he and Dani were going to marry. The teenager was an unknown quantity. They'd never actually had a conversation about anything, yet suddenly Evan was going to be his stepfather. Joanna had recommended that Evan treat him the same way he did Ross. "I think Spence has a good relationship with his mother, despite the fact that he isn't living with her. He's simply looking for some father time. You can relate, right?"

Evan could relate.

After Spence opened his gifts, the three of them chose a pizza restaurant near the Naval Academy on the premise that college kids knew good pizza. What they discovered was that college kids like noise, flat screen TV's and football games with their pizza. It wasn't the easiest venue for a serious conversation.

When Evan asked Spence's permission to marry Dani, "You're her closest male relative," Spence looked proud and embarrassed.

"Am I supposed to ask you questions or something?"

"If you want."

"Um, do you love each other?"

Dani blushed and Evan reached for her hand; together they answered *yes.*

"What's your favorite baseball team?"

"Red Sox."

"Good choice. I pronounce you engaged." Spence almost giggled as he said it. Dani remembered his little boy giggle. She hadn't heard it in a long time—he was too grown up. But at this moment, he'd turned back into her little boy. She was so glad Evan had thought of asking him for her hand. Spence's family was changing, and he needed to feel that he was part of the changes.

Evan had slipped the ring box into his jacket pocket before they left the motel room. He took it out and set it in front of Dani. "Now that I have permission to marry you, let's make it official before the pizza comes." He winked at Spence, and the giggle returned.

Dani opened the box hesitantly and stared at the ring, tears cresting in her eyes. "Oh my. It's lovely." She lifted it out of the box, holding it between her thumb and forefinger, admiring it. Ben hadn't been able to afford an engagement ring. They'd had to pool their cash just to buy plain platinum bands.

"It was my Grandmother Murray's. Abby helped choose the setting. Let's see if it fits." Evan took it from her, slowly slid the diamond on her ring finger, then kissed the ring into place. Dani couldn't think of anything to say. Such a perfect moment.

After eating most of two pizzas—the ham and pineapple one that Spence loved and the everything-but-anchovies one that Dani preferred—they told him about Clarissa.

"So now it's okay if she teaches me to play poker?"

Dani wanted to laugh. Spence hadn't missed the irony in the situation. "Yes. You may, however, be the only one she's speaking to."

"She's not happy about you guys getting married?"

"Absolutely furious would be more accurate."

"She was always nice to me when she was doing the teas."

"Clarissa's not doing the teas anymore."

"Why not? I mean she was kind of fussy about getting everything just right, but I think she liked doing them. Made her feel important or something." There was Spence's warm heart.

"Since my ankle's healed, I don't need her to manage the teas."

"You fired her?"

"Not exactly. The job was only temporary." Good Lord, Spence was taking Clarissa's side. What was so awful about letting her go? The whole episode was becoming larger than life.

Even more disturbing, if she and Evan did adopt, then Clarissa would be the child's great-grandmother. Dani didn't begin to know how to handle that. Almost to herself, she said, "When I was deciding whether to buy the house and let Clarissa stay, I asked Margo Waters *How much trouble can she be*? I think I have the answer."

New England's fall color was on schedule. It crept south from Canada, spilling paint box colors over the hillsides, a yellow-orange-red extravaganza. Leaf peepers followed the nightly *Best Color Spots for Tomorrow* TV reports, turning the local roads into parking lots while they took endless pictures of the annual color pageant.

Lee hit its color peak the weekend after they visited Spence. The Maples—framed by its own bright red trees—was fully booked every night. Dani could almost see black ink at the end of the financial tunnel she'd been traveling through for the last year. If there were any other Ruth Schmidt defections because Clarissa was no longer doing the teas, Dani didn't know about them. As soon as the garden faded, Evan hired Ross to dig up the annuals and separate the bulbs to be stored in the basement until spring.

A whole year in this house. Dani had begun to learn its rhythms, to interpret its peculiar creaks and groans. A four bedroom friend. She had done what she set out to do, but she knew adjustments would have to be made after she and Evan were married. Right now, they were living in her cottage, Evan commuting to the farm to work. Though Polly was on night duty three evenings a week, Dani still did all the breakfasts, teas, bookkeeping and shopping. They divided up the cleaning, Polly doing the upstairs, Dani the downstairs. She and Polly had gotten more efficient, but Dani's daily schedule didn't allow much time for Evan and there was certainly no way she could take care of a baby and manage a B & B. Decisions were on the horizon.

Her love affair with The Maples had taken up residence in her life gradually, just as her love for Evan had grown slowly, steadily, deepening to a delicious richness. Now these two loves were competing for her heart and attention. Evan had been understanding about the demands The Maples made on her. He kept crazy hours too. But if they were going to establish a family, something would have to give. She knew she loved him, knew he was more important than a house or a business. Yet it was difficult to imagine walking away from The Maples, turning it over to a manager or—selling it.

She loved everything about the house. The new porch, the stairway, the mood she'd created. Her guests were quick to compliment The Maples, the food, the service. Appreciation was heady stuff.

But, when Evan wrapped his arms around her, she knew that all she wanted was to blend her life into his and have his blend into hers. She didn't want to make the same choice—mistake—that Clarissa had made.

Clarissa hadn't admitted to any of her friends that Evan Murray was her grandson. However, knowing how easily gossip percolated through Lee, Matt's indiscretion would, at some point, be public knowledge.

At the end of October, she received the wedding invitation.

Evan Andrew Murray
and
Danielle Ann Springer
invite you to witness their wedding vows
Saturday, November 28, 2009
1:00 p.m.
First Congregational Church
Lee, Massachusetts
Reception at the Church Hall
Regrets Only
413-555-4693

Clarissa slipped the invitation back into its envelope and buried it beneath the stack of quilting catalogs on her kitchen counter.

She would not go.

Would not watch her only grandson marry the woman who had taken over her house.

An impossible situation.

Besides, if Clarissa attended the wedding, people would begin speculating about what connected the two families. The Murrays and the Hamiltons had never socialized.

A few days later, Lorraine noticed dark circles under Clarissa's eyes. "Aren't you sleeping well?"

"None of your business." Clarissa snapped, unwilling to admit she'd lain awake trying to figure out how to save face, how to answer questions about Evan—if anyone asked. So far she had no plan.

"You can't decide what to do about the wedding, right?"

Cornered. Clarissa hated that Lorraine read her so easily. "Wrong. I have decided. I'm not going."

"Too bad. Aileen and I are going, and Rose and her husband are driving over from Boston for the day."

"He invited Rose and Aileen?"

"Cynthia too, but driving from Philadelphia with three young ones seemed too daunting."

"Where is Aileen staying?"

"With Grant and me. Bart can't leave the resort right now; they're expanding."

Clarissa's family was coming, yet no one had told her. They'd left her out of the loop.

"Mom, you can't change the fact that he's Matt's son. Go to the wedding. There'll be about thirty or forty guests, a simple ceremony with the reception at the church. Joanna and Monique are doing the food, Sam's providing the flowers, and Dani's closing The Maples for ten days so they can have a short honeymoon."

All these plans that Clarissa knew nothing about. "I repeat, I'm not going."

"And that"—Lorraine told Evan the next day—"is that. At school we call it sulking."

"We want her to come."

"Arguing won't help. Once she's committed herself, backing down is almost impossible for her. She needs a compelling reason—generally in her own self interest—to change her mind. And her feelings are hurt because I didn't tell her about Aileen and Rose."

Dani and Evan had spent hours weighing the virtues of eloping versus getting married in Lee. But when Sam said he'd do the flowers and decorate the church, and Joanna and Monique offered to do light refreshments, the church wedding won. Lucilla volunteered to make the cake. "As a thank you for your business."

It would have been foolish of them to turn down all that generosity.

Dani bought a pale peach, full-length dress with an A-line skirt at a discount boutique Abby knew about in Springfield. Evan already had a dark suit. Sam would be the best man and Abby would be maid of honor. "An excuse to get myself a new outfit." Spence asked if he could walk her down the aisle, and Ross had been tapped as usher. Polly was going to take care of the guest book at the door.

Of course there had been no reply from Clarissa. The few times Dani had encountered her, both of them nodded and kept walking. Safe silence. Dani would have been lying if she said she wanted Clarissa to accept because, wherever Evan's grandmother went, trouble followed. The problem was that Evan sincerely wanted her there.

The day that the Memorial sculpture was delivered to Evan's studio, he called Dani. "When tea is finished, do you have time to come over and take a look?"

"I do. I'm dying to see it. Polly's studying in her room, so I can get away for an hour or two. I'll let her know."

Evan had given Dani daily reports about what was happening at the two construction sites—an elaborate rock-walled garden adjacent to the dining room at the golf club and the Memorial. Juggling two projects was really pushing him. The flaws in his one man operation were beginning to surface. The paperwork, as well as driving between the sites, was taking a toll. He couldn't continue to accept this much work without extra help. He'd always resisted expanding his company; now he might have to rethink the balance between needing more income and trying to do everything himself.

The sculpture was in the center of the barn, an eight foot bronze of three male faces and one female face, representing the major military branches; they blended into and out of one another in such a way that it was hard to tell where one began and another ended. A compelling collage.

"Evan, it's—heart stopping." Dani circled it several times, studying the details. "Have you ever thought about doing this kind of work full time?"

"Think, yeah. But it's hard to make money designing sculptures. This is the first big commission I've had. The rest of the business, which I really do enjoy, feeds Zack and me and now you."

"When will it be installed?"

"Thanksgiving week. It takes a crane and lots of logistical stuff; then we'll cover it with plastic so it doesn't tarnish before the park is dedicated on December 18. I can hardly wait to see how it looks once it's in place."

"You love your work." She loved that about him.

"No argument, but not as much as I love you."

For a few minutes, they ignored the sculpture.

One arm tight around her, "While we're here, let's look at the farmhouse." He switched off the studio lights and grabbed a flashlight to guide them across the barnyard. "Jacob's men finished painting the outside, so it's ready to face the winter."

"What's the color? It's too dark to tell."

"The same as before, a soft yellow—something called Creamed Corn. Who makes up those names?" He unlocked the front door and turned on the inside lights. It was the first time Dani had been inside the house he'd grown up in.

"Which room was yours?"

"The one at the top of the stairs, on the left."

"Can I go up?"

"Sure. Everything on the inside still needs painting. How much else I do to it depends."

They were both at the top of the stairs. "Depends on what?" She turned into his childhood room, fairly large by California's tract house standards, a double window looking onto the side yard, but no trace of the young Evan.

"Depends on whether we eventually live here. Your cottage is pretty small, especially when we add a child, and Spence should have his own room."

"I hadn't gotten that far in my thinking. I know we're going to have to make changes."

"This house has three bedrooms, but only one bathroom. That could be problematic. I looked into adding a second bath before I rented to Cathy's family. The cost is prohibitive. Lots of rebuilding, moving walls. The plumbing is pre World War II."

They discussed whether they could fit in the upstairs rooms; the bathroom definitely needed upgrading. The country kitchen was spacious and, in daylight, probably brought in plenty of sun. The appliances were vintage 1980's. Whether he rented it or they moved in, the stove would need replacing, and there was no dishwasher.

Living at the farm didn't feel quite right to Dani. It was a long way from town, necessitating schoolbus rides. Rather difficult to manage after school activities and play dates with school friends. So many decisions all at once—all good—but decisions nonetheless. First they needed to get married.

Chapter 27

The question of moving to the farmhouse stayed on the back burner. Dani couldn't get past the nagging possibility that she might have to close down The Maples and sell it. That possibility was stealing some of her joy.

At the same time she had been sending out wedding invitations, she began consulting Abby about the financial options. She and Evan were, at the moment, real estate and small business poor. The Maples and the farm were good investments over the long haul—not so good short term. Running The Maples required huge chunks of Dani's time. Evan's work required equally large chunks of his. Though he hired a variety of laborers to do the actual construction, he still had to oversee their work.

Dani and Abby brainstormed various scenarios. Abby loved making spreadsheets and solving financial puzzles. "This is why I get paid the big bucks at Lego."

Abby had once accused her of having caught Clarissa's *I love my house* virus. Dani was finally ready to admit she was exhibiting some of the symptoms. She was proud of having taken a nice house and turned it into a beautiful business; in a year or two, she might even make a profit. Success, even a little success, felt good.

But keeping The Maples open would mean years of working her butt off and having to put Evan, and perhaps children, second.

Not going to happen. Her life with Evan came first.

This house did not own her. But she did own it and its sizable mortgage, which had to be paid every month. Yet the prospect of taking down the sign in the front yard and replacing it with a For Sale sign was keeping her awake nights.

Abby showed up on a Saturday morning with spreadsheets and questions.

"Have you and Evan talked finances?"

"Only in the most general sense. Right now, he's busy with two jobs, as well as having the farmhouse painted."

"Do you know what the farmhouse rents for?"

"No."

"Is the farm free and clear?"

"I think so."

Abby was definitely in managing mode. "Make sure."

When Dani asked about the rent, Evan explained that he'd been renting the house to Cathy below market because she helped out with Zack and looked after his mail when he was out of town.

"Do you mind if I ask Margo what it should rent for? She's now doing property management for Krag & Krag."

"Okay by me. What's going on?"

"I'm trying to make some plans about my house and the business. Abby's helping. Is the farm clear?"

"Yeah, just taxes and insurance. The rent for the house covers those and keeps me in hamburgers between paydays. Are you in financial trouble?"

"Not yet, but I need to figure out how not to work seven days a week and still avoid bankruptcy. My alimony stops the day we say I do. So there goes my hamburger money."

"You hardly ever eat hamburgers."

"Metaphorical hamburgers."

"So where does the farmhouse fit?"

"I don't know exactly. Abby did spreadsheets. She's very good at financial analysis, helped me work through several knotty problems when I was getting ready to open The Maples."

"So long as we're in the same house at the end of the day—that's all I care about."

He said the nicest things at the most unexpected moments.

"We're in the same house now. And it's nearly midnight."

He pulled her close. "I should have included in the same bed."

Abby came up with several financial scenarios for The Maples.

Scenario #1: If they lived in the farmhouse and Dani turned her cottage over to a manager, she might break even. That scenario was predicated on having very few vacancies. Dani would probably still be handling the paper work. The taxes and insurance for the farm would have to come out of Evan's business.

Scenario #2: If they stayed in Dani's cottage, which was really too small for a family, rented the farmhouse and the new manager lived elsewhere, then the manager's salary would have to be higher, and Dani would need to be on site at night. The farmhouse rent would still go to taxes and insurance for the farm—and hamburgers.

Scenario #3: She could sell the house, though there might be a capital gains penalty on a short term ownership. A tax accountant would have to do the math. In the current economy, finding a buyer would take some time. With this scenario, they would be living in the farmhouse and might have some cash after the sale of the house. But then the house and everything she'd put into it would belong to someone else. That possibility was oddly upsetting. The Clarissa virus perhaps.

Dani read Abby's figures over and over, finally going for a long walk to clear her head. Getting married was beginning to look like financial suicide.

When Evan came home about eight o'clock, he found her sitting in the garden, her down jacket barely blocking the November wind chill.

"Hey, you do know it's cold out here?" He sat beside her, giving her a quick kiss. "Ummm, salty." His fingers brushed the tears on her cheeks. "What's wrong? Please tell me we're still getting married in nine days."

"Of course," her voice trembled.

"Why are you crying?"

"Because I might have to sell this place. I can't see any other option."

He took her hand. "You're freezing. Come inside so we can talk."

She showed him Abby's spreadsheets, explaining the columns of numbers. "Scenario #4 would be closing The Maples and keeping the house—but the mortgage is pretty big."

"I didn't realize you were so worried."

She knew she should have confided her fears. Keeping the problem to herself was much the same as Evan not telling her about Matthew. They both had a lot to learn about communicating. "You've got plenty going on with the sculpture and everything."

"Doesn't matter. I want to know what's on your plate too."

"Sorry."

"Dani, new rules. I get to help you with your business, and you get to help with mine. We should do this kind of thinking and worrying together."

"I know. I do know." How nice to share the problem. It had been a long time since she'd had anyone to share with. His love was miraculous.

He held her against him until she was calmer, then reminded her that his business was growing, might grow even more once the Memorial was open. "I don't get paid every week, sometimes not every month, but I do get paid. I promise we won't starve."

Aileen flew into Hartford on Thanksgiving afternoon, rented a car, and arrived at Lorraine's just after dark. It had been Bart who talked her into attending the wedding.

"Honey, you can't hide from your mother forever. You're all grown up. It's okay to go eyeball-to-eyeball if necessary. Might clear the air."

"Easy for you to say," she grumbled.

Not at all put off by her response, "Remember the scene in *The Wizard of Oz* when the curtain is finally pulled back to reveal that the frightening noises coming from the Wizard are really made by a machine and a pudgy little man pulling its levers? Once the Munchkins saw the truth, they weren't afraid any more."

"My mother certainly does make frightening noises."

"Shall I rent the movie?"

"No need." She laughed. Bart had that effect on her, helping her see her foolishness. "You're right. I'll go."

"Tell her she's welcome here any time. Maybe you should invite her to come back with you."

Aileen wasn't ready to go that far.

Though it had rained most of Thanksgiving Day, on Friday the sun was out, everything washed clean for the outing Lorraine and Aileen had spent the previous night planning. Evan provided them with the locations of some of his design projects, and Lorraine plotted them out on a local map.

At nine, Aileen was at Clarissa's front door. She hadn't wanted to give her mother any warning; she needed surprise on her side. And Clarissa's expression told Aileen that her mother was, indeed, caught off guard.

Score one.

"Good morning, Mom. May I come in?"

Clarissa stood aside. Ignoring her mother's frown, Aileen walked into the living room. "I haven't been in here since Dad converted the workshop. It seems quite comfortable." She looked around, recognizing some of the furniture from her childhood.

"It serves." An answer somewhere between martyrdom and sulking. "You didn't come for Thanksgiving."

Not willing to let her mother sidetrack her, Aileen cut to the chase. "Mom, Lorraine and I want to take you for a drive this morning, then have some lunch. Get your coat and purse, go to the bathroom if you need to. We have places to see."

Clarissa didn't have time to formulate an argument and, for once in her life, did what she was told, much to Aileen's amazement.

Not until they picked Lorraine up did Clarissa ask, "Where are we going?"

"On the Evan Murray Design Tour. We all need to learn a few things about your grandson—our nephew."

For the next two hours, they visited the six sites Evan had suggested. The fishing pier, the playground in Stockbridge, the town park in Allenville, and two small sites in Great Barrington. Last on the list, the Veteran's Memorial.

"These are all places your grandson has designed and built, the grandson you don't want to acknowledge because you're ashamed." *And such a snob.*

The Memorial was a small, formal garden built around a graceful, stylized sculpture—a collage of faces. Two workers were drying off yesterday's rain, getting ready to wrap the sculpture in heavy plastic. The women arrived just in time to get a good look at it.

Lorraine explained that Evan had done the drawings for the sculpture, then had it sculpted and cast by a young artist in Amherst. "It was installed a few days ago. The Pittsfield Art Council is planning to submit the sculpture for the Annual Arts Prize at the U of Mass."

The three women walked around it, studying it from all angles. Aileen took several pictures with her cell phone. "I love the way all the faces merge—yet are separate. I want Bart to see it."

All morning, while Aileen and Lorraine had been doing a running commentary on Evan's work, their mother had hardly uttered a word. When they stopped for lunch, she ordered a turkey and Swiss cheese sandwich, but that was the extent of her conversation. The word stonewalling had been created just for her. Aileen had no clue what her mother was thinking.

After lunch, Aileen dropped Lorraine off at the church in case Joanna needed help, then drove her mother home, followed her inside and, without being asked, sat on the couch.

Puzzled that Aileen wasn't leaving, Clarissa sat down too. Neither woman removed her coat.

Aileen cleared her throat. "Mom, you cannot pretend this marriage isn't happening. It won't go away, and you're hurting your grandson."

"I'm not hurting him. I don't hurt people."

The opening was too good to pass up. It was time to confront her mother about the letter. Aileen had carried the pain around long enough—she should have gotten rid of it years ago.

"You hurt me with that letter you sent."

"Those were facts and figures. You're the one that did the hurting. Running off to please yourself. You always pleased yourself. Never paying any attention to your family."

"You mean not paying attention to you, not pleasing you. That's what all of us were supposed to do. Please you."

"You didn't even know Matt was dead."

Not fair, Mom, not fair.

After all this time, the mention of Matt's death tapped into Aileen's tears. When they were growing up, Matt had been her best friend, despite their age difference. He had understood why she bolted, and he would have understood that she had no way of knowing he had died. She'd been devastated when she finally heard about the crash. His death was why she returned to the States. Since then, she'd tried to stay in touch with the girls, knowing Matt would have wanted her to give them a connection to his family. When her father was at The Court, he spent time with his granddaughters; her mother, on the other hand, had quickly written Suzanne off, paying attention to Rose and Cindy when it suited her purposes.

Aileen stood up. Trying to exorcise the past was fruitless. Her mother would never change. Better to stick to the issue of the wedding.

"Evan has done nothing to hurt you. He's a fine man. Matt would be so proud of him. And the fact that he's found love with Dani is wonderful for both of them, a second chance at happiness. Did you know his Scottish fiancee was killed in that terrible 2004 tsunami? Luckily he survived but, if he'd been swimming with her, he'd probably have died too, and you'd never have known Matt had a son. Evan's a talented, caring man who works hard and has been really nice to you—even before he knew you were his grandmother. And here you are, standing on some sort of moral high ground, boycotting his wedding."

As though Aileen hadn't said a word, "He's marrying—*her. She* fired me." More fourth grade sulking.

"Get over it. You don't like her because you haven't been able to bulldoze her like you have the rest of us."

"You have no right to talk to me this way."

"Someone needs to tell it like it is, and today I'm the designated hitter. You've been terrorizing Lorraine for years. So—here's what's going to happen. Tomorrow, you are going to get dressed up—something you love to do—and I will pick you up at twenty minutes before one. Then you and I, along with Lorraine and Grant, will attend the wedding. And you will look happy. His Thai friend, Kanya, is flying all the way from Bangkok. Be nice to her. Don't worry about a gift. We put your name on the one from the family." Aileen paused. "I can't believe I'm actually saying this, but we are still a family, warts and all." She who had avoided all things family. "We want you to join us."

Without waiting for a response, Aileen fled before the emotions she'd been hiding from most of her adult life made her say things she'd regret.

Chapter 28

$\mathcal{H}$is wedding day.

Evan was awake early and, by six, he was driving toward Albany to meet Kanya's commuter flight from New York. Thaksin had agreed she could attend the wedding on her own. When Evan had called her in Bangkok—he didn't trust that the invitation would arrive in time, given the vagaries of the Thai postal service—she'd been wonderfully excited for him. "I wouldn't miss it for the world."

"What about Thaksin?"

"He will agree."

"Thank him for me."

"I look forward to meeting Dani."

Having Fiona in his life had been a blessing. Marrying Dani was a new blessing, and now Kanya was going to meet Dani, pulling some of the disparate pieces of his life together. In the last few months, he'd been retrieving scattered parts of himself, attempting to become complete. Getting all the pieces in the same place at the same time was tricky. Today he was close.

He spent the rest of his wedding morning showing Kanya what he'd done with the farm and the studio, introducing her to Zack, telling her what he'd discovered about his father. At 11:30, he excused himself to take a shower and get dressed. She helped him with his tie, "I like the color," and made sure there was no dog hair clinging to his suit. "You're gorgeous. Dani's lucky."

"I'm lucky too."

"Be happy, Evan."

"I am."

At the church, he hugged Kanya and left her in Polly's care. When he walked out of this building, he'd be a married man. He loved the sound of it.

Her wedding day.

After her divorce, Dani discovered she didn't remember who she'd been before marriage. Once she was single again, finding all the pieces of the original Dani Springer became an excavation project, searching through the buried layers of herself.

A year ago, she'd hardly known Evan, yet the invisible thread of attraction had quickly begun spinning them together. This afternoon, Spence would walk down the aisle with her. Not exactly giving her away—but acknowledging that he approved of this new layer. And when she walked back up the aisle, Evan would be holding her hand.

Sam Senior had picked Spence up earlier. Both Sams, Drew, Spence and Ross had been drafted by Joanna and Monique to help set up the church hall for the reception. Then the men would get dressed at the church. That arrangement gave Dani and Abby the cottage to themselves so they could take their time getting ready, fixing each other's hair and make up. High school all over again.

"What's Evan doing this morning?" Since Spence was staying with Dani at the cottage, Evan had slept at the farm last night. Abby had been at Drew's.

"He picked Kanya up in Albany early this morning. She flew into New York yesterday and planned to catch an early commuter flight. They're probably talking nonstop. I'm looking forward to finally meeting her."

"Weddings do bring the past and present together. Not always an easy mix."

"Speaking of past lives, did I tell you that Ben's new orders are sending him to Florida in July? When we were married, I hated moving all the time. Packing, fixing up new quarters, finding a new school for Spence."

"How does Spence feel about Florida?"

"Not interested in going. He's already told Ben he wants to move back with me. Since he's over twelve, he gets to make that call. The perfect wedding present. He knows a lot of the guys on Lee's high school soccer team, and the coach watched him play last summer, so it's not like going into a whole new school and sports program. I think Beth's proximity may also be a factor."

"Who's Beth?"

"Ross's younger sister."

"Now the parenting fun will really begin."

At 12:30, they drove to the church in Dani's car because Abby's sports car didn't have room for Dani's long dress.

At exactly 12:40, Aileen was again on her mother's front porch, but this time there was no answer to her knock. After a minute or two, she walked around to the parking lot. The Lexus was gone.

So much for ordering her to be dressed and ready to attend Evan's wedding. Aileen should have known better. Her mother had rarely taken directions from anyone. Occasionally from Judd, and then not graciously. Lorraine had cautioned Aileen not to assume their mother would obediently fall into line. Her sister should know.

At once aggravated and disappointed, she drove to the white clapboard church that had faced The Green for a century and a half. The one other time she had been in this church was when her fifth grade class had been given a tour as part of a social studies unit. The only thing Aileen remembered was watching a man wind the historic clock that still marked the hours for the town. As she climbed the church steps, its bell tolled the hour. Just inside the door, a pretty blonde girl, "Hi, I'm Polly," asked her to sign the guest book, then turned her over to a redheaded teenager who carefully took her arm and escorted her into the sanctuary. Lorraine and Grant were seated on the left side of the aisle, fourth pew from the front. "I'll sit with them," she told the boy, and he retreated up the aisle.

"She escaped, didn't she?" Lorraine asked.

"Don't gloat. You were right."

"Rose isn't here either. Great family turnout."

"I guess we can't decree instant bonding."

She surveyed the guests, probably thirty in all, but she didn't recognize anyone. After all these years, why would she? Undoubtedly, they were wondering who she was too. Aileen'd never regretted her decision to stay in Europe and then settle in Florida. Lee had always made her claustrophobic. She'd wanted to see the world, figure out how she fit into it, without anyone— especially her mother—telling her how she ought to live her life. Coming back to Lee these last two Thanksgivings had been interesting but not at all tempting. How Lorraine had tolerated living here all these years, Aileen couldn't imagine.

At 1:10, the minister, followed by Evan and a redheaded man who was undoubtedly related to the young usher, walked in single file from the side door, stopping at the right of the lectern, facing the audience. Evan was wearing a dark suit, white shirt and a blue paisley tie. He looked very different from the Levi-clad young man that had visited her in Florida.

A minute or two later, the organist switched from the medley of love songs she had been playing to *The Bridal Chorus*. A tall, blonde woman in a pale yellow suit, her hair pulled up with a silver clip, walked slowly down the aisle to where the men were standing, taking her place on the left.

Waiting at the back of the church, Dani watched as Abby reached the front, turned, then smiled at her. It was time for mother and son to begin their journey.

The moment the music announced the entrance of the bride, everyone stood to watch Dani and Spence walk down the aisle. Her floor length, sleeveless dress had a jewel neckline, her only jewelry, a single stand of pearls and drop pearl earrings that had been her mother's. When Spence answered the minister's question *Who giveth this woman?* with his firm "I do," Dani leaned over and kissed his cheek, then handed her bouquet of miniature white roses to Abby. As Dani and Evan faced one another, he took her hands, briefly raising the left one to his lips.

The ceremony was simple. Evan stumbled over one or two words in his vows—apparently more nervous than he looked. Then they exchanged yellow-gold bands. While Evan was repeating the *With this ring* speech, Dani watched his face, not the ring, and saw tears lurking in his eyes. She loved that he could show his feelings for her in front of everyone.

When the minister finally said, "You may kiss the bride," Evan kissed her—and kissed her until Sam tactfully touched his cousin's shoulder. Laughter rippled through the church.

As soon as the laughter subsided, the minister turned them so they faced the audience. "May I introduce Mr. and Mrs. Murray."

The Wedding March joyously proclaimed their marriage as Dani and Evan walked hand-in-hand out of the church into the cool autumn sunlight.

Only when Aileen turned to watch the bride and groom leave the church, did she see her mother sitting at the back of the sanctuary alongside Rose and her husband Justin but, by the time Aileen reached the last row, her mother had disappeared. "Hi Rose. Where's your grandmother?"

Rose hugged her aunt, then slipped her arm through Justin's. "She said she was too tired to stay for the reception. I promised we'd drive her home, but you know grandmother. She does what she wants."

Words that should be carved on her mother's tombstone.

"Did the three of you come together?"

Rose nodded. "Justin and I arrived early to visit with her before the ceremony. When we got to her place about ten, she said she had something to show us. We left our car in the parking lot here, and grandmother drove us to the Pittsfield Memorial Evan designed. Even with plastic wrapped around it, his sculpture takes your breath away. I had no idea a landscape architect did artistic things like that. She told us about his other jobs and drove us to a park in Stockbridge. You know how she loves to brag, loves knowing something you don't know. She went on and on about how nice Evan always was to her, how much he looks like Dad, what an important sculptor he's going to be. Then we took her to lunch and, by the time we finished, it was almost one; we slipped in at the back of the church just before the processional began."

Aileen was tempted to tell her niece that she'd just taken the same tour her aunts had forced down her grandmother's unwilling throat yesterday. What a difference twenty-four hours made. She went to find Lorraine. Only her sister could fully appreciate the utter perfection of the way their mother was able to turn even the smallest things to her own advantage.

When Grant came looking for them to say the cake was being cut, they were both laughing, tears running down their faces.

Clarissa managed to keep her emotions in check until she closed the front door of her guesthouse. She turned the deadbolt, pulled the curtains, and sat on the couch, submitting to her anger and frustration.

Her sadness.

And quiet disappointment.

She wasn't precisely sure what the tears were for. They'd been collecting inside of her all week. Now, they were running over her cheeks, streaking her make-up, dripping onto her hands, which were clenched in her lap. She would be eighty-five next week. At this age, she should have something to show for—for her life. Instead, she was huddled in this workshop while her grandson and her family celebrated his marriage, undoubtedly toasting the happy couple, never missing his grandmother—probably grateful she'd chosen to absent herself from the reception.

Self pity was new for Clarissa. She'd been in the habit of pitying others who didn't have the standards, the lifestyle, the status that the Hamiltons possessed. The Hamilton name had given her that power. Of course, she wasn't really a Hamilton. Still just a Malone masquerading as a Hamilton. No matter how she pretended, no matter how hard she worked to convince others that she wasn't a Malone, she was. She'd been successfully lying to herself for over sixty years. Judd had let her get away with it. In spite of all her nagging and putting on airs, he'd somehow always loved her. And she'd loved him. That was the one true part of the past. Her children, however, hadn't always loved her. Tolerated her, yes. JT might have been the exception. He'd easily seen through her, teased her, kissed her on the cheek. *Hi beautiful.*

In many ways, Evan was more like JT than like Matthew. Though life had been hard for Evan, he had JT's sweetness. Aileen had told her about Fiona, about the tsunami, about the Thai woman who would be at the wedding. Clarissa didn't want to meet her, didn't want to publicly be Evan's grandmother yet. Judd would be furious about her missing the reception. He'd have made the first toast, would have embraced Evan's wife, sincerely welcoming her to the family. But then Judd had always been a better person than she was. Too late now to be something she'd never been.

It was nearly six o'clock when she called Aileen's cell number. "I'm taking Bart up on his invitation to go to Florida with you. Can you get me a ticket?" The fact that she was accepting her son-in-law's suggestion—Aileen had delivered Bart's message about visiting Florida yesterday—told Clarissa how lost she was. She who had always been sure of what was right, of what she wanted—didn't know any more. It had started with *that damned woman* taking over the house. Now *she'd* taken her grandson. Clarissa didn't want to be on the premises when the newlyweds returned from their honeymoon. That was too much to ask of an old woman.

"I'll call Bart. He'll manage it. I'll call you back when I know the details. Throw some things into a suitcase."

Clarissa carefully packed two suitcases and, on Sunday morning, she and Aileen drove to Hartford to board the flight to Miami. Bart had promised to pick them up at the airport.

Chapter 29

On the last Monday in February, Lorraine called Dani to tell her Clarissa was returning from Florida. What had begun as a convenient escape to Aileen's had extended through the holidays and into February.

"I tried to convince her she should wait until the worst of winter was over, but she was adamant. I suspect she and Aileen are beginning to get on each other's nerves. I'm surprised they've lasted this long."

Dani sighed. The months of freedom were over. "When?" She hoped her voice didn't reveal her dismay—though now that she'd gotten better acquainted with Evan's aunt, she suspected Lorraine felt much the same way.

"Thursday. Grant will bring her car over before then. He's having it serviced and washed."

"Thanks for the heads-up. I'll call Evan. He's at the studio today, interviewing for a combination secretary, bookkeeper and office manager."

"So the loft is now his office?"

"Yes. And the farmhouse is rented. All we have to do is get my cottage ready to rent and our living arrangements will be settled. When spring comes, he's planning on leasing the rest of the farm's acreage. He doesn't want it to lie fallow."

She called Evan's cell, but it went directly to voice mail. He was probably in the middle of an interview. Since the dedication of the Memorial in Pittsfield, he'd been deluged with jobs. No longer could he do everything himself. The upside was that he could pick and choose which jobs he wanted to do, joking that there'd be no more fishing piers. Sam had come on board to take over all the planting, leaving Evan more time for designing, and he was trying to tempt Drew into taking over hiring the crews and overseeing the construction sites. Since Jacob was making noises about retiring in a year or two, Evan was fairly sure Drew wouldn't feel disloyal about leaving Jacob's firm.

Dani spent the rest of the afternoon packing up the towels and linens she wouldn't need on a day-to-day basis. She probably had enough to last them for several years. Turning The Maples back into a home hadn't been as hard as she'd imagined, but it had entailed endless trips between the cottage and the house, adding some of their personal possessions to what was already in the main house and putting the rest in the basement. The movers would come tomorrow to deal with the heavy pieces. Spence's bedroom furniture would replace the furniture in the blue bedroom. That furniture and the furniture in the yellow bedroom—now the twins' room—would also be stored in the basement. She and Evan needed to shop for furniture for the children's room so the woman from the Department of Children's Services could see where the children would be sleeping. She'd already paid one visit, reminding them they needed safety gates at the top and bottom of the stairs. The elegant stairway with its beautiful newel post had been labeled a hazard. Most of the background checks and volumes of paperwork were done. All for two small children named Faith and Joshua. If Dani were actually giving birth, no one would ask about sleeping arrangements or baby gates.

So much had changed in the last three months. Evan's business taking off, then hearing from the adoption agency in early January that there were mixed race, year old twins who needed parents. The children had been in foster care since birth, but it was getting harder to find foster parents who would take them both. Would the Murrays be interested in adopting them? The Murrays would. Since then, everything had been on fast forward. The people at the agency had originally told them it would be a year, probably longer, before a child would be available.

After their first visit with thirteen month old Faith and Joshua— there had been many visits since—she and Evan were certain they wanted these delightful children, who had almost been adopted twice before. Milk chocolate skins, thick black hair with a slight curl, and smiles that stole Dani's and Evan's hearts. Faith had immediately snuggled into Evan's lap, successfully making him her slave. His face seemed lit from within. Dani knew that, whatever else they faced with these children, the moment of watching Evan's face become a father's face was worth everything else.

Putting The Maples out of business had ultimately been painless—even joyous. Polly would stay in her attic room until the semester was over. When Spence moved back in July, The Maples would be fully booked—in the nicest way possible. Dani could hardly wait to fill the house with children instead of overnight guests.

Clarissa came home because she was curious. Lorraine hadn't been at all forthcoming about what was happening at The Maples, about Evan. All she would say was "Things are about the same" and switch to discussing what a hard winter it had been, how lucky Clarissa was to be in Florida. She could tell Lorraine was sidestepping something, though Clarissa had to admit the weather on Big Pine Key was amazing. For years, she'd scoffed at people rhapsodizing over Florida's weather, but they were right. She didn't have to deal with the ice and snow. Bart owned several cars and told her to use them whenever she wanted, none of Lorraine's driving restrictions either. He was a generous host, making peace whenever she and Aileen argued. He was easy to like.

In Aileen's sprawling house, Clarissa had a lovely room and bath all to herself, she swam in their pool almost every day and occasionally helped out with special events at the resort. She was fairly sure Bart created jobs for her—to keep her out of Aileen's path—but she loved meeting people, so she played along. Clarissa's favorite sentence had become, "My son-in-law is the owner."

But it was time to go home. Her quilting students would be missing her and, despite Lorraine's silence, Clarissa knew in her bones something else was going on. Besides, Aileen would probably be glad to see the back of her.

When Lorraine turned into the driveway, the first thing Clarissa noticed was the absence of The Maples' sign in the front yard, yet there were lights on in the main house. In the winter twilight, it looked invitingly familiar.

Lorraine pulled the suitcases—there were now three—into her mother's bedroom. "I put some supplies in the fridge and there's fresh bread. That'll get you by until you go to the store." She turned to leave.

"What happened to the sign?"

"Dani took it down last month."

"Did the business go under?" Clarissa knew she'd asked too quickly, was too eager to assume failure. Had her reviews had anything to do with this?

"No. She and Evan have made some changes in their lives. I'll let them fill you in. I need to get home and check math quizzes for tomorrow."

And Lorraine was gone, having told her mother nothing.

As soon as Dani heard Evan's truck drive into the parking lot, she hurried out the back door to meet him. She loved watching him let Zack out, reach for the briefcase he carried when he needed to work at home in the evening, loved the way his eyes smiled as he lifted her off the ground and kissed her. If someone wanted her definition of pure joy, this was it.

They walked into the house, calling for Zack to get out of the garden, delighting in each other and the new rituals they were creating.

"I see the Lexus is back. Have you seen her yet?"

"Only through the French doors when Lorraine dropped her off."

Evan closed the back door, kissed Dani again, and hung up his jacket. "Wine, yes?"

"Wine yes."

He opened a bottle of Merlot, and she pulled two wine glasses out of the cupboard. They settled on the couch.

"I'm so glad you're home."

"You say that every night." He slid his arm around her, pulling her close.

"I mean it every night. You brought your briefcase—do you need to work tonight?"

"Nope—it contains children's furniture catalogs, compliments of Aunt Joanna. She thought we should look at them before we go crib shopping."

"Not at all excited about being a great aunt is she?"

"She'd move into the other bedroom if we gave her the chance. She's circled the ones she approves of."

Dani laughed. "You do have a lovely family."

"All of it?" He grinned.

"You know the answer to that."

"Dani," he took his arm away and sat forward, "we need to end this state of war between the two of you. She's not going away and neither are we."

"Tell her that."

"You don't have to love her. I'm not sure I'm ready to love her either, but we need a truce."

"She's the one who believes I'm trespassing."

"It's our home, and we're about to put children in this home. We don't want them feeling all that hostility."

"How do you propose to change things?"

"First, we need—"

"We!"

"We need to tell her about the twins."

"You can tell her—with my blessing."

"No. We. A united front. You've outmaneuvered her lots of times. What's changed?"

"First, I'm tired of having to outmaneuver her and, second, now she's your grandmother."

"I'm not sure that matters."

"It does to me."

"Let's invite her over for coffee and pie tomorrow night and get the discussion over with."

"Evan—"

"You know it has to be done."

When Clarissa accepted Evan's invitation for coffee and pie, she feared he was going to tell her that she couldn't live in the guesthouse any more, that *that woman* had convinced him Clarissa was no longer welcome. Not that she'd ever been welcome.

Instead, they'd served her chocolate pecan pie and coffee and told her about the children. Now she found herself in the uncomfortable and unexpected position of having to rethink what her relationship with Evan—and *his wife*—was going to be. She'd been put on the spot, backed into a corner. The rules had changed. The Maples was gone. About that, Clarissa was not sorry. She only hoped they would never find out about the reviews she'd sent. She suspected Phoebe knew but had kept the secret.

The house was again a house that would have a family. A good thing.

Twins, born of an African-American father and a Native-American mother. Dark-skinned children who'd be her great-grandchildren. She wasn't sure how she felt about that.

Evan had walked her back to her place and given her a key to their house. She hadn't expected that. As he bid her goodnight, he kissed her cheek. She hadn't expected that either. "And please call Dani by her name—you avoid it every way imaginable."

Clarissa didn't reply.

"Three weeks from tomorrow, we're scheduled to go to Springfield to pick up the children. We'd like you to go with us. Make it an occasion." He probably should have consulted Dani before he issued the invitation. But including her suddenly seemed like a good idea.

"Do you have room in her car?" That sounded like an acceptance, but she hadn't meant it that way.

"Absolutely. We traded it in for a mini-van."

On a sunny Friday in March, they picked the children up at the home of their most recent foster family. When Faith saw Evan, she raised her arms, wanting him to pick her up. He kissed her cheek. "How's my princess?"

Joshua, quieter than his sister, stood very still beside the social worker who was overseeing the transfer of custody, studying Clarissa. Dani gently took his hand, walked him over to Clarissa, and knelt down. "Josh—this is your grandmother." Great-grandmother was too much right now.

He continued his evaluation of this new person, then held out his other hand for Clarissa. She took it, looking down at him just as intently as he was looking at her.

"I'm Nana," she told him. That's what Cindy's brood called her, not that she saw them often enough for them to remember who she was.

Dani released Josh's hand and let him walk to the car with Clarissa. Evan was already buckling Faith into her car seat. Once Joshua was settled in his seat in the middle, Clarissa sat beside him, and Josh reached for her hand again.

Before Evan put the key in the ignition, he stole a glance in the rearview mirror, wishing someone could snap a picture of this moment. His son and daughter and his grandmother—together.

"Everyone okay back there?"

"Yes. But it would help if Danielle could move her seat forward a little."

Danielle did, and Evan started the engine.